OTHER

breakable

THINGS

ALSO BY KELLEY YORK

HUSHED
MADE OF STARS
MODERN MONSTERS

OTHER
breakable
THINGS

kelley york · rowan altwood

Entangled Publishing, LLC
2614 South Timberline Road
Suite 109
Fort Collins, CO 80525

Entangled Teen is an imprint of Entangled Publishing, LLC.

Visit our website at www.entangledpublishing.com.

Edited by Stacy Abrams and Tara Whitaker
Cover design by Kelley York
Interior design by Toni Kerr

ISBN: 9781633755949
Ebook ISBN: 9781633755994

Manufactured in the United States of America

First Edition April 2017

10 9 8 7 6 5 4 3 2 1

*Dedicated to those whose
health has escaped them.*

"Ever has it been that love knows not its own depth until the hour of separation."
—*Kahlil Gibran*

Prologue

The rain is coming down in sheets. It has reduced visibility by 50 percent, but damn if it doesn't make for great mood lighting for two people driving down the freeway near midnight with only the glow of the dashboard for company. Every now and then a streak of lightning foreshadows the boom of thunder that follows. It makes him jump, which in turn makes her smile. She's aware of this little-known secret of his, that he hates the sound of thunder, or fireworks on the Fourth of July.

She asks if he wants her to drive, not for the first time. He rolls his eyes and laughs. "I'm not letting a little rain scare me out of the driver's seat." But the fact that she offers makes him smile, because she's always thoughtful like that.

He removes a hand from the wheel, extends it in her direction, and she places her small palm against his and locks their fingers together.

The next strike of lightning illuminates the moving truck veering into their lane.

The thunder that follows mutes the sound of metal on metal as the truck drives the smaller car off the road and into the muddy embankment, and no one's brakes do anything on the rain-slicked asphalt.

When they finally slide to a messy stop, no one moves.

The air is filled with smoke. Not from the engine—but from the airbags. His throat burns, ears ringing. The truck's horn is going off and won't stop. He can't see the other driver.

Instead he looks over at her, his whole world, and realizes the passenger's side airbag didn't deploy.

Luc

(3 years ago)

Mom bursts in like a hurricane, slamming on lights and cracking her knee against the dresser. She swears loudly. I'm instantly awake, blinking bleary-eyed into the sudden onslaught of brightness.

"What the hell?"

"Get up, get dressed," she whispers, as though there's anyone she's going to disturb with a normal voice, and like she wasn't being loud enough already. Her hair is still twisted up into a messy bun that she'd never be caught dead with out of the house. "Your dad's waiting downstairs. Jesus, I still have to change…"

I sit up and swing my legs out of bed. Mom pulls jeans and a T-shirt from my closet and throws them onto the bed beside me. Ordinarily I'd be worried, but this energy she's giving off doesn't feel like that of an emergency or anything bad. "Mom? What's going on?"

She stops at the door. Turns. Smiles brightly at me. There's a nervous edge to it, though. "There was an accident. Pileup on the freeway. One of the girls was pronounced brain-dead and she's an organ donor."

All of a sudden, I want to throw up what little I ate for dinner. Shit. "Why are you happy about that? Someone's dead."

That makes her smile falter, but only briefly. "The surgeons want you brought in immediately and prepped for surgery, Luc. You're getting your new heart."

ONE

Evelyn

Mom says falling in love is the most incredible thing in the world. She would know; she's done it as many times as I am years old. Sometimes they're weeklong whirlwind romances, flings with soldiers who come into town during an off-duty stint, who promise to write after they leave and never do. Sometimes they're a married firefighter who calls things off after he decides he and his wife really need to *work it out*. Mom takes every one of these relationships—and breakups—very seriously.

To be fair, for a while even *I* was pretty convinced Robert was the one who would last. It started out as many of Mom's relationships did, and I thought it would end the same as all the others, too. Except this time, Mom came home to Grandma Jane's late one night, gently shook me awake, and said in an excited whisper, "C'mon, Evelyn.

We're getting out of here." This was new. This was different. I went into it thinking, *hoping*, that Robert might be some missing piece to our family dynamic.

Oh God, how wrong I was.

Three years. That's a long time for a woman who normally doesn't have a relationship beyond three months. Yet here we are back at square one, with our suitcases in hand in Grandma Jane's living room, and she's sighing as she shakes her head. "Go on, then. Get unpacked."

That's that. Three years in a podunk town in Arizona, and now we're back in California. Back in Fresno. It's like no time has passed at all.

Grandma wanted me to go back to public school. "A seventeen-year-old girl should be making friends," she insists. "Going to prom and all that."

A few years ago I might have agreed with her. But it's not like I have any friends here, and I really don't think I'm going to be making any. Online independent study has gotten me through the last three years just fine, and I don't see why I can't let it carry me the rest of the way.

Besides, back then, I'd always thought when I went to prom, Luc would be the boy at my side.

There are things I missed about this stupid town, though. The movie theater where Luc and I spent a lot of our weekends, for instance. We'd start out bright and early in the morning, hitting up whatever movie was playing first. When it ended, we slipped into our respective bathrooms, gave it fifteen minutes, and met back up to sneak with the crowds into the next movie. We never did get caught.

There's also the mall, the park, Emperor's Pizza

Palace that does karaoke every Tuesday night. We always went but never sang. It was more fun to sit in the back with a pizza between us and watch everyone else, laughing to each other over the horrible singers and commending the occasional decent one. We were both good at that. At watching.

All the things I missed about California are Luc-centric. Which makes sense, I guess. I mean, it wasn't like I really had any other friends. Neither did he. The difference being…I think Luc could have made friends if he'd ever *wanted* to, but I was awkward and shy and no girls—or guys, for that matter—my age really took any notice of me.

Our second day back in Fresno, just for kicks, I drive by the high school. I was only there for six months before we moved, but obviously it's fresher in my memory than middle school. Students are running laps out on the track, so school must be in session. If the bell schedule hasn't changed, they'll be going to lunch in about fifteen minutes.

I see the bleachers Luc and I used to hide behind when we ditched classes, when I got overwhelmed and just wanted to be away from everyone. It didn't matter what class Luc was supposed to be in; he always went with me.

As I'm heading home, I take a detour into one of the much nicer neighborhoods, only a few blocks from mine. I stop at the curb in front of a large, beautiful two-story house that might be a different color than I remember. Maybe they had it painted.

Luc's house.

Unless he's moved. Which is a possibility. Or his

parents still live here and Luc himself is off on his own somewhere. His family has the money for things like that, and Luc would've turned nineteen two months ago, old enough to have his own place.

I'm psyching myself out, I realize. Trying to come up with excuses to not approach and knock. The driveway is empty, but that doesn't mean anything; they could park in the garage for all I know.

What would I say to Luc if he answered, anyway? *Hey, thanks for being a shitty friend when I left!* Somehow I don't think that would end well, and it wouldn't make me feel any better.

But there's no denying how much I've missed him. How much I want to hear his voice, see his face…

I also don't want to be the one to initiate it. It feels like I've chased after Luc for the last three years, trying to get him to talk to me, to keep in touch. The number of nights I spent crying myself to sleep over it borders on ridiculous.

After sitting and debating for a while, I twist around to rummage in the backseat, which still contains a few boxes Mom and I haven't unpacked yet. I find a scrap of paper and begin folding. When I was little, Mom took me to a bookstore and let me pick out a book of my choice. I found myself drawn to one on origami, and it started a lifelong love of creating life out of a single piece of paper. I leave the crane I create on Luc's doorstep. When—if— he sees it, he'll know that it's me. And if he wants to see me, *really* wants to see me, he'll do it.

As I'm driving home, I can't shake the looming sense of hopelessness that he won't.

•••

Mom hasn't left her room all day, Grandma says. Go figure. She takes a casserole out of the oven and I bring a plate of it upstairs. Mom has not, in fact, gotten out of bed, and her eyes are bleary as she stares at the old TV with its fuzzy picture of basic cable. Grandma would never invest in anything more than that.

She lifts her head to look at me and manages a smile. "Hey, baby girl."

I wish I could tell Mom that we dodged a bullet with Robert. That I'm glad we left. That I don't know how much longer I could have handled living under the same roof as him, and that even the thought of him makes my stomach twist into unbearable knots. I bite the thoughts back, though, because the last thing I need to try to explain to her are my own issues and how badly I want to leave Arizona and Robert as a distant memory.

"Hungry?" I set the plate on her nightstand even as she's waving it off.

"Bah, I can smell the onions. Mama likes to make that crap to spite me. She knows I won't eat it." Mom sighs, rolling onto her back. "C'mon over and sit with me a bit. You were gone for a while. Have a good day?"

I crawl into bed beside her, drawing my knees up to my chest. "It was fine." My default answer for everything. Mom was always so stressed or unhappy that I never wanted to tell her when school was hard, or when I was lonely because I didn't know how to make friendships last, or when I fell in love with a boy named Luc and she made me leave him behind so she could chase after Robert.

So…*fine*. It's a safe word. Not *good*, not *great*, but

things could be worse and therefore it isn't a lie.

"You're always good." She chuckles, lifting a cool hand to brush the dark hair back from my face. "I swear. One day you were my baby, and then I turned around and you had grown up. When did that happen?"

I just smile. I settle down with her to watch TV in silence and wonder what it means that when I say *fine*, she always hears the words I'm specifically not saying. Like *good*.

Is she really listening?

Luc

Grocery day is Dad's favorite day. Or at least, it would be if I didn't usually go with him.

Dad's been in immaculate shape for as long as I can remember. Broad-shouldered, solid but not overweight. He isn't some muscle-head but he does work out, keeps himself healthy. Exercises enough that he can grab a bag of chips and a quart of ice cream with a big, cheesy smile on his face. His diet consists of *whatever I want so long as I burn off the calories later.*

My diet consists of caloric restrictions, low sodium, low cholesterol, low carbs, low salt, and low fat. Basically, low everything that tastes good.

Going shopping together means Dad picking out foods he loves, while I'm reading over labels to make sure I'm getting things I'm supposed to actually be eating. When we're shopping together, though, I see him hesitate with his choices, stealing glances at me as though he feels guilty. Half the time, he puts his food back. Which makes me feel like crap. Other people shouldn't have to suffer just because my body is stupid.

I've stuck rigorously to the diet the nutritionists suggested. For all the fucking good it's done.

When we get home, Dad hoists all but two small bags into his arms. I grab the remaining two, shut the tailgate to his pickup, and follow. I find him standing on the porch, stepping back a few inches to look at something at his feet. "What's that?"

I unlock the door for him before stooping down to pick it up. The moment I'm close enough, I instantly recognize it.

An origami bird.

Only one person in all the world would leave something like this on my doorstep. Seeing it, holding it, might be the first time I've felt like I could breathe freely in months, while constricting my chest painfully at the same time.

Evelyn's back in town.

When she moved to Arizona, she wrote me damned near every day at first. I wrote back once a week. Her emails tapered off to once a week, mine went bi-weekly. As of this exact moment, I haven't written to her in nearly four months and I have four emails sitting read and not responded to in my inbox.

It had nothing to do with her.

That is, it isn't because I didn't *want* to keep in better contact. It wasn't that I didn't *want* to talk to her. I liked getting every email she sent—at the time, she didn't have her own cell phone so we were restricted to writing—but I never knew what to write back. With her gone, I did a whole lot of nothing. When you cut out my transplant and the extensive recovery process that followed, I really didn't have a lot to talk about.

Besides, what sense would it have made? I was sick. I *am* sick. A new heart didn't change that. Evelyn didn't need that kind of shit in her life. I never should have let her get close in the first place because it made her leaving all that much harder. My hopes for Evelyn after she moved had been for her to live a happy family life and meet some nice guy who could give her everything and treat her the way she deserved. She was smart, she was beautiful, she was kind; if she would *realize* that, she'd have no problems meeting people who would love her the way I do. And I—well. I might be six feet under by that point.

Who knows? I'm already halfway there.

TWO

Luc

Three days should be enough time to let the whole thing go. Some girl I hung out with when I was younger is back in town. Big deal. Nothing has changed. Or rather, maybe everything has changed.

So I don't know why I'm standing on Evelyn's doorstep. It's been years, after all, and I don't think I'm the same person anymore. Various family members tell me I've changed…and not for the better. Too much time spent in hospitals, too much pity, too much of the unknown. It doesn't help that I went through that stupid transplant and I'm still on a leash when it comes to what I can and can't do. I feel like an old car that constantly needs attention and oil and coolant to avoid breaking down on the side of the road.

I wonder if Evelyn has changed, too. Maybe she's grown out of her awkwardness, her loneliness. For all I know, she's morphed into the stereotypical blonde cheerleader with a clique always in tow. (I can't picture that, though. Evelyn? Not if her life depended on it.) Writing the occasional email is way different than seeing someone in person, so I really have no idea what she's like anymore.

Regardless of whether or not I understand the reason, here I am. I spent the drive trying to play out what to say, how to stand, how to act, anticipating what to expect when I see her.

Thankfully, it isn't her mom or grandma who answers the door. It's Evelyn herself. For every inch of her that's changed in some way, I would have instantly recognized her anywhere without a second glance. She's...grown into herself, almost. Taller, sure. Curvy. But she looks less like the awkward, frizzy-haired outcast and more like—I don't know. Soft and beautiful in her pajamas with a hole in her sock and I can't look away because holy hell, it strikes me just how gorgeous she is and how much I've missed her.

Her brown eyes widen the instant they land on me, and I can only imagine what she's thinking. I look different, too. Taller, skinnier. Unhealthily so. Without thinking, I nervously say, "Looks like you took all my weight."

That...probably could've come out better.

Evelyn's face twists into an expression that is all too familiar. Unimpressed and unamused, and yet... unsurprised. She purses her lips. "Mm-hmm. I'm going to close the door and let you try that again."

"Fair enough."

She shuts the door. I exhale heavily through my nose and roll my gaze skyward. This was a terrible idea. But

I'm here, so…I knock again. This time when Evelyn answers, I try a simple, "Hello."

Now her expression is torn somewhere between pained and sad and hopeful. I kind of want to grab her cheeks and pull them into a smile. Suits her better. But we just stand there, staring at each other, at a loss for what to say, like three years has robbed us of all our words.

Evelyn finally steps outside, shuts the door behind her, and folds her arms, trying to look more relaxed than I suspect she really is as her gaze roams over me. "I did take all your weight."

Not that I was ever well built or that Evelyn has turned into a whale, but… "You look good."

"Good to see you, too," she says. "What are you doing here?"

I mirror her posture of crossing my arms over my chest. It's a defensive stance, but whatever. "You left me a bird. And I could ask you the same thing." Probably could've sounded less accusing there.

"I live here."

"You used to."

"I used to, and I do now." Her shoulders lift and fall, head dipping so she can stare at her feet. "Is that why you came over? To find out why I'm back?"

"Maybe," I respond, because I don't know what else to say. Admit I have no idea what I expected when I showed up here? I'd prefer to at least pretend to know what I'm doing.

She squints. More awkward silence. "I haven't heard from you in a while."

"No, you haven't." Guilt edges into my voice. I could tell her why I didn't write—awkwardness, health issues, uncertainty—but again, that's not my style. It opens the flood-gates for too many questions I don't know how to answer.

The tension that slides across her shoulders is visible. "Did I do something wrong?"

Ah, typical Evelyn. Blaming herself. I'd hoped she'd skip that route this time, but I should have known better. "What? No. I've just been busy." Yeah, good job, great answer.

Her voice is tight. "Too busy to drop an email once a week? Or even a text, maybe a phone call? I gave you my number as soon as I got a phone."

My eyes close. "I was...*really* busy." What a lame excuse. But it's partially the truth. Both before and after the operation, I've been in and out of hospitals. Tests. Therapy. Never mind the number of times I looked at the phone or sat at my computer to contact her and never knew what to say.

"You were too busy for *three years*," she says, incredulous. "Why are you here, Luc? Really?"

Why *am* I here? The whole point of avoiding close contact with Evelyn was to prevent hurting her in the long run, and showing up at her front door isn't helping things any. Being here is a selfish move on my part; I so badly wanted to see her. Guilt starts to settle in fast. "I can leave if you want."

"Don't you do that," she says quietly. "I waited for you. I waited for every little scrap you would throw me while I was out there." She breathes in deep, and it's obvious she's trying not to cry. "If you hadn't wanted to talk to me, you could have said so. I would have understood."

I stare at her for a long moment, trying to adjust to an Evelyn who would stick up for herself. Evelyn was always a quiet presence, not afraid to defend others but still reserved and careful with her words. It's a good change. A great one, even. I used to worry about how she let everyone walk all over her.

God, I want to tell her the truth just so that maybe she'll understand that I did it to protect her, but I brush that idea off as quickly as it comes. The last thing I want is pity from Evelyn. Isn't it bad enough that I get it from everyone else? I can't stand the idea of her treating me like a delicate flower. I'd rather have her angry and think I'm a jerk than that.

"I can tell you that I'm sorry and I would mean it," is what I offer, and it's sincere. "But I really… I don't have a reason. I was an ass." But she's getting upset now, I can tell that much, and I suddenly don't want to be here, so I turn away. I can walk off without a second thought, except— "I left something for you," I find myself saying before I go. "In your backyard."

Evelyn straightens, chin inclining, her anger melting into confusion. "Where?"

I lift a hand in a sort of vague wave good-bye. "You'll figure it out."

Evelyn

I left something for you in your backyard, he said. I have no idea what I'm going to find aside from spiders, dirt, maybe an old hose, and broken gardening tools.

Miraculously, Mom has emerged from her room and is coming downstairs when I sink onto the couch. "Who was that boy you were talking to?"

Oh yes. A boy. Naturally, Mom would want to know. Not because her daughter is possibly making friends, but because she jumps all over the idea of my having a boyfriend. She was probably spying from her bedroom window. Maybe she wants to see me succeed where she's failed so many times. I don't know.

"His name is Luc. He's a guy I met at school before we moved," I mutter, flipping on the TV. Even basic cable channels are crackly. Someone needs to explain to Grandma Jane the benefits of upgrading to something that doesn't require bunny ears to work. I've tried going over the concept of HD to her, but she didn't get it.

"A guy from school who comes to see you at home after all these years?" Mom sits next to me, nudging an elbow into my ribs. "Is that the one you used to go places with all the time after school?"

"That would be him."

"So…tell me more!"

I sigh. It's complicated, and the last person I want advice from regarding boys is my mother. "Just a friend, Mom."

"Really?"

"Really." Are we even that anymore?

"Oh." Her expression falls, and my insides twist guiltily. I wish I could throw her a bone just so we would have something to talk about. I've made the attempt before. Hell, I even invented a fake boyfriend when I was thirteen just because of how excited Mom was about the idea. How she sat down with me at dinner to get the details, to instill in me the way a proper significant other—because Mom didn't care if I had boyfriends or girlfriends—should treat me, the things I should never put up with. When I turned sixteen, Mom insisted I go to the doctor for birth control pills and gave me a box of condoms. That won the award for the most humiliating moment of my life. She said while she didn't condone sex at my age, she knew "how teenagers are these days" and wanted me to be safe. Just in case. I appreciated the sentiment, but still—*awkward*.

Mom doesn't last long in the living room before she ditches me to retreat upstairs again. Grandma comes home from her Bunco group, and the sound of clanging pans and the scent of roasting chicken waft in from the kitchen. My stomach is in so many knots that I can't decide whether it smells delicious or nauseating. Once the sitcom I'm watching begins to roll credits, I kill the TV and make my way for the stairs.

Just a guy, I had told Mom. She never officially *met* Luc face-to-face; I made sure of that. Luc rarely came over. The most Mom would've seen him was outside on the swing set with me, but she was typically too wrapped up in her own thing back then. Those were the early days with Robert, back before everything went wrong. Back when I could be in the same room with Robert without feeling like I was going to be sick.

But Luc had never been *just a guy*, had he? He was… quiet, sarcastic, even mean sometimes. We mixed like oil and water, not blending so much as rolling together. I was pliant where he wouldn't budge. I pushed where he pulled. We could run circles around each other. Nothing he said fazed me, and there were times when I would say or do something and Luc would pause and grin at me, as though he'd asked a question and I had given just the right answer. I adored every little thing about him.

I left something for you, he'd said.

So I go outside.

Grandma's backyard doesn't consist of much. It isn't even fenced in, and it backs up to an empty field that was probably once home to crops of some kind and is now overrun with tall brown weeds and grass and the sad remains of a swing set whose seats haven't seen a butt in years, probably since Luc and I used to sit out here. Only a small six-by-six patch of actual green surrounds the back porch.

The porch.

Yes. It's honestly the only place to put anything. A brief look around tells me Luc didn't leave anything sitting in the grass, and so...the porch it is.

Years ago, Grandma had the porch steps boarded in along the sides to keep animals and small children from crawling under the house and getting stuck. "Had a skunk die down there once," she had grunted. "Most horrific smell you ever saw."

"How do you see a smell, Grandma?" I asked.

"Don't get smart with me, Evelyn."

At any rate—the guy she paid for the work didn't do an amazing job. By the end of that summer, the planks of wood along one side of the steps had started to bend and give way. I can't crawl under the stairs, but I can easily fit an arm in there. Spiders and darkness and dirt, oh my. I sigh, push up a sleeve, and slide my hand inside and down. My fingertips brush damp dirt, and then come into contact with something hard and slick. I pry it up by one corner until I can get a decent grip and pull it out through the hole.

In my hand, I have a blue CD case. It's covered in condensation and filth. Let's not think about the way my heart aches at the thought of fifteen-year-old Luc cramming this under my back porch after I moved three years ago. No way.

I clutch the dirty case tightly as I duck back inside long enough to grab Mom's car keys and then escape into the garage. The only CD player in the house is... well, in the car. I slip inside, give the key a half turn in the ignition, remove Mom's CD of country songs that she listened to our entire ride back from Arizona, and slip in Luc's CD. The display says there's only one track. I frown and force myself to lean back and close my eyes while the music plays.

I'm not a music pro. Everything I do know, I probably learned from Luc. He loved it. He could name any song on the radio; the older or more obscure, the better. I loved that about him. His ability to close his eyes and hum along perfectly in tune with anything.

The song is a familiar one. Elton John. Even I can recognize that voice, though I doubt I could name much of his work off the top of my head. Except for this one, because I remember Luc playing it for me years ago.

I'd cut out of school early one day, upset over some dumb comment a girl made in the hall about my hair. I can't even remember what she said anymore. Just that it had struck a nerve and, in tears, I'd ditched my last two classes—including the one I shared with Luc—and ran outside to the track in order to hide like a baby behind the bleachers.

Luc found me.

He dropped his backpack onto the ground and plopped down at my side as he asked, "What's wrong?"

At the time, I'd felt *so dumb* for sitting there in the dirt, crying my eyes out. Maybe it was hormones, maybe it was that I felt alone, not pretty, unwanted, out of place. I didn't know, but when all I did was sit there with tears rolling down my face, Luc pulled off his jacket and draped it around me. He retrieved his phone from his backpack, popped an earbud into his ear and another into mine, and slipped an arm around my shoulders to hold me against his side while he scrolled to a song, "Tiny Dancer," and pushed play.

This was the song we listened to on repeat for the better part of an hour, because I liked it, because Luc hadn't known what to say to make me feel better but he'd *wanted to,* and that meant more to me than any poetic, pretty words he could have conjured up.

Even if my fingers are numb from being outside in the fall weather, even if I didn't turn the heater on in the car...I'm warm all over from the tips of my toes up to my ears. I picture every moment with Luc. All the things I wanted him to say and he wouldn't. The simplest sign of affection seemed beyond him, but his kindness when it came to me...maybe it was subtle, but it was perfect.

Always perfect.

I open my eyes and blink back the tears as the song ends for the second time. We've been apart for three years.

Why would he have me listen to this now, and what does it mean? People can change a lot in three years. What if he's entirely different than I remember? What if *I'm* different? We were kids so why do I still feel this way?

After everything that's happened between us, I refuse to let him lift my hopes anymore. No. Absolutely not.

I listen to the song again.

It's only polite, I decide, to tell him thank you. It was a gift. Obviously one that was sentimental to him. Still, it takes me four days before I work up the nerve to swing by Luc's house. Mom had me running up to the store in her car for some groceries, and the decision to park outside Luc's large home is a spur-of-the-moment deal.

I approach his front porch with caution. Although I've been to his house before, I've never been inside, and my palms are sweating as I lift a hand to ring the doorbell.

A slender woman with shoulder-length dark hair and wearing a suit opens the door a moment later. She smiles with a quizzical tilt of her head. "Hello?"

I've only ever seen Luc's mother from a distance, but Luc looks like her. Same sharp features, same bright eyes. "Um, hi. I'm Evelyn. Is Luc home?"

"Yes. He's— Oh, right here." As she speaks, Luc's lanky form appears in the doorway behind her. He blinks once, seeming puzzled by my presence. I try not to look as uncomfortable as I feel. Luc's mother is oblivious. "I was just heading out to a luncheon. It was nice to meet you, Evelyn." She plants a kiss on Luc's forehead, ruffling his hair, to which he grunts and frowns. Then she's slipping past me and heading for the driveway, leaving Luc and me to stand there on opposite sides of the threshold, awkward and silent.

"So," I finally say.

He leans against the door frame, hands in the pockets of his sleep pants. "So."

"I found the CD. It was nice."

"Good. I was aiming for that."

"Right." Deep breaths. "I just…wanted to say thank you for it. That's all."

Luc studies my face. I hate how he's capable of being so still and silent while I'm wanting to fidget and squirm into the floor so he stops staring at me like that. He asks, "What brought you guys back to town?"

I tuck my hands under my arms and shrug. I guess I'm feeling more cooperative today. At least enough that I'm willing to give him answers. "Mom's relationship went down the drain. Grandma Jane's was the only place we had to go, so."

"That sucks."

"Not really. Arizona was boring. Which you would have known if you'd read my letters." It's an intentional barb. One that doesn't seem to affect Luc much at all. He simply watches me until he answers, "I *did* read your letters. I read every single one of them."

I swallow the lump in my throat, struggling to keep my tone even. "You just didn't want to write back."

Another sigh. Like this conversation is somehow exhausting him. Luc pushes a hand back through his dark, unkempt hair and looks at me again. "I said I was sorry and I was being an ass. You're here now; can't we focus on that?" He glances down, scuffing his bare foot against the threshold. "Do you want to come in and hang out?"

Come in. Hang out. Not *come in and we'll talk about it* because I know Luc and he hasn't changed so much that I think he wants to sit down and hash out our feelings over coffee. I want to grab him and ask what the hell the point of that CD was if he can't open his mouth and *say something.*

My heart hurts.

"No, I don't," I say, defeated. And because I can't help myself, because I can't think of how else to convey every emotion rolling around inside my chest, I hold on to his gaze for a moment longer and hope he can feel even a fraction of it through a simple stare. "You know, I really, really missed you," is all I say before I walk away.

THREE

Luc

Two in the morning. Another sleepless night. That's nothing new. It's not even that I can't sleep—I have meds for that, after all—but rather that I don't *want* to. I like the peace and quiet that can be found only in the middle of the night; it helps me balance out the noise and irritations of the day.

Usually, my routine is pretty consistent: I lay in bed, headphones on, and stare at the ceiling. I don't think of anything beyond the song I'm listening to, the sound of the music, the tone of the singer. Nothing special, right? No thinking about doctors or medicines or my parents' concerns or how shitty I've been feeling lately. Just me and Jim Morrison or Paul McCartney or whoever else happens to pop up randomly on my playlist.

Tonight, though, things are a bit different. I keep trying

to let my thoughts drift off, keep trying to focus on nothing other than the rise and fall of "In the Lap of the Gods…Revisited", but instead of Freddie Mercury singing about what people might have wanted from him, I find myself thinking of Evelyn. I wish I wouldn't. I don't want to. What good can it possibly do me? I know by now that it's better—for me, for everyone—if I keep my distance from people, and yet…

And yet, I've never really listened to my own advice when it comes to her. At school, before my transplant, I had no interest in friends or girlfriends or whatever. Too much damage to be left behind when I kick the bucket. But Evelyn managed to worm her way in, and I hadn't been able to stay away. She was smart and cute and so painfully shy, a prime target for some of the other girls at school, and all I wanted was to protect her. Had things been different, had I been *normal*, I'd have asked her out in a heartbeat. As it was, she deserved so much better.

Keeping my distance was so much simpler when she moved away. Ignoring a text or a letter was easy. But ignoring her when she's in town? When she's close enough that it would be a ten-minute drive at most and I could actually be *with* her? Suddenly she's not so easy to brush off anymore.

Maybe it's because she was really the only person in my life to ever treat me like…well, like me. Granted, that could be because I've always made such a point to keep my illness and the transplant from her, but—some part of me dares to hope that she'd treat me the same even if she knew. You know, that small part that I won't allow to surface.

Whatever the case may be, whatever my reasons might be, she's on my mind and it doesn't look like she's going anywhere anytime soon. I sigh and roll onto my side, curling up a little around my iPhone. Maybe I should just take my meds and go to sleep, try again for peace and quiet tomorrow. If I were smart, that would be what I would do. If I knew what was best for me, I'd follow my instinct. Especially with how shitty I've been feeling physically, and how I have a doctor's appointment tomorrow to find out *why*, and these sorts of things never bear good news for me.

Maybe that anxiety, that nervousness, that fear, is why I do find myself eventually killing the music to make a call, eager for the sound of her voice. Before I have a chance to talk myself out of it, I've dialed Evelyn's number. She gave it to me in an email and I saved it, even if I never used it. The phone is against my ear, and I'm not thinking about how late it is or that she might be sleeping. Although it takes a few rings, she answers with a sleep-ladened voice that makes me smile to myself because I'm envisioning her in her pajamas and socks with her hair a mess.

"H'llo?"

I should hang up. What do I have to say to her? A casual *hey* seems a bit much for two in the morning. Yet even as I'm thinking that I don't know what I'm doing, I guess some part of me does, because I blurt out, "I missed you, too."

On the end of the line, Evelyn takes a deep breath, in and then out. The sound of it is stupidly soothing because I can hear her tension exiting with it. There's a heavy pause before she asks softly, "Are you *actually* sorry? Did you really have a good reason?"

I let out a slow breath. A good reason? I wonder idly if she'd think so. If she'd understand why I couldn't, why I *wouldn't*. Why I had to constantly keep her at arm's length and why I should still be doing that even now. Could she understand that I never expected to live, that I didn't want to drag anyone down with me? I don't honestly know. It must be hard to imagine for someone who's never been in that situation. "I *am* sorry, Evelyn. More than you'll ever know."

More silence. I'm not used to Evelyn being silent on the phone with me. She used to be able to carry on a conversation for an hour while I kept my answers limited to *uh-huh, really, is that right.* This is almost unnerving.

"Okay. I guess I forgive you, then."

My eyes close. That's good, isn't it? Maybe, maybe not, but I've come this far. Might as well go full idiot, right? Because I have missed her. And maybe, just maybe— "You want to meet up for dinner tomorrow or something? I have errands to run, so I'll be out already."

The way her voice brightens is almost tangible. "Yeah? Okay. What time?"

My doctor's appointment—the "errands" I have to run—is when? I think about it for a moment, because all of them honestly blend together, and…right. Three. Assuming the results from a biopsy I had a few weeks ago don't reveal that I'm, like, dying all over again or something, an hour should be plenty of time. "Four? I can pick you up from your place." Evelyn agrees and we say good night and hang up.

I have no idea what I'm getting myself into.

•••

There are a lot of reasons I could have been feeling crappy the last couple of months. An infection, a cold, a need for an up in my meds... Any number of things that could be fixable to get me back to feeling as close to 100 percent as I'm capable of feeling. Yet the following day, the entire time I'm in the waiting room, my leg is bouncing a mile a minute and I can't seem to calm the rising anxiety eating at my insides.

Years and years of this, you'd think I'd be used to it. Maybe no one ever gets used to preparing for potentially bad news.

Mom had wanted to come with me—she always does—and I managed to talk her out of it. I know she or Dad would come with me to any appointment I asked them to, but that's just the thing—I *don't* want them to. They've spent enough time in hospitals and doctors' offices; now that I'm old enough to do it on my own, I don't want to waste any more of their time.

One of the nurses—Allison, I think her name is, from previous visits—pokes her head out from a door. "Luc? Come on back."

I wipe my palms on my jeans as I stand and follow her, going through the standard procedures of taking my weight, blood pressure, answering the typical slew of questions about how I've been feeling.

Dr. Nadeen is a middle-aged woman with bright red hair and freckles to match. I've always liked her, all things considered. She isn't my surgeon, but she is a specialist, and one of the primary doctors I've dealt with for years. I like to think we've got a pretty good doctor-patient relationship going, and I've gotten pretty good at reading her.

So when she steps into the room and takes a seat on her stool with a heavy sigh, I know this is not going to end well.

"Okay, Luc… I think we need to talk."

Four o'clock rolls around and I am nowhere near Evelyn's house. I have no plans of picking her up, no plans of going to dinner. Just the thought of eating makes me feel sick to my stomach. And seeing Evelyn? I don't want to be near anyone right now, especially her.

All I want to do is exactly what I'm doing—still sitting in the parking lot of the doctor's office, "A Day in the Life" on steady repeat. As though Lennon and McCartney can somehow drown out the echo of the doctor's voice, the test results. I mean, sure, I hadn't been feeling well, but I'd never thought…

You're going to need another transplant. Out of everything Dr. Nadeen said, that's really the only thing that sticks with me. Something about the transplant rejecting, some sort of medical mumbo jumbo that meant nothing to me, just—well, that. Like nothing I'd been through meant anything. Starting from scratch, going through it all over again…

I don't want to think about it. I can't. If I do, my throat tightens and my stomach knots and I feel my body teetering into panic-attack land. Thinking about it just leaves me torn between crying and laughing, but overall uncertain and so tired. I don't want to think about doing it all over again. Months and years of my life, medicines and treatments and surgeries and so much time lost in the hospital, so much time lost waiting and seeing.

"If I choose not to, how long do I have?" I'd asked.

"It's hard to say. Could be a few weeks, could be a few months."

But not even a few years.

Of course, she had said, it depended on a lot of varying factors. How well I take care of myself. If they could find some other medications to stabilize me and slow down the process. She prescribed me a new one and an upped dosage on another that I picked up at the pharmacy downstairs before I left.

Chances are, though, it would hit all at once. My heart would stop, and I'd be dead.

All I can think is that I'm going to throw up.

Eventually, I go home. There are questions from Mom and Dad, of course, about how my doctor's appointment went, but I shrug them off. I'll have to tell them eventually, but the longer I can keep from saying it out loud, the longer it won't have to seem so real to me.

Truthfully, thoughts of Evelyn don't pop back into my mind until later that evening. Not the middle of the night this time—only eight—but I'm tired and drained enough that instead of being able to push it back, I feel guilty when I think of her. We were supposed to have that dinner today. And I could tell, just from the tone of her voice, that she was excited. Stupidly hopeful. I let her down, didn't I? No, I don't even have to ask. I know I did. I let myself down. Seeing Evelyn, having her near, being able to reach out and take her hand like I used to do when she was upset about something, might have even made me feel better about the shitty news. Those were little, intimate things that always helped when we were in school.

I debate it for a long time, but eventually I pick up my phone and dial her number. In the grand scope of things, it seems stupid to be bothered over something like this, but—maybe it's something easier to focus on. Something that isn't quite as complex, isn't quite as life and death.

When she answers the phone, I don't even wait for her to speak. "I'm sorry," I say.

I'm not sure what to expect as far as her response. People aren't my strong point, and Evelyn is both the most predictable and unpredictable person I've ever met. Every time I have her figured out, she surprises me.

Like now. When all she responds with after a moment of quiet is, "What happened?" There is no anger or annoyance in her voice. Simply gentle concern.

I let out a breath. "It was…a bad day," is the only explanation I offer her. If I'm not saying anything to my parents, after all, I'm certainly not saying anything to her. I don't want to.

I can't bring myself to.

Evelyn breathes in, slow and deep, but she sounds almost wary. "All right. I guess you can make it up to me later."

I make a noise at that, noncommittal. I don't even know if there will be a later. I don't know if I want there to be. "Don't expect that anytime soon." Might as well be honest this time around. With the news I got today, I doubt I'll be feeling up to outings-I-don't-want-to-admit-are-dates for a while.

Evelyn sighs, bordering on annoyed. "Someday, you'll learn how to use your words and talk to me. Why don't you get some sleep? You sound like you need it."

Words. Talk. Yeah, sure. I'd love to be able to say that I was really looking forward to seeing her today, but I can't even begin to know how to open my mouth and make it cooperate. But she's right about one thing: I *am* tired. More tired than I've been in years, actually, which is why I just say, "Yeah, good night," and end the call. Conversation over, I put my phone down and reach instead for my headphones. "Desperado" for a desperate situation. Sometimes the most cliché music is exactly what you need, though. Something to close my eyes to, something to listen to other than the silence and my breathing.

Alone in the dark with my music, I finally force myself to think about things. I could almost cry from how tired I am, an emotional and mental thing more than anything else.

How long have I been playing this game? The first time around had been complete hell. Honestly, I don't even know how I survived it, and now—well, now they want me to do it all over again. And I worry, what if this isn't the end of it? What if it happens *again*? Though they had promised something different, I'm wondering if this will be my life: to be sick and chained to my own health. Doctors and nurses and medicines and procedures—what kind of life is that? I can't do any of the things I want to do, any of the things that other people can do. I'm worried that I'll never get to, either.

Part of me, a large part of me, I realize, doesn't want to go through it a second time. I mean, I don't *have* to, do I? I have to consent to treatment and all that. I could just tell them no, say that I don't want to, that I want to simply enjoy whatever time I have left. Not that my parents would take that lying down. I know they'd do everything in their power to force me into it, and I understand their line of thought with that, but...

Well, what are my other options? Waiting on a list again, waiting to see if anyone else dies so that I can live, or skipping out on it entirely. I think briefly about suicide, but I push that thought away as quickly as it shows up. With how my luck has been going lately, I'd probably survive it with another handicap to add on to what's already there. Not to mention my parents, who've stayed strong and resilient through all my medical problems, my anger, my resentment, would be devastated. How could I do that to them?

When I finally drift off to sleep, I'm still uncertain, still trying to figure out what I should do. I need to come up with an answer and I need to come up with it fast, I know that much.

I'm not made of much time and never have been.

FOUR

Evelyn

A lot changes in three years. I'm no longer secretly into watching My Little Pony or wanting to wear shirts with kittens and sequins. Luc—who was always kind of jaded and grumpy to begin with—seems to have sunk more into that mindset. I wish I knew why. But even after all this time, I still feel like I have a good hold of his moods, of his level of sincerity, and something in Luc's voice last night on the phone sounded so very off. Maybe it's just me. Maybe I'm looking for some excuse to forgive him because I have every right to be pissed off and admittedly my annoyance level is fairly high, but…

Something's nagging at the back of my head.

I debate it all through my schoolwork the next day. The online lessons are a blur; I have to play the videos and read the instructions twice just to get the gist of what I'm supposed to be doing. As soon as I'm done, I pop my head into Mom's room to let her know I'm going out. I drive to the store up the street, buy a bag of pretzels, and then head to Luc's house.

My heart is in my throat when I knock. It takes a few tries before I hear Luc's voice—"I'm coming"—and he opens the door. His expression twists into confusion when he sees me. The shadows beneath his eyes are more prominent today, and the way he squints against the offending sunlight suggests he's been cooped up for a while. "What're you doing here?"

I promptly hold out the bag of pretzels (his favorite—or, at least, they used to be) and a paper crane I folded out of my receipt. "I came to check on you."

Luc doesn't reach out to take them. "I'm not a kid who needs to be checked up on, you know."

"When I had the flu," I say, "you came to check up on me. I'm returning the favor."

"It's not a favor if I don't want it."

"You're a pain in the ass. You know that?"

He lifts his thin shoulders in a shrug. "I know."

I stare at him for a long moment, contemplating how much to say. That I know something is going on with his health even if he hasn't told me? Luc has always been kind of sickly and missed a lot of school. I figured he'd grow out of it. And since he hasn't…well, maybe he has lupus. Or HIV. Or something chronic. None of that would bother me. I'm also not going to blatantly say that I'm aware he's hiding something because he doesn't want me to know.

Instead I hold up the paper bird. "It's a crane."

His eyebrows slowly lift. "I can see that."

"Did I ever tell you the story about these?"

"No, but I bet you're going to." He smiles faintly, stepping aside. "Are you coming in?"

Oh! Inside? I've never actually been inside Luc's house before. I shrug and move forward to follow him down a long, clean hallway and past a living room to a set of stairs. We must be going to his room. My excitement is rapidly turning into vague nervousness. Not because I mind being in a boy's room, but because it's *Luc's* room, and the idea makes my stomach do a bunch of weird little flip-flops. I don't say anything, but I'm insanely curious to see what the bedroom of someone like Luc Argent looks like.

Luc opens the door and steps aside, allowing me to enter. His room is remarkably normal. Bed, desk, bookshelves, nightstand, dresser. The music posters adorning the wall don't surprise me. The Beatles look down from above his bed.

What does catch my eye are the butterflies. There must be a hundred of them, all pinned in display cases on the walls and the desk. Awed, I instantly forget all nervousness and go to them for a better look.

I don't know the first thing about insects. What I do know is that Luc told me years ago that he liked butterflies, collected them, but I'd never really put much thought into what that meant. There are butterflies in all shapes, sizes, and colors, and despite being under glass, they all look like they could lift their wings and fly away at any second. "These are beautiful. Where did you find them all?"

Luc pockets his hands and shrugs, walking over to my side. "Around. Most of them from various family members. Dad brings them home from business trips sometimes."

I abandon the pretzels on his desk, careful not to disturb any of the cases there. "I didn't realize so many types of butterflies even existed. Which one is your favorite?"

"That one." He points to a display case on the wall that has only a single butterfly inside. "*Papilio crino*. A Banded Peacock. Dad got it from a trip to Australia."

The Banded Peacock is a beautiful blend of black with emerald green markings. I can see why he likes it. I touch my fingers to the display case frame, letting my eyes wander across the others, pausing on a larger specimen that is easily as big as my hand. "I like that blue one up there."

"That's a Blue Morpho. Ordered it online from South America."

"Cool." I'm fascinated. This is a side of Luc I didn't know anything about, and his tone of voice is soft, content, like this is a topic he speaks about with ease and so I'm comfortable asking questions. "What made you get into it? How do you do it?"

Luc shrugs. "I don't know. I was probably around seven. It's—uh. You know. It's a long process."

"I'm listening."

"Well, you basically get the butterfly from wherever and put it in a humidity box. To loosen it up."

"Loosen it up."

"Right. Because bugs get really brittle when they die." The words are coming easier now. A hint of excitement and interest is burning at the edges of his voice. "So you put them in that box for a few days and when you take them out, they're pliable. You pin them through their thorax on this special type of board, spread their wings out, position them. When they dry out again they look like that." He gestures to the cases.

I like this. In this moment, I've forgotten about the last few years. It's just Luc and me, and I'm standing close enough to him that I could reach out and touch him if I wanted. If I were brave enough. But like every time when we were younger and the urge to lean in and kiss him presented itself, I totally chicken out. Instead I try to satisfy myself by staring at his mouth. "The next time you do it, would it be okay if I watched?"

The upturn of Luc's lips seems to fade a little. "Maybe."

"We should go to one of those butterfly houses," I say thoughtfully. "I went when I was really little. I cried because none of the butterflies wanted to land on me, though."

"Uh-huh."

I glance sideways at him, his expression softening before looking away. I stare at the origami crane still in my hands. I was going to tell him the story about them, wasn't I? "I had pneumonia really bad when I was younger," I start. "There are legends that say if you make a thousand paper cranes when you're sick, that you'll get better. I was still teaching myself to fold so, I mean, they looked pretty pathetic at first, but I did it. I made all one thousand of them." I hold out the crane to him.

Luc is watching me intently, but his expression has

morphed into a deep-set frown. "That's a nice fairy tale, but you can't actually believe it."

"Maybe." I take a deep breath. "Look. I don't know what's going on with you, and I'm not going to ask you to tell me, since you obviously don't want to. But I will ask you not to push me away anymore. Please? Even if I can't help. I just…" I gesture vaguely, lowering my gaze. "I just like being around you."

He averts his gaze. "That's a terrible idea and I can't help you with that."

"It's not a terrible idea and you *can*." I look back up at him. "Why come see me if you were going to turn around and ignore me again?"

His shoulders roll into a stiff shrug, but his voice catches, like he's forcing the words out. "Things change. I don't think this is a good idea."

I hold my ground, shoulders squaring. Refusing to budge yet. "I know you're sick."

Luc's gaze hardens; the temperature in the room seems to drop several degrees. "Conversation over, Evelyn."

"I don't care, you know." I don't move. "I mean—I *care*. But it doesn't change things. It doesn't change that I want to be near you, or that you've always been my best friend. It doesn't change anything."

The muscles of his jaw tense and for half a second, I wonder if Luc would really throw me out. He doesn't. Instead, he turns and storms out of the room himself. My eyes tear up as I follow after him. "It isn't *fair*! Why can't you just talk to me? Why won't you ever let me help?"

He laughs and turns to face me, halfway down the stairs. "Because there's *nothing you can do*, Evelyn.

There's nothing anyone can do!"

I come to a halt, staring at him. He's never yelled at me. Not once. Then again, I've never pushed him about anything like this, either. A first for us both. Maybe a last. I don't know whether to be angry or sad and I think it's a little of both, because I hate this.

In this second of existence, I hate him in the same breath that I care about him so much it aches.

The split second he's finished yelling, I can see the regret and the guilt etch across his features. "Evelyn…"

I swallow hard and keep my chin up as I push past him on the stairs. I don't say anything as I leave.

I go home and try not to think about it. I refuse to waste any more time on Luc Argent. I'm an idiot for thinking things would be like they used to be, or that I was important enough to someone who couldn't even be bothered to respond to my emails more than once in a blue moon.

I don't understand it. I don't understand him. As much as I try not to, I dwell on these things.

But I have other stuff to preoccupy myself with over the next week. I concentrate on getting through as much of my schoolwork as I can. It's senior year, I've done most of my credits already, so if I stay on track and work hard, I can finish early.

I find myself reading up on butterflies. Not because of Luc, but just because it's interesting. I color a piece of paper to match a Banded Peacock and fold it up, then crumple it and throw it into the nearest trashcan.

That part of my life needs to be over because apparently I didn't get the memo that it ended three years ago. Maybe I'm too old for making stupid animals out of paper anymore. Except that it's one of the few hobbies I've ever had, and abandoning it now leaves a sizable hole in my life. While running errands for Grandma a few days later, I bring home a stack of scratch paper from one of the recycle bins at the library and sit on the floor of my bedroom, constructing paper cranes, frogs, cats, rabbits, and anything else I can think of.

Anything but butterflies.

Mom has started coming out of her room more, a smile on her face. What this means, I don't know. Either she's finally getting over Robert, or she's been talking to him. I'm heavily suspecting the latter. Especially when she says at dinner one night, "So, Robbie and I... We've been talking."

Grandma gives a long-suffering sigh and lowers her fork. "Really, Violet? Really?"

"What?" Mom says, innocent. "You told me I should be trying to work things out."

"I meant while you were out there. Before you moved back in," she grumbles.

The rest of their words fade into the back of my brain. Mom is talking about moving back to Arizona. That she thinks they can resolve their differences and Robert says he misses us. Not just Mom, but us. Me and her.

Me.

I have to go back there. I have to go back to *him*.

I'm cold all over.

I'm going to be sick.

This, too, I try to take in stride. Try to ignore. At least until Mom comes into my room that Friday afternoon to tell me, "I'm really sorry, sweetheart. I know moving you around has got to be difficult. But I'm sure you miss Arizona, don't you? We'll be going back next weekend."

My throat constricts. We've been back in California barely three weeks. "I don't want to," I try telling her, on the verge of tears. "Why can't I stay here with Grandma?"

Of course she takes it the wrong way. That I don't want to be with *her* as opposed to not wanting to step foot in the same state as *him* again. Grandma can't really afford it long-term and Robert has the connections to get me into a better college despite the fact that Mom has never seemed to give a damn about me going to college before.

I don't want his help for anything.

I don't care about any of it. I can't go back. I can't even tell Mom why. Maybe in part because I'm terrified she won't believe me. When has she ever listened? *Really* listened?

Arizona it is, then. In one week. And I'm at Luc's door late that night, having walked all the way here after sneaking out of my room, and I feel like an absolute idiot. He doesn't want to see me. But in the end, I didn't know where else to go. I don't know who else to talk to.

With it being this late, I can't exactly knock. So I text him instead, knowing this isn't likely to go over well. *Outside* is all I say. Hoping he knows I would not have walked all this way close to midnight if it weren't extremely important.

Praying that he *cares* that I need him.

●●●

Luc

*A*nother long night. The more time passes, the worse I feel and—well, the less time there is for me to decide. Either go on a list and risk dying on it, or make my own path. For once in my life, take control of myself and decide how I want things to be. No doctors telling me what I can and can't do, no parents shadowing me to make sure I'm resting and taking my medications. No more wondering, waiting, terrified by the thought of my own mortality, dreaming that I might not wake up in the morning.

Since Evelyn stormed out of my place a week ago, I've been doing research. The upped med dosages aren't doing shit. The doctors had suspected that something was up months ago, and they put me on additional medication and adjusted what I had back then, too, to keep my body from rejecting the transplant more than was to be expected, but—nothing. No signs of improvement. Just me getting sick all over again.

I've decided I don't want to do this anymore—slowly deteriorating while I wait on a list to see if I get lucky again. I'm tired of living my life on anyone's terms but my own. There has to be another option.

I have options. I need to keep telling myself that, make myself believe it. Yes, sitting on the transplant list is one option. Putting a gun to my head is another. Simply riding out the storm and making the most of what I've got left is also on the table.

My research leads me to Oregon. Human euthanasia. The Death with Dignity Act. I've heard about it before, of course—Doctor Kevorkian and all that—but never really thought much about it. Turns out, it's legal in Oregon. Suffering from a terminal illness? They'll let you put yourself out of your misery with dignity and, I have to say, the idea appeals to me. To go before the going gets bad with a method that's guaranteed to work and be, from what I've read, painless.

Of course, there're all sorts of hoops you have to jump through and I wouldn't qualify for a bunch of them, but there're always ways around that. Always pockets to be greased, always someone who's greedy enough or sympathetic enough that they can be convinced to turn a blind eye. The point is that the medicine cocktail is legal there, which means it can be bought. Maybe not legally in my case, but it's something, and something is better than what I have right now.

Setting the record perfectly straight, I'm not thinking about killing myself.

At least, not entirely. Not yet.

But *options*, right?

The idea is there, in the back of my mind, and while I'm thinking over the choices I have, I want to get the hell out of this city. Regardless of which road I choose, I'm not going to sit in this room wasting away more days and weeks of my life.

Getting out of here is what I'm thinking about when I get the text from Evelyn. I stare at it for a long moment, taking off my headphones and frowning. I haven't seen or heard anything from her since that afternoon. For however much it bothers me sometimes, for however lonely I can feel…yeah. It's easier. Not just for me, but for her. (And, yes, I *will* make that decision for her because she has *no* idea.)

I think, of course, about ignoring her. Except what the hell is she doing outside this late at night? It's not like her at all, and that tells me something's up. Something that has me crawling out of my bed, slipping on my shoes and jacket before I head downstairs.

When I open the front door, Evelyn is seated on my front porch steps, shoulders slumped, head down. I step up behind her, uncertain, even more so when she speaks without looking at me and her voice has the barest tremor to it.

"We're going back to Arizona next week."

I slip my hands into my jacket pockets. That's for the best, isn't it? I ignore the lonely twinge in my chest. "Oh."

She presses the heels of her hands against her face, breathing in deep, before lifting her head to look at me with puffy red eyes. "I don't want to go."

Something in her expression and her tone makes me pause. My spine stiffens. "Why? What is it?"

"I don't want to go back. No—I *can't* go back. I need to…I don't know. I need to figure out a way to stay or to talk her out of it."

"What's so wrong with it? I get it's not the most exciting place, but…"

Evelyn opens her mouth, but the words don't come out. Her face has always been an easy one to read. Open and raw and honest, and what I see in her now is worry and a hint of fear. "I don't want to go back there with *him*."

The words weigh on my chest like a bag of bricks. Evelyn sounding this distraught over the situation doesn't suggest she simply doesn't care for this guy because he dresses funny or he's annoying. No. I'm getting an entirely different vibe off her right now, and it makes every bone in my body ache with anger. But just to be clear: "Are you saying what I think you're saying?"

She only stares at me. Her silence is really all I need.

What do I say to that? What am I supposed to *do*? How can I help her, protect her? Sit down and talk to her mom? Offer to let her stay here? It's not like I'm going to be sticking around for long, and my parents would have a million and one questions. I'm at a loss, and I want to reach out and wrap her in my arms, to promise that whatever was going on, I won't let it happen again. "What can I do?"

"I don't know." She looks away. "I just… I don't know. I'm sorry. This is stupid. I meant to come say good-bye."

"No, you didn't. You came here hoping I'd be able to help you." And I want to, if I could figure out how.

Evelyn rises to her feet, hugging herself tight. "Yeah, I guess. But I shouldn't have. I just have to ride it out until I'm eighteen in a month."

It's not that easy, though. No one really turns eighteen and just moves out of their parents' home, especially when they come from a family who isn't particularly well off. There's a lot more to consider than that. She would need to get a job that could support her living on her own and, let's face it, the financial world isn't friendly to people our age, especially in California. It could be months or even a year or more before she could get out on her own, and that thought…yeah, it bothers me. Evelyn means more to me than that, to simply throw her to the wolves.

"I have an idea," I say after a long moment, "but I can guarantee you won't like it."

Fuck. What am I thinking?

A small frown touches her face as she turns to look at me. "What?"

I have to avoid her eyes. "I'm going to Oregon in a couple of days."

"Okay…"

"So, you could come with me."

"Mom would never let me," are the first words out of her mouth. As soon as they've flown off her tongue, she pauses, gets it, and says, "Oh. What's in Oregon?"

I shrug. "I've heard good things, so I'm plotting out a whole road trip from here to there. I can't promise you'll enjoy it, though." What am I doing? I don't know what this trip is going to mean. What if I *do* make that decision to not come home? What if my heart gives out while we're on the road? What would something like that do to Evelyn?

Still, my desire to not see Evelyn looking so desperate and afraid, to somehow make this situation better for her, is overriding everything else.

She mulls over my proposition, biting her bottom lip. "As long as we're somewhere with wifi, I could keep up with my homework, and I don't have a lot left…"

"See? No problem."

Her hands wring together. "What happens after Oregon? It sounds like a short-term solution."

"It is a short-term solution," I admit. "But it gives us time to figure something else out."

Evelyn turns away. I study the rise and fall of her shoulders, the nervousness in her stance. Asking someone who has never done anything worse than cutting a few classes to just up and run away from home is a big deal. I get that. But she has to weigh her options. Besides, from what I've learned of her mother, she has a thing for meeting idiot boyfriends and taking off with them. The way I see it, this is fair play.

When she turns back to me, Evelyn's eyes are warm and hopeful. Without a word, she closes the gap between us and puts her warm arms around my neck. I can feel the entirety of her pressed up against me. Comfortable and soft, and it makes my heart hurt in a very different way than I'm used to as my pulse kicks up a notch. I reluctantly touch a hand to her back, closing my eyes. "Don't get mad at me if it doesn't turn out like you think it will."

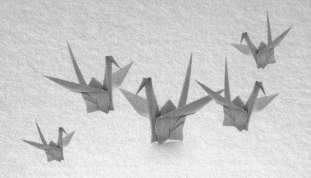

FIVE

Evelyn

Running away from home.

With a boy.

Those are phrases that describe my mother. Not me.

No, I was always the one who followed Mom wherever she went. Did whatever made her happy. I stayed behind and took care of the house while she went on dates. When she had her heart broken, I was the person who sat at her side and watched television while she lamented her loss and how alone she felt.

I never voiced to her how alone *I* felt.

Maybe that was because I told myself as long as I had Mom, nothing else mattered. She was the center of my world, even though I don't think I've ever been the center of hers.

Which is why I hope she'll understand that I can't bring

myself to go back, but that I would never want to stand in the way of her happiness with the man she repeatedly said was the love of her life.

I'm scared she wouldn't believe me anyway. I'm scared she would still choose Robert.

Tuesday night, the night before Luc and I are scheduled to leave, I sit on my bed to write her a letter. I'm leaving. I'm safe. I'm in good hands. This has nothing to do with her and everything to do with me, because I *can't* go back to Arizona and the reasons are ones I can't express to her right now. I'll have my phone, and I'll call her if she promises not to freak out or send the cops after me.

I'll be okay. I love you.

Wednesday is spent staring vacantly at the TV with Mom. I try to enjoy dinner with her and Grandma Jane. For all their flaws, these women are my family and I know they love me. I have to remind myself this isn't the last time I'm going to see them. Just a few weeks. Maybe a few months, if Luc and I can manage it. I'll be eighteen in less than two weeks and then anything Mom says or does to try to coax me back will have nothing to do with the law and everything to do with my decisions.

My choices. *Mine.*

I've done so much trying to make Mom happy. I'm not sure I've ever really made a big choice on my own that didn't involve keeping her best interests in mind.

I lie in bed close to midnight, listening to the sounds of the house settling around me. This old place is home, and I'm going to miss it to some degree. I'll miss Grandma's knitting and Mom's hysterical laughter at the same tired shows she's watched a hundred times. I'll miss her coming into my room in a pretty dress to ask how she looks right before a date. I'll miss a lot of things. But again, I remind myself, this isn't *good-bye*. It's *see you later*.

I leave the letter on the driver's side seat of Mom's car. This way she won't see it right when she wakes up. Chances are, she won't find it until she comes looking for me. It'll buy me a little bit of time to get out of town.

With a duffel bag over my shoulder, I slip through the side garage door, around the backyard, and hurry down the street to where Luc said he'd park to wait. He's standing by his car, hands in his pockets, staring at his feet. He doesn't lift his head to look at me as I approach. "You ready to go?"

All I've brought along is what I could fit in my backpack. Necessities. Clothes. Toiletries. What money I had in my savings, which isn't much. I have no clue what this trip entails, how long it'll take us, what Luc is bringing. "Yes. No. I think so." I manage a smile. "Are you?"

Luc lifts his head and peers at me, mouth twitching up weakly. "Ready as I'll ever be. You *sure* about this?"

"I'm here, aren't I?" I take a deep breath. "When have you ever known me to take a risk without thoroughly thinking it through? I should be asking you if you're sure you want me to come along."

To that, Luc only shrugs and pushes away from the car to open the driver's side door. "Let's go."

Not much of an answer. I get into the car and push my stuff to the backseat where Luc has his things. He takes a deep breath. Is he as nervous as I am? Is he wondering why he's doing this? (Why *is* he doing this? I know he won't tell me.) Is he thinking the same thing I am?

Because I think we're both crazy.

The dashboard clock reads a little after three a.m. when the car rolling to a stop in a grocery store parking lot wakes me up. I straighten in my seat, my back and neck sore from sleeping slouched against the window. We've only been driving a little over three hours. I don't remember falling asleep. "Where are we?"

Luc turns the car off, places his cell on the dashboard, and reclines his seat. "San Jose."

"We're stopping already? We didn't get very far."

"Uh-huh. But I'm tired, and we have some things to do here in a few hours."

"What things?"

He grunts, reaching behind us to grab a blanket from the backseat, which he drapes over us both. "You'll see. Get some more sleep."

I'm still tired. I'm a girl used to her eight hours of sleep every night, and I've had less than three. For that matter, the last few nights haven't been particularly restful for me, either. I settle down, nestled beneath a blanket—the same blanket as Luc, I think idly, not without a faint flutter in my chest—and close my eyes. It's cold, but I can feel Luc's warmth from here, and I can't resist the urge to reach my hand out for his beneath our covers. He sighs comfortably and doesn't pull away.

The sound of his breathing pulls me under.

SIX

Luc

What do you say in a good-bye note to your parents? I debated not saying anything, but I didn't want Mom and Dad thinking I'm dead in a ditch somewhere and reporting me missing.

I kept it short and sweet, to the point: *I really need some time to myself. Please don't worry about me.*

They'll worry anyway; that's what good parents do, and mine have always been just that. Good. Kind. Worried. *Always* worried about me. About how much I moved around, the medications I took, my diet, my happiness. I can't count the number of times before my transplant where I laid in bed, exhausted and feverish, while Mom hummed to me and petted my hair.

My phone rattles and buzzes on the dashboard as the alarm goes off, chasing away the nice memory. I bat at it tiredly while Evelyn makes a groggy noise beside me. My joints are killing me from sleeping in this position. The windows are frosted over and I can see my breath in the October air when I exhale. Ugh. "Time to get up, Evelyn."

She sighs and forces her eyes open. "Ready to hit the road?"

I pull my seat up into position, trying to stretch my cramped spine. "Ready to get breakfast. What do you like?"

Evelyn's face scrunches up into something worried and uncertain. "Whatever's cheap?"

It's not like I expected Evelyn to be able to fund half of this road trip. I have a few credit cards I'm more than willing to max out, plus money I pulled from my savings account that has been accruing interest since I was five. A college fund is pretty pointless right about now. Whether I choose to end things in Oregon or my heart gives out on its own, I doubt school is in my future.

"What do you *like*?" I ask again. Thinking back to high school, Evelyn always had a bagged lunch. We would sit shoulder-to-shoulder behind the gym, away from the general population of the school, while we ate our lunches. She always offered me her cookies or chips, and I always declined. The days I felt too unwell to eat at all, Evelyn would watch me worriedly, seeming almost reluctant to eat her own lunch.

She opens her mouth, cheeks pink, and looks down at her hands in her lap. "Um. I'm not picky. Anything is fine."

Well, that's helpful. I guess we'll stop at the first place we run into. At least, the first stop that isn't fast food, because I really don't need to be deviating too much from my diet right now. So instead our eatery of choice is a local hole-in-the-wall diner. Evelyn crawls out of the car after me, fussing with her sleep-mussed hair. I kind of like that look on her. Disheveled. It's sort of sexy.

"So"—she yawns—"it's like a twelve-hour drive to Oregon, right? But we aren't driving straight through?"

"No." I push the door open and hold it for her. "We have plenty of stops to make."

A waiter greeting us keeps Evelyn quiet long enough for us to be seated, with menus, near the window. Then she asks, "Where are we going?"

"Why don't you wait and see?"

Her nose wrinkles. "You're a pain." She picks up her menu and I do the same.

When our waiter returns, we place our orders and I lean back in my seat, eyes closed. I wish I could have slept in longer. In a bed. I'm still trying to figure out a hotel situation that isn't going to make things weird, though. I have money, but not unlimited funds, and so booking two rooms every stop of the trip is out of the question. So...a room with two beds? Is that weird, sharing a hotel room with her? Is it any different than sleeping next to each other in the car? Less privacy in a car. I don't know. We're running away together; maybe we're beyond worrying about crap like that, and I sure as hell wouldn't mind an excuse for being that close, but I don't want to make her uncomfortable.

Throughout our meal, I watch Evelyn's hand repeatedly go to her cell phone, turning it on, checking for messages or missed calls despite that it hasn't gone off once. She's nervous. I can tell by the way she bounces her leg and plays with her hair, the way she looks around and, on the occasion that our eyes meet, tries faintly to smile. Hopefully it wears off the farther we get from home.

When we're done eating, Evelyn disappears off to the bathroom while I pay for our meal. She returns looking refreshed, with her hair brushed and clipped up. I can only imagine what my shaggy hair looks like and the dark shadows under my eyes. I can't be bothered to care at this exact moment.

"I can drive if you want to sleep more," Evelyn says in the parking lot.

"No point. Our next stop isn't far from here."

In truth, our next stop is less than thirty minutes from the diner. Evelyn peers out the window at the surrounding neighborhood. I pull into the parking lot where only a handful of other cars are lined up. She's out of the car before I am, curiosity spurring her on.

"The Winchester Mystery House," she says. "I didn't realize it was so close to home."

Of course she didn't. That would require her family to ever *do* anything. Not that I've ever been here, either, but that was because Mom and Dad had issues with taking me out in public. Too afraid I'd get sick. "Well, now you know. Come on. First tour starts at nine."

Evelyn looks to me with wide eyes and childlike excitement, mouth spreading into a smile. You'd think I had taken her to Disney World. Before I can think twice, she's grabbed hold of my hand and is leading me toward the front doors and to the main desk.

Eighty bucks later and a brief explanation from our tour guide about what we're going to see, and Evelyn still hasn't let go of my hand.

I can't exactly say that I've pulled it away, either.

Evelyn

"After the death of her child and husband, Sarah Winchester fell into a deep depression and sought the help of a medium. The medium said her bad luck was due to the guns her family built, and the spirits of those who'd been killed with those guns were seeking revenge." Lowell, our tour guide, takes our little ragtag group of six down the hall, pausing at a set of portraits here and there while explaining the history of the house.

As he leads us down the halls and up a set of very small steps, I'm forced to release Luc's hand in the narrow stairwell. We're lagging at the back of the crowd, but that's okay. I can still hear loud and clear.

"These stairs feel like they're made for a five-year-old," Luc mutters, taking them three at a time.

"This whole house is kind of sad, when you think about it." I reach the top and look over my shoulder at him. "To think someone was so lonely, so depressed. To have lost all her family that way. I would think plenty of people would go a little nuts."

"Doesn't hurt that she had millions of dollars to blow on whatever she wanted," Luc drawls. He hasn't pocketed his hands, and I'm itching to take one of them again. Just to hold on to him. Before I can, he surprises me by taking my hand first and heading around the corner. "C'mon. We're gonna lose the group."

He doesn't let go for the remainder of our walk through Sarah Winchester's home. A hundred and sixty rooms, two thousand doors—some of which lead to absolutely nowhere—forty-seven fireplaces... And we don't even get to see a fraction of it. What I wouldn't give to sneak away from our tour to investigate all the areas that're closed off to the general public. I can't say that old, creepy houses are a passion of mine or anything, but I'll admit that while in Arizona, I may have snuck into an abandoned building a time or two, just out of curiosity.

Maybe the best part of the whole tour is how I don't think to check my phone even once. I've been antsy since I woke up, looking to see again and again if Mom has called. Should I call her instead? I've asked myself that fifty times today...up until Luc brought me here.

I've never really gotten to do something like this. The most traveling my family ever did was to visit other family, maybe once or twice to the zoo, or when Mom dragged me along on trips to see new boyfriends. Never for a vacation. Never just us.

But now Luc's fingers are wrapped around mine and although he's quiet, it's a calm sort of quiet. He's interested in this strange home as much as I am. What's more, I feel like we're here *together* as opposed to just me tagging along at his heels like I've done with everyone else in my life. I'm wanted. At least, I hope I am.

Running my thumb over his knuckles is a reassuring gesture for me, especially when I feel his fingers give mine an absent squeeze and he glances at me, eyebrow raised curiously. I shake my head and offer a sincere smile.

If the inside of the house could be called interesting, then the rest of the estate is simply exquisite. We're left to our own devices while we wander the original pathways Sarah Winchester constructed, stopping to look at the variety of plants, flowers, and fountains we come across. I don't know anything about plants, and neither does Luc, but we can appreciate the beauty of it.

Lowell wanders up to us while we explore with a smile on his round face. "Are you two enjoying yourselves? Any questions?"

"Just looking," Luc says in his typical short way without even glancing at Lowell. He's too busy studying the flowers we're standing in front of, although I have a feeling he's so intent on them for the sole purpose of avoiding having a conversation with this guy. Which makes me feel a little bad, so I offer him a smile.

"I think we're good. Thank you, though."

Lowell nods. He isn't exactly the most handsome of guys, but he has a comfortable smile. "Great. I just wanted to say, you two are really cute together. It's always wonderful to have young couples come here to keep the history alive."

Cute together? Oh. Well, the hand-holding probably would hint at something, wouldn't it? I notice Luc looking vaguely awkward, but he doesn't correct Lowell, and he doesn't pull away. So I keep my nervous smile in place. "Um, thanks."

He nods once, lingers awkwardly as though expecting us to magically come up with some questions for him, and then he turns to wander over to the other people who were in our tour group.

"You're so rude," I say to Luc, but it's without malice. Just an observation.

He straightens up, turning to lead me deeper into the gardens. "He shouldn't interrupt tourists when they're trying to enjoy something."

"He's just doing his job."

Luc looks at me in this patient way of his and I can't help but laugh. These little things…they're just Luc being Luc. I don't think he means to be *rude*, he's simply being him. Putting up a wall because he doesn't know what to say or how to act and he doesn't want to be bothered.

"You really want me to be nicer?" he asks.

"Hm. Can you be?"

"Of course I can."

The look I give him is nothing shy of disbelieving. *Polite* and *Luc* don't typically go in the same sentence.

I figure that's the end of the conversation. But when we pass through the gift shop, Luc stops. "Pick something out."

"What?"

"A souvenir. Pick something." He shoves his hands into his jean pockets and waits.

I frown and glance around. I can't say I'm interested in having a fake Winchester rifle or a flattened penny or whatever, so instead I pick up a book with more in-depth information on the house and Sarah Winchester herself. "Um…this?"

"Cool." He takes it from my hands and heads to the front counter. The girl working the register can't be much older than us. Hair pulled into a French braid, glasses, slender. Pretty. Her name tag says KAREN. Luc slides the book to her to ring it up and—to my surprise—flashes her a smile. It's tight and forced, but maybe I only see that because I *know* Luc. Karen behind the counter doesn't seem to notice he doesn't mean it.

I immediately see the transformation from bored gift shop clerk to intrigued female eyeing a potential catch. "Oh, hi. Is this for you?"

Instantly, my stomach somersaults into knots like a clumsy gymnast. It isn't her words that mean anything out of the ordinary; it's the way she's leaning forward on the counter to draw attention to the low V neck of her shirt, and the eyes she's giving him. If Luc notices she's flirting, it doesn't show. Honestly, he's so oblivious I doubt it dawns on him at all, and the fact that he's not glaring at her and giving short, one-worded answers suggests he's taking my advice and trying to be nicer. Damn it. This has spectacularly backfired. "No. It's for her."

"That's cool." Karen smiles at me, but her glance is brief. There's too much to enjoy about Luc's face to look anywhere else for long, what with his pale gray-blue eyes, the dark hair framing his cheekbones, and the angular line of his jaw. I don't blame her, but it does rub me the wrong way that she acts so dismissive. What if I *were* Luc's girlfriend, and she's fluttering her eyelashes at him like I don't exist?

Karen takes her sweet time scanning my book. "I'm

guessing you don't live around here."

Luc's brows twitch together, uncomfortable. "Uh… sort of. I guess. Not that far." He glances at the register, fishes out his wallet, and hands over a credit card.

"Is that right?" Karen scribbles something on the back of Luc's receipt and hands it to him with his card and my book, lashes half lowered. "Give me a call next time you're in town, then."

Finally, it seems to dawn on Luc just what it is she's doing. He takes the receipt, glancing at the phone number like he's never seen one before.

I can't help it. I whirl around before Luc has even turned to me and hurry out of the gift shop, wanting to get to the car. Angry at Karen, but mostly angry at myself for being so stupidly jealous over *nothing*. Luc is my friend. Not my boyfriend. Even if he had shown interest in her, it's not like I have some kind of claim on him.

I'm angry at myself for suddenly wishing that I did.

I reach the car, pull on the handle, and realize it's locked. And armed. The sound of the car alarm blaring fills my ears, and it's all I can do to stand there like an idiot with my hands pressed to my ears while Luc trails to the parking lot and fishes out his key to stop the noise. He's disarmed it but not unlocked it, so I lower my hands and stare at the ground.

"Did I do something wrong?" he asks, stopping in front of me. "I was trying to be nice."

I squeeze my eyes shut and breathe in deep. I can be mad at myself all I want, but I can't justify being upset at Luc. "No, no, you didn't do anything wrong. I just…"

When I look up, Luc is frowning. Not out of annoyance, but bewilderment. He tilts his head. It almost sounds like a question when he says, "You're jealous?"

"I am *not*."

For a moment, Luc just studies me. Then he holds up the receipt between pointer and middle finger and I see clearly Karen's name and number written on it, along with a little heart and a smiley face. He reaches out, tucks the receipt into the front pocket of my jeans, and then offers me the book with a slight smile.

Reluctantly, I take it.

Luc reaches behind me to open the car door for me, eyebrows raised. "Don't worry so much, Evelyn. She's not even my type."

I don't have the courage to ask him what his type is, or if I fit the mold.

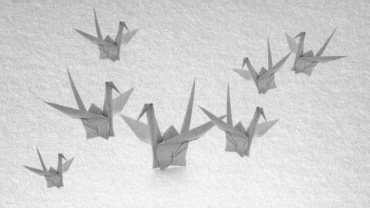

SEVEN

Luc

Lunch consists of deli sandwiches from a café and then relaxing in a nearby park. Well, I relax, anyway. Evelyn spends her time near a pond feeding the remains of her sandwich to ducks. I'll admit, watching her is fun. For as sensitive and self-conscious as Evelyn can be, she's oblivious to the world around her. She doesn't care that she looks ridiculous, picking apart her bread scraps while the ducks and geese surround her, then panicking when they venture too close and she throws the crumbs to distract them while she gets some distance. I don't blame her. Geese are assholes.

The rest of the afternoon is spent window-shopping. I ignore the fact that I'm starting to feel worn out. This is the most I've been on my feet since as far back as I can remember. I went into this trip knowing it would be physically taxing with my failing heart, but I'm not about to let it stop me. What if I die on the way to Oregon? That's going to put a damper on the trip.

Let's not explain that bit to Evelyn just yet. At some point, I won't have a choice. Especially if I choose to stay there and end my own life—which is still a very real option on the table and looking better the worse I feel. But for now, I like things as they are, seeing Evelyn this way. Smiling. Laughing. Happy. It's selfish to think I want to make the best of this and give her some good memories. I don't know if I'm going to die in a week, a month, three months...but if I were to die tomorrow, at least I could die knowing I'd given her a few good things to remember me by.

I'm regretting not doing the same with my parents. Sure, I had a last meal with them. Gave my mom a hug and a kiss good night. But I wish I'd taken her out to lunch somewhere, maybe a movie. I wish I'd gone grocery shopping with Dad one last time.

I haven't had the heart (ha) to look in-depth at my phone yet, although I've kept it on; I have unopened text messages and voicemails. Until I get a little farther from home, I don't want to risk having Mom and Dad guilt me into coming back. I don't *think* they'd come after me unless they knew exactly where I am or seriously thought I was in danger. But just in case, I'm careful about where I use my cards and instead take out cash to make my location a little vaguer.

We don't hit the road again until sometime in the early evening, which is planned; our next stop is only a few hours away. Without something to constantly distract her, Evelyn has gone back to looking at her cell every ten seconds while I drive, until I finally say, "Why don't you call her?"

Evelyn promptly shoves the phone between her knees. "What?"

"Your mom. That's who you're waiting for, right? Just call her and get it over with."

She turns partway in her seat to stare out the window. "She probably hasn't even noticed I'm gone yet."

I'm not sure what to say to that. All I know about Evelyn's mom and grandmother are what she's told me. Honestly, I think her mom's a selfish moron, but Evelyn doesn't seem to think so, and I'll keep that opinion to myself. I'd deck anyone who said a bad word about my parents, after all.

Instead I fish my iPhone out of my jacket pocket and offer it up. "Here. Put on some music."

She fumbles with the controls for a bit while I turn on the Bluetooth to the car stereo, so when she finally picks something, it comes through the speakers loud and clear.

"You have the weirdest taste in music," she mumbles thoughtfully, still scrolling through the collection of artists. "I haven't heard of most of these."

"Because you probably weren't born when they were released."

"Oh, you're so cool and edgy because of your music taste."

"I'm cool and edgy for a lot of reasons. I suppose my music taste included." I grin over at her, wiggling my eyebrows, and she responds by laughing and smacking me lightly on the arm. I don't tell her I spent all week compiling these playlists for myself. Maybe a little for her, but mostly for me. This, which will be the first and last road trip I ever take, will be immortalized by the music I've chosen to be my soundtrack. Queen and Janis Joplin and Freddie Mercury. Artists who got me through long hospital stays and doctors' appointments and countless deliverances of bad news.

It will get me through this, too, no matter what waits for me at the end of the road.

As I glance at Evelyn beside me, her eyes closed, her breathing even, I wonder if music will help her. After I'm gone, will she need songs to remind her that everything will be okay, that even as I know I'm going to break her to pieces that I've only ever wanted what's best for her? I have no idea if bringing her along was right or not. Just that it was a spur-of-the-moment decision. That it was possibly, at least in part, a selfish move, but that I'd rather her hate me for the rest of her life than go back to Arizona.

I want to ask her more about that. About Robert. About whatever it is that has her terrified to go back there. Sure, I can put two and two together and make assumptions, but that isn't enough. I just can't figure out how to get the words to roll off my tongue, or decide if it's the right thing to do. Would talking about it make her feel better? Or would reliving something traumatizing make it worse?

The whole thought process gives me a headache. I focus on the music instead, occasionally looking over at Evelyn. She doesn't sleep deeply, but I can tell by her soft breathing she's drifting in and out on the drive from San Jose. I use that as my excuse not to bring up Arizona just yet.

We don't reach our next stop until after dark. Evelyn stirs and opens her eyes as I pull off the freeway and take a few seemingly random turns into what looks like the middle of nowhere. No street lights. No homes. Just a stretch of neglected roads and abandoned buildings slouching in the night.

Evelyn sits up straight, instantly alert. "Where are we?"

"Mare Island." I pull off the main road and park behind one of the buildings. "Ever heard of it?"

"No." She peers out the window with a frown.

"It used to be an old naval base." I turn off the car and hop out, stopping to lean in and peer at her. "Now, well, it's obviously nothing."

I pop the trunk to rummage for a flashlight. Evelyn circles around to the back, hands tucked under her arms and the ocean breeze from the nearby shipyard whipping her hair into her face. "Cool. Although it looks like a dumping ground for bodies."

"That's why we're here," I drawl. "No one will ever find you."

She rolls her eyes. "Ha."

I only have one flashlight, but I doubt Evelyn will leave my side anyway. I flick the switch and a beam of light slices through the darkness. "They've been in talks for ages to reuse this whole peninsula. Figured I might as well see all of it before they kill its magic."

stays close while I lead us in the direction of the nearest building, but her eyes are wide and she lingers now again to study the graffiti-riddled walls in fascination. Given her interest at the Winchester house, I'd hoped she'd enjoy this place, too. Seems I wasn't far off.

The steps along the side are collapsed, so we head for a set in the back. I hand her the flashlight and begin scaling the stairs, keeping to the right to avoid where the rotted wood has caved in on the left.

"This is insane. You're going to hurt yourself," she hisses.

I hiss back, "Why are you whispering? Worried about ghosts?"

She plants a hand indignantly on her waist. "*No.* I'm more worried about the structural soundness of those stairs, or people who are *actually* here to dump bodies."

I give a short laugh, reach the top of the steps, and open my hands. She tosses the flashlight up to me and carefully starts to climb up. I inch two steps down in order to catch her by the elbow and help her the rest of the way.

At least inside, the flooring is steadier, though maybe not by much. The wind makes every board and windowpane creak and groan. It really does look like one day the Navy just decided to walk out and not come back. There're still rusted file cabinets in some of the rooms, old paperwork weatherworn and scattered across the floors. There are newer signs of life, though: random articles of clothing from homeless people. Condoms. One of which Evelyn stares at and wrinkles her nose.

"Oh gross."

"What, don't think this is the perfect place for sexy times?" Still, gross. We take one brief look into the bathroom and decide that was a terrible life choice, and continue on our way.

The second story to the office building involves a treacherous trip up a crumbling flight of stairs. Evelyn grips my hand when I head for it. She shakes her head.

"No way. Nuh-uh. We're high enough off the ground."

I give her a flat look and shrug out of her grasp, pushing the flashlight into her hands. "Remember when we snuck into the gym early in the morning before school?"

That coaxes a smile from her lips. "Because I wanted to see up close the Romeo and Juliet set the drama class made? I remember."

"You were so scared about getting caught or some-thing happening. I told you it would be fine, and it was fine, wasn't it?"

"That was a little different. Those set pieces weren't going to cave under our feet."

"You wait here, then. I want to check it out."

Evelyn purses her lips and stays right where she is. Probably for the best, since halfway up the steps, I'm practically on all fours trying to duck beneath falling beams and stepping over missing stair slats and I'm thinking Evelyn really isn't coordinated enough for this. Though, honestly, I think the view up here is totally worth it.

Upstairs is much less violated than down. Probably too much of a pain for the homeless to crawl up here to sleep. The holes in the rooftop don't offer much shelter from the elements and, for some reason, it's ten times chillier than it was outside. But it's so fucking cool. Long after I'm gone, everything I'm looking at now will continue to shine on. Kind of appropriate how something so endless can make a person feel so ridiculously small and insignificant. Yet I have the gift of free will. That's something the stars don't have. The free will to keep struggling to live or the free will to end it all.

"Luc?" Evelyn calls worriedly.

"I'm good." I lift a hand, tracing a line of stars. I probably shouldn't leave Evelyn down there alone in the dark for too long while I'm busy contemplating my own existentialism. When I descend the steps, Evelyn is clutching the flashlight for dear life.

"I swear I keep hearing people outside."

"Maybe. It's no big deal, though, yeah? No one's ever been murdered here or anything." That I know of, anyway. I take the light from her and head back the way we came. Half the building is inaccessible thanks to a fire set by some idiot guys exploring a few years ago, according to one of the online forums.

We start to move from building to building, with Evelyn pointing out interesting pieces of graffiti and taking guesses at what some of the unlabeled structures used to be. They're set far apart, not clustered together like any regular city road. We creep through old warehouses and through a wing of the hospital until padlocked doors obstruct us. Across the road is another building, pitch black inside thanks to the boarded-up windows, and seems to have been some sort of cafeteria or hall for events. I stop in the middle of the wide, linoleum-covered room, turn to Evelyn, smirk…and turn off the flashlight. She lets out a startled yelp, and I jog back a few steps as she reaches wildly for me.

"That's not funny!" she shrieks, but there's a laugh at the tail end of her words. I hear her footsteps coming toward me and move away, keeping just out of her grasp.

"Sounds pretty funny to me. C'mon. Hide and seek and we don't even need a hiding spot." As long as I can hear her voice, as long as I know she's not actually freaking out, this can be fun.

We dance around the room in the dark, calling to each other and making our voices echo into the abyss. She tags my arm and runs away, leaving me to chase after her this time. I can envision her in the darkness, her hair starting to fall down from its tie, and now and again when I reach for her, I feel the arch of her back, the curve of her hip, before she twists away from me again. I let her stay out of my grasp until I'm at my physical limit. When I catch her, it's with an arm latching around her waist and dragging her to me so quickly our legs tangle together and we tumble to the floor in an attempt to regain our footing.

Evelyn sags back against me, full of breathless giggles. I click the flashlight back on and shine it in her face, refusing to focus on the fact that I can feel the rise and fall of her chest as she catches her breath. "See? Told you it would be fun."

"What would you have done if I hadn't come along?" she asks, twisting around and batting at the flashlight to get it out of her eyes. "Played tag by yourself?"

"Maybe." I redirect the beam onto my face instead. "I

would've been a better opponent to play against."

She laughs and gets up, offering her hands to me. My chest is tight and my lungs hurt a little. Today has definitely been pushing it too far. It's the only reason I actually take the offered help to get to my feet.

"Did I wear you out?" she teases.

"You have no idea." I motion for her to follow. It's getting late and we still have driving to do tomorrow when the sun comes up to cover as many miles as we can. We've been messing around for hours. I lost track of time.

Except I don't head straight for the car. Close by is one last building I want to check out: a series of dorms where the Navy Seals used to stay. At least eight floors of tiny apartments smaller than the size of my bedroom back home. We trek upstairs to the top floor and Evelyn pauses at the railing, tilting her head to look up at the sky. We have the same beautiful view as I had from the second floor of the first building we explored.

All stars. All sky. Nothing else.

"It's so pretty. Makes you feel a little small," she murmurs.

"Yeah." Funny, I thought the same thing when watching it earlier, and yet with Evelyn next to me…it doesn't seem so intimidating. This moment is a "first" for me, but I don't want to dwell on what it would be like for it to be a "last." The last time I contemplate the beauty of the world with Evelyn…

I linger at her side for a minute longer, then glance behind us.

"Why don't we sleep here?"

She twists around, looking to the dorm room at our backs. *"Here?"*

"Sure, why not?"

"That's inviting someone to murder us in our sleep."

I step to the door and mess with the handle. "The lock still works. No one is coming in through the window without us hearing them. I bet we could see the sky through the glass."

She bites her bottom lip. "Guess it would be more comfortable than the car."

No doubt about it. "Then it's settled."

We march back to the car and drive it closer to the dorm building, parking around back just in case any security guards wander by. Upstairs we bring a few blankets and pillows. The floor of our "apartment" isn't the most comfortable thing in the world, but once we've made two little pallets positioned just right so we can look out the window, it isn't so bad. Evelyn settles a foot or two away from me, wrapped up tightly in her blanket, and I watch her watching the window.

"I had fun today," she whispers.

Deep breath. My whole body is tired and protesting all the day's physical exertion. It's only going to get worse. But Evelyn is within reach, so close I could bridge the gap between us and touch her face, her arm, her hair... I'm exhausted and I'm more content than I can remember being in a long while. "Yeah. So did I."

EIGHT

Evelyn

I dream of Arizona. Of blistering hot afternoons. Opening all the windows to let in some air while I made dinner, hair pulled back, leaning over the stove. Mom is in the shower. Robert comes into the kitchen behind me and I say, "Food will be done in ten."

He says nothing. Stops behind me. Braces his hands on the counter on either side of the stove. He's so close I can feel his breath falling across my ear and neck and it makes me go still. He leans into me, the entire length of his body pressed against the back of mine. This nearness makes my brain stop working because I don't understand it, because it makes my skin crawl.

"You're a really good cook," he says.

I'm fifteen. Old enough to understand this doesn't feel okay at all. But when I try to rationalize, what he's doing isn't *technically* wrong, right? He isn't touching me anyplace inappropriate. He's fully dressed. He isn't saying anything out of bounds. Yet every nerve in my body is wound tight and if I had room to edge away from him, I would.

He pulls away just as we hear Mom come down the hall before turning into the kitchen. But I can still feel him there. Pressed against me, breathing me in…

I wake to the sound of a creaking door and can't fully chase the nightmare away because it wasn't a nightmare, but a memory. A recollection of the first time something happened with Robert that I couldn't explain. Things escalated so subtly and slowly that, toward the end, I still wasn't sure if it was all in my head.

I swallow hard. Luc is moving around the room and I sense him stopping, leaning over me. When I open my eyes, a bearded man in a fisherman's cap is inches from my face.

A scream tears out of my lungs on pure instinct.

I scramble back. Adrenaline courses through every inch of my body as he advances, wildly waving his hands. I pinch my eyes shut and kick out as hard as I can.

"Hey!" Luc's voice cuts through the room like a knife. My attacker backs up, shoves his hands in the air and stammers, "I-I was just making sure she was alive!"

Luc rushes to my side, and I scramble to my feet, gripping hold of his arm. Never mind this guy is bigger than Luc and probably outweighs him by a good hundred pounds, Luc's shoulders are squared and tense and he's trying to push me behind him.

"Yeah, I'm sure."

The homeless man bobs his head as he backs for the door, apologizing over and over until I'm starting to believe him and I feel bad. Then again, I don't know of anyone who wouldn't be a little freaked out to wake up to a complete stranger invading their personal space. When he's gone, Luc turns, looking me over with a deep-set frown. "Are you okay?"

I sigh, hands still trembling from the rush. "Yeah. Sorry. I think I overreacted. He just startled me. Where did you go?"

"I went to grab some snacks from the car. You sure you're all right? You're white as a ghost."

I glance past him at the door. "Actually, I think I feel a little bad. Maybe he wasn't trying to hurt me."

Luc grunts. "Maybe. Let's get out of here. We slept later than I meant to."

Together we pack up our sleep stuff and carry it to the car. The homeless man is peeking out at us from one of the first floor dorm windows, and I would say he's probably scared judging by the way he ducks out of sight when we make eye contact.

Maybe he isn't all there. Maybe he would've tried to hurt me, but I don't really think so. I have a feeling my nightmare didn't help matters. I glance at Luc, who's busy getting everything to fit back in the trunk. He isn't going to agree but…well…

I dig around in the front seat and compile a baggie of snacks, a bag of chips, and two bottles of water. Not much, really, and I feel vaguely guilty considering Luc is the one who paid for it, but I'll make it up to him. When I open the dorm door, the man shrinks away a little and shakes his head.

"Wasn't tryin' to hurt anyone. Honest. Just seen guys bringing gals out here and leaving 'em before."

"I'm sorry I screamed." I offer up the food. He slowly lowers his hands and stares at me, uncertain, but that doesn't last long before he reaches out and takes it. He doesn't say thank you but that's okay. I figure we're kind of even now.

When I emerge, Luc is standing by the car with his arms crossed and eyebrows raised. "You're something else, you know that?"

My cheeks grow hot. "He was hungry. I felt bad for scaring him."

The way Luc watches me is somewhere between exasperated and amused. If I didn't know any better, I would think there's some sort of sentimentality in the way he says, "Of course you did."

We slide into our respective sides of the car while I ask, "What's that supposed to mean?"

"It means you would forgive someone for throwing you into a beehive if they said they didn't mean it."

I slouch back in my seat and buckle in, trying not to pout. "I would not."

"You so would." Luc laughs and starts the car.

"Maybe you should consider yourself lucky. You're a douchebag, and we wouldn't still be friends if I didn't forgive you as many times as I have."

"This is true. It's also why I think you should be meaner."

I hadn't realized I left my phone in the car. While Luc is taking us down the street away from Mare Island and onto the freeway, I dare myself to turn it on. Not sure whether to be surprised or not to see missed calls. Twenty of them, in fact, all from Mom. I close my hands around the phone, debating what to do. I don't say anything to Luc. I won't call her while he's sitting here because I don't know how the conversation will go. I was so wound up in wanting Mom to care about my leaving that I didn't actually put much thought into what to say to her when we finally spoke.

We stop outside Sacramento to grab some food and take a brief stroll around Old Town Sacramento, watching the Delta King Showboat cruise down the river, and admire all the old architecture and history the town has to offer.

Luc leaves me outside for a few minutes while he ducks back into a costume store called Evangeline's, and I take the opportunity to slip around the corner and fish out my phone.

I stare at the screen. I'm not any surer what to say to Mom now than I was this morning, but I need to let her know I'm all right.

The phone rings only once before Mom's voice is on the other line. "Evelyn?"

"Hey, Mom." And I add quickly, "I'm fine."

"What in heaven's name has gotten into you?" I hear the strain in her voice, the fact that she's been crying. "Where are you?"

I glance at a WELCOME TO OLD SACRAMENTO sign hanging nearby. "We drove through San Diego about an hour ago." Lying is not my strong point, but I think it sounds convincing.

"We? We *who*?"

"I'm with a friend." Speaking of—I see Luc coming out of Evangeline's and heading toward me. "Look, I just wanted to let you know I'm okay. Nothing's wrong. I just…I need you to trust me and let me do this, okay?"

Mom scoffs. "You're with that *guy*, aren't you? The one who came by the house. What would make you think it's okay to run off on me with some boy?"

The way she says it makes tension slide through my shoulders. *Some boy*. I don't feel like she's worried about me at all. She's more affronted that I left *her*.

"*You* did, Mom."

I hang up just as Luc stops in front of me.

He raises an eyebrow. "Everything okay?"

I'm blinking back tears as I turn off my cell and put it away. Let her call back. I'm not going to answer. Even as I'm struggling not to cry, I'm trying to offer Luc a smile. "Yeah. Everything's good."

He says, "Uh-huh," because he doesn't believe me. But I'll say it's one of the nice things about Luc: he rarely pushes when he knows I don't want to talk about something. It's a favor I try to repay, but then again I tend to be a lot more forthcoming with information than he is. There's so much I don't know about him, about his family, his life, and I feel like he has a much better grasp on me and mine.

I try to change the subject and avert my train of thought. "Where're we heading next?"

Luc shrugs. "Redding."

"Where's that?"

"About three hours north, if traffic is okay."

We cross the cobblestone street to where we left the car along a row of parking meters. There's still an hour left on our meter, but I guess it'll be nice for the next person coming along. "What's in Redding?"

Luc shakes his head, smiling. "You are the most impatient person I know. Stop jumping ahead. Enjoy what we've got here and now."

I get into the car with a thoughtful frown. "Here and now is a three-hour drive."

He starts the car and gives me a long look whose meaning I can't place. "Enjoy it. Sometimes, it's all you have."

With traffic and the rain that hits us just outside Sacramento, it takes us closer to four and a half hours to reach Redding. We pull into the parking lot of a hotel called the Thunderbird Lodge and head inside. I point out, "We passed four other hotels and yet you chose this one." The oldest-looking one.

Luc glances at me and shrugs. "Why do you think that is?"

Honestly? "Probably because you thought the name was cool."

He grins and steps inside. "Sounds legit. Figured it'd be nice to have a real room and a shower. We smell like car air freshener."

I don't doubt that, but Luc pointing it out makes me blush self-consciously. I won't argue the idea of having a real bed to sleep in, at least.

The lobby is moderately sized and is cozy, just old. The rugged stone fireplace reminds me of Grandma Jane's house. The clerk at the counter is a graying woman with a friendly smile. "Hello, there. Welcome to the Thunderbird Lodge. How can I help you?"

Luc doesn't waste time before offering his driver's license and credit card. "Just a room. Two nights."

It'll be strange staying in one place for more than a few hours, but I can't say I'll miss being cooped up in the car and on the road.

"Absolutely. Just so you know, all rooms have coffee-makers and cable TV. There're on-site laundry facilities just down the hall, and I'll write down the wifi password. I know how you young people can't live without the wifi."

Luc snorts, and I can't help but smile. "We do like the wifi," I agree, somehow managing to keep my voice even.

She gives us our key and directs us to a first-floor room at the back of the building. Luc circles around with the car until we spot our room number. We carry our bags inside and in sync we pause, both studying the room's single bed. Luc didn't specify how many we needed, but then again, the clerk didn't ask.

"Should we ask for a different room?" I ask slowly.

He sighs and dumps his duffel bag on the bed. "Nah, forget it. I'll sleep on the love seat."

"You paid for the room. No way."

Luc shrugs. "Not a big deal. I really just wanted a shower." He unzips his bag and pulls out a clean set of clothes. Given that we've been wearing the same things for a few days, I'm more than eager to peel out of my T-shirt and jeans. The whole sharing-a-room-with-a-boy thing is going to make this a little weird, and I'm going to have a hard time not picturing Luc—naked—in the adjoining bathroom.

Okay, rephrasing. Were it any other guy, it would be weird. With Luc it's just...nerve-wracking. And a little embarrassing. I'm not going to sit here and imagine him naked in there. Nope.

"Go get a shower, then." I sit on the edge of the love seat that I do not intend to let Luc sleep on. "I'll get one when you're done. Are we staying in tonight?"

He shrugs and heads for the bathroom. "Might as well relax. We'll grab dinner and go to our destination tomorrow morning."

I open my mouth to ask what our "destination" is, but the bathroom door closes before I have the chance. Not like he would tell me anyway.

Luc

The shower is heaven. The heat chases some of the ache from my body, and it's a relief to scrub my scalp until I feel like I've worked loose the last few days' worth of grime. Sleeping in a place like an abandoned military dorm didn't do much for either of us keeping clean.

Funny how stupid things like this make me think about home. Before I left, I tried to remember all the details of everything that would be my "last time" in case I never made it back home. The last time I ate dinner at the table with my parents. The last time I slept in my own bed. The last time I sat at my desk and worked on a butterfly, adjusting the position of its wings and pinning it with precision.

Now that I think about it, I don't remember relishing my last shower. I don't remember the last thing I ate before leaving or the last time I played a video game or read a book. All little and insignificant things, but I kind of regret not paying closer attention now, just in case I never see or do them again.

What will my other "lasts" be like, I wonder? The last time I see the sun rise or the last time I go to sleep, sure that I'll wake up. The last time I hear my parents' voices. The last time Evelyn will smile at me and hold my hand.

God, it pisses me off when she does things like that. When she looks at me like I'm a real person. Someone she finds interesting and enjoys being around. It infuriates me not because it's bad, but because of how it makes me feel. I hate that she's the most forgiving girl I've ever met, because it means I have no real reason for keeping my dying heart a secret from her.

I just don't want to see her cry.

I never wanted to give a damn about anyone. Least of all her. Now I'm dwelling on how it's going to feel the last time I see her face.

Am I really capable of doing that willingly? Of looking at Evelyn and saying, *this will be the last time*, and ending my life?

The hot water is fading, and I don't want to waste it all so she gets stuck with a cold shower. I finish rinsing and get out, toweling dry to the best of my ability. The mirror is defrosting, leaving me to stare at my own reflection. Messy dark hair in need of a cut (says my mother). Too skinny body. Long limbs.

For a while after my surgery, when I started the recovery and therapy phase of having a new heart, I looked pretty good. I *felt* good. I had energy and I could get through a day without feeling feverish or tired. Those good days are getting fewer and fewer and the doctors said it was a bad sign. Rejection is a normal thing with organs but they give you some meds, run some tests, get your body stable, and send you home again. But when it happens again, and again, and again—a long-term loss of function over time—it becomes chronic.

Wait for another heart despite that getting the first one was a stroke of luck…or wait for the time I go into the hospital with symptoms and don't get to leave again? With no definitive timeline of how long I have left, it's unsettling.

It's terrifying.

Fuck that. I'd rather run myself into the ground enjoying what time I have left.

I slide my fingers along the upraised scar down the center of my chest. Evelyn has never seen it. I want it to stay that way. I want to keep all this as far from her as I can, for as long as I can. Which is why I pull on a clean shirt with my sleep pants and socks before emerging.

Evelyn is sitting at the foot of the bed, shoes discarded on the floor, her knees pulled to her chest and arms wrapped around them. She looks like a kid, staring at the TV like that, so absorbed and smiling to herself at the sitcom she has playing. I find myself watching her long enough that she notices I'm there. Her eyes meet mine, and she draws her bottom lip into her mouth.

I clear my throat. "Shower's free."

She gets to her feet, grabbing an armful of folded clean clothes and trotting past me into the steamy bathroom. I exhale. Need to get myself together and stop thinking about things I shouldn't think about. Like how in a few seconds, Evelyn is going to be naked with nothing but a thin wall separating us and—yeah. Let's not let that thought go any further.

Though that leaves room for other thoughts. Like how it would be to live a normal life. How things might be different if my body wasn't letting me down. Maybe I'd be in college and Evelyn would come to my place for dinner. I could take her out on dates. Maybe take her to stupid Senior Prom or whatever at school. Because she would probably like things like that, wouldn't she? Maybe I'd even enjoy it a little, even if only to see her happy. I could make my parents proud and *be* something other than a past-due medical bill.

I rub at my eyes and make my way over to the bed, flopping down with a sigh. Not as comfortable as home but it sure as hell beats the car. Maybe it's because I'm feeling tired and *not right* that I finally grab my phone to see what messages I have been ignoring from Mom and Dad. I miss the sound of their voices.

I have fifteen voicemails, twice as many missed calls, and a ridiculous number of text messages.

Luc we're worried about you

Please call home

Let us know you're okay

Sweetheart this isn't funny please call

We need to know you're okay.

Vallejo???

Right. They're smart; they probably pulled up my credit card activity to see where I've been. I had a feeling they'd do something like that. Ultimately, I hadn't thought that it mattered. I left a note. They know I wasn't kidnapped or something.

I swipe my thumb across the screen and breathe in deep. My chest hurts. It's a deep ache that might not even be anything to do with my heart and everything to do with the anxiety that's been building behind my ribs since my biopsy results came in.

When I call, Mom answers on the first ring. "Luc!"

"I'm okay," I say quickly, wanting to alleviate that worry right away. "I'm sorry. I just wanted to let you know that."

"Do you have any idea how worried sick we've been?" she asks, voice choked with emotion. "Your dad and I have been driving all over town, calling all the hospitals… Baby, what are you *doing*?"

My eyes squeeze shut. My doctors can't legally tell my parents anything anymore now that I'm over eighteen. But I have a feeling if they pushed hard enough, they could get Dr. Nadeen to spill enough information to put the pieces together. "I don't honestly know, Mom. I'm trying to… I just had to get away."

"Is this about your doctor's appointment? Your results?" Can't blame her for sounding afraid to ask. "What did they say?"

I'm a great liar, but lying to Mom isn't something I want on my conscience right now. "I think you know what they said."

Mom drags in a shuddering breath, and I know what comes next. Between my parents, Mom is always the one who squares her shoulders, stares bad news in the face, and begins tackling it head-on. No time for feeling sorry for yourself. "Okay. All right. I have phone calls to make. We need to get you in to Dr. Nadeen and see if there's—"

My stomach lurches. "No, Mom."

"What?"

"I can't. I just…" I run a hand down my face. The shower has turned off in the bathroom. "I'm not…in a good place right now, okay? Just need some time to myself to figure things out."

"You shouldn't be going through this alone." Mom sounds desperate to keep me on the phone, to keep me talking. "This affects all of us as a family. Let us help you."

"You've always helped," I assure her. "But not this time."

"Luc—"

"I love you, Mom. I'll call back in a few days, okay?"

Before she can argue, I hang up and stare at the ceiling, willing my heart not to give out like I feel it's going to. Was calling selfish? By pushing my parents away, am I making it worse for them? As much as I want to limit the casualties of my death, I'm feeling less and less confident in how to go about doing that.

The bathroom door opens and Evelyn emerges, dirty clothes folded just as neatly in her arms as the clean ones were…and I'm staring at her.

Don't get me wrong: even when we were younger, I *liked* how Evelyn looked. She was awkward, wore clothes that never flattered her, and her hair was always frizzy and dull. But I liked the curve of her face and the way she smiled. And I liked her big brown eyes because she always looked at me so intently, like nothing else existed in the world. She's put on some weight and filled out in the years she was gone. Her hair is longer but better taken care of; soft-looking, wavy, still a bit out of control, which is probably why she wears it up most of the time. She still has a warm smile and a way of looking right through a person.

I don't know what it is about this exact moment, whether it's because I was so caught up in depressing thoughts, because I'm homesick, because I'm just *sick*, or whatever, but I'm looking at Evelyn as she steps into the room in old, worn pajamas and her hair hanging in long wet tendrils down her back and around her face, her socks don't match and…I think she's beautiful.

She sets her clothes on top of the dresser—I figure we'll do some laundry on-site before checking out of the hotel—and catches my gaze, a frown worrying at her brow. "Why are you staring at me like that?"

Telling her she looks nice would go against this whole keeping-her-at-arm's-length thing I've been going for and failing miserably at, so I shrug it off. "You smell better now."

She snorts. "Too bad you don't."

"I smell like a princess," I say with a yawn, stretching out until I can grab a brochure for some of the local eateries on the bedside table. "What sounds good for dinner?"

"We still have snacks in the car." Evelyn takes a seat beside me and then lies back so we're shoulder-to-shoulder, looking through the menu together.

"Boring. Might as well make the most of it while we're here." I skim through the selections, which aren't anything terribly exciting; typical diner food, for the most part, but at least a few of them deliver and it means we don't have to go back out.

We pick two dishes to share and Evelyn places the order, and while we wait, neither of us moves from each other's side, lying there staring up at the ceiling. If I turn my head just slightly, I can almost smell her shampoo.

She finally rolls onto her side to ask, "What made you decide to take this trip?"

That's a tricky question. One that I can't really answer without it being a direct lie or incredibly vague. *I'm dying and I wanted to do something on my own before it happens. I want to figure out* how *I want to die.* "Seemed like the thing to do. I've never gone off and done something like this by myself."

"You aren't by yourself, though; I'm with you."

"You weren't supposed to be," I point out. "But I more meant without my parents."

Her lashes lower. She absently toys with the hem of my sleeve. "Oh. Because they worry about you?"

I'm not entirely sure how much Evelyn knows and chooses not to bring up. When we were younger, she knew something was wrong with me. Although I know she wanted to, she never asked questions. Never pushed me for answers and certainly never worried or fussed over me like Dad and (especially) Mom do. It was something that drew me to her, the fact I could be myself without being treated like some kind of fine china.

The urge to tell her everything is overwhelming but

extremely brief before I cram it into the recesses of my head. Like hell I'm going to say anything. Evelyn is the only one I can be normal with. The only one I can chase around Mare Island in the dark, the only one who would hold my hand just because she wants to be near me while we wander the halls of the Winchester Mystery House. I can't stand the idea that she might ever look at me the way my parents do. It makes my chest hurt in a very different way.

"Yeah, I guess so," I say, not looking at her because sometimes the way she looks at me is too difficult to make sense of.

"You don't want to talk about it, do you?" she asks.

I counter with (perhaps unfairly), "Do *you* want to talk about Arizona?"

"Touché." She plays with a loose thread on my shirt while we listen to the silence until our food arrives with a knock at the door.

Typical diner food, like I suspected. We sit on the bed with the television going, sharing each other's meal while watching a movie I ordered on pay-per-view. By the time we're done, I'm exhausted but pleasantly full and the dull ache in my body from earlier today has mostly subsided.

Evelyn clears off the bed while I grab a spare blanket from the closet and head for the love seat. I'll have to let my legs rest on the arm of it, but that's okay. Still beats the car. I can feel her eyes on me as she says, "I told you I would take the couch."

My shoulders roll into a shrug as I drop down onto the cushions. "I said it first."

A glance in her direction shows her frowning even as she pulls back the covers. "You know, we slept next to each other in the car. This really wouldn't be any different."

I consider that, but don't point out that in the car, we had an entire console separating us. In a bed? Nada. "Yeah, it really would. Get some sleep, Evelyn."

She slouches down, pulling the covers up to her chin. "Yeah, well. Just so you know, I wouldn't care. There's plenty of room."

I give her a look. "Are you *asking* me to sleep next to you?"

Her toes wiggle beneath the covers as her gaze flicks to me, away, to me, away again. "Maybe."

I sigh and roll my eyes, but only because I don't want to openly admit that sounds like a *fantastic* idea. The couch isn't comfortable anyway. "All right, all right." She doesn't even try to hide the smile on her face as she draws the blankets back on my side of the bed. I'm careful to keep on my half, not touching her, even though I want to. I definitely want to. I think she would even be okay if I did, but boundaries, right? "Better?"

"I should be asking you that," she says, rolling onto her side to face me.

Well, it is more comfortable, yeah. So long as I don't dwell too much on the idea that a girl I'm attracted to is within easy touching distance, in a bed, which sort of naturally leads to other thoughts. "Go to sleep."

After she has flicked off the bedside lamp and—just like she did in the car—slipped her hand over mine and closed her eyes, I watch Evelyn in the dark. The way her breathing evens out as she drifts off, the shape of her mouth and how soft it looks, like it'd be perfect for kissing. Eventually, I let my fingers curl around hers.

I try not to let myself feel guilty for enjoying these little things.

NINE

Luc

In the night, Evelyn gravitates toward me, steadily closing the gap between our bodies. I don't want to admit maybe I inched closer, too; it's not like I tried to get away or anything. When I open my eyes, I see her curled up at my side, my arm being hugged against her chest and her cheek resting on my shoulder.

I'm not surprised. I'm also not sure what I'm feeling but—warm, content, happy and…sad, maybe?

For a while longer, I let her sleep. I check the messages on my phone, since it doesn't require me to move, and text Dad to check in. *Still fine. Please tell Mom to stop worrying. I'm ok. Love you.*

In the same breath as I'm doing that, I'm pulling up the browser on my phone to do some more research. I started searching things on euthanasia—in Oregon, specifically—

before this trip. The Death with Dignity Act, they call it, and I wonder why anyone thinks there's anything dignified about dying no matter how you go about it.

The idea of killing myself is the second most terrifying thing I've ever faced.

The most terrifying thing is death claiming me out of nowhere, of having no say over it.

I'm scared of suffering and having my choice taken from me.

A forum I come across has a pinned post at the top of the page linking to several blogs of people who have either chosen euthanasia, or have family members who have. Most of them are middle-aged or older, but not all. People terminal with AIDs, Parkinson's, MS, cancer, a ton of other diseases I've never heard of. I don't see anyone else in the same boat as me.

One of the blogs I read through is written by a sixty-something woman named Marilyn. The header to her page is a photograph of herself and her husband, diagnosed with ALS two years ago. He decided he wanted to die on his own terms, before he became a burden on his wife and children and grandchildren.

The entries read so much like a private journal that I feel almost awkward reading it. Marilyn doesn't skimp on the unpleasant details, like the loss of his bodily functions or the end of their sex life due to his condition. She writes about her thoughts of frustration, of loss, grief, hopelessness. Of how horrified she was when he came to her with his decision to utilize the state's laws regarding medicinal suicide. She writes about how he changed his mind at the last minute.

Psych evaluations were passed. Medicine was obtained. And he changed his mind.

Once I've gone through the blog from beginning to end, I select the *contact* link at the top to bring up a blank email. What should I say? By the blog entries, it's only been a month since her husband passed naturally. I'm likely prodding at fresh wounds.

I keep it short and simple. Introduce myself, tell her how I found her blog, that I'm sorry for her loss, and that I'm considering ending my life as well and would she be willing to answer some questions for me and share her experiences.

I turn off the screen and exhale through my nose, looking at Evelyn and watching her for a long moment, resisting the asinine urge to reach over and brush the hair out of her face, or to lean in and press my lips against her forehead. Wondering how she would feel if I *did* choose that path, if she would understand.

"Hey," I say softly, "it's time to get up."

Evelyn

Luc's voice doesn't wake me right away. It etches into the corner of my dreams, a gentle reminder I'm asleep, and I make a soft and plaintive noise as I burrow my face against his arm. "Hmm?"

"Let's get a move on," Luc murmurs. His tone is milder than usual and brings a smile to my face.

My eyes flutter open. I say, "Oh," when I realize exactly what he's said, and then "Oh…" again when I realize just how close we are. I lift my head off his shoulder, too sleepy to be fully embarrassed. "Good morning."

"Morning." He tilts his head, studying me. "You hungry?"

I push myself to my elbows, still trying to chase the sleep from my brain. Luc is so warm that I really don't want to get out of bed yet. "I guess a little."

"I'm starving." He rolls away from me and out of bed in one fluid motion. I close my eyes, already aching for the warmth of having him near.

"Okay. They have that diner, if you want. Or I think we passed a grocery store a few blocks away."

"Diner," is all Luc says as he grabs his bag and trots for the bathroom, disappearing behind a closed door.

I watch him go until the door is shut before rolling onto his side of the bed. It's warm. I curl up there, pressing my face into Luc's pillow that smells of damp hair and shampoo and soap. I could fall asleep here all over again, but…right. We have plans, even if I have no idea what those plans are. Luc mentioned back in Sacramento that we'd be coming back to the room at the end of the day so I can look forward to another night of sleep like last night.

Reluctantly I roll out of bed, catching sight of myself in the mirror above the dresser. Yikes. How did he not laugh at my hair? I shove my fingers through the waves, trying to make some sense of it, and end up settling for tying it up instead.

Luc emerges a few minutes later, freeing up the bathroom for me. After I've changed, we drive to the diner and enjoy a very diner-y breakfast of eggs, bacon, sausage, and toast. Luc sips his water while I down two glasses of ice-cold milk. He says we're going to Turtle Bay. I leave our waiter's tip folded into origami turtles.

Big surprise that he doesn't tell me what exactly Turtle Bay even *is* as we're pulling into the parking lot. Turtle Bay Museum is what the sign above the front desk reads. Luc pays our admission and I grab a pamphlet. Entertaining and stimulating exhibitions and programs, including a nursery, gardens, some special kind of bridge, and rotating exhibitions. Actually, it sounds like my kind of place.

As we walk deeper into the building to begin our day, I show Luc the brochure. "Hey, look. Part of the year they have a butterfly house."

Luc stops in his tracks, frowning. "It's open now, right?"

"No. It's closed until May." I pause. "Judging by the look on your face, I'm guessing that's why you wanted to come here."

His pout is kind of cute, really. "One of the reasons, yeah. Whatever. There's other stuff to see."

I feel bad, even if it's not my fault. We wander the halls of the *Art of Man's Best Friend* exhibit, which seems to cheer him up a little and takes my mind off the butterflies. I've never been a creatively inclined person, making stuff out of folded paper not included. So the detail put into some of these pieces is fascinating to me. Fur strokes and colors I never would have thought to use.

The museum itself takes us a few hours to get through,

since I insist on playing with every interactive piece they have. We skip the nursery but hit the botanical gardens where we at least get to spot a few wild butterflies among the flowers.

"What's this one?" I ask, pointing to a brown-winged one. Luc comes up behind me, leaning over my shoulder.

"A California Sister. They're common to central California."

"Oh. What about the flower it's on?"

Luc makes a face. "Do I look like a flower expert to you?"

I turn my head just slightly, startled by how close it puts our faces. "You never know. You don't look like a butterfly expert, either."

"Touché. What do I look like?"

He's so close. I could lean in half an inch and kiss his jaw. It brings me back to sitting behind the gym with our lunches, shoulder to shoulder, looking to my left and finding Luc engrossed in a book or a homework assignment. The number of times I've desperately wanted to kiss him and have had the opportunity to do so has to be up in the hundreds by now. "Like someone who listens to a lot of old music. Like Luc."

"Like Luc," he repeats, vaguely amused. "Well, you aren't wrong."

We meander through the rest of the gardens, and I'm starting to notice what's felt off today. Luc has his hands in his pockets, making it impossible for me to hold one of them. I don't get the impression it's because he's trying to keep his distance from me, exactly, but more...

"Are you feeling okay?"

His spine straightens at the question, like he's become self-aware that he's slouching and looking fatigued and is trying to play it off. "Yeah, I'm fine. Just a little worn out."

Fair enough. We've had a busy few days, although I can't say I'm tired enough to have it show. Still, Luc's never been the healthiest person, and I can't help but wonder if it's starting to catch up with him. He probably won't like me asking, so I just reach a hand out to brush the hair back from his face without thinking. "We can head back to the hotel, if you want."

He shakes his head. "I want to see the rest of the gardens first. And the Sundial Bridge."

Arguing with him isn't going to get me anywhere, so I decide we'll keep at it. We walk the rest of the gardens, stopping to admire some of the plants and read the informational plaques. When we leave, it's only to get into the car and drive to the nearby bridge, which is, in fact, shaped like a gigantic sundial.

"I guess if the world ever does have a zombie apocalypse and we lose all electricity," I say as we sit on the hood of the car and watch the traffic go by, "we can count on the good old bridge to tell us the time."

Luc makes a tired but amused noise. "Uh-huh. Because wind-up watches aren't good enough."

"Shut up."

He nudges me with an elbow, a lazy smirk on his face. "I think the sundial is telling us it's dark outside and we should be heading back."

I slide off the car hood, turning to face Luc and offering my hand. Surprisingly, he takes it and gets to his feet as I say,

"You've been quiet today. You sure everything's all right?"

"Everything is fine." He looks down at our joined hands like he isn't sure how that happened. "I'm just… tired, you know? No big deal."

My fingers squeeze his and then release. Luc drives us back to the hotel. We had a late lunch and he seems drained, so we skip dinner all together. I offer Luc the bathroom first but he waves me off. When I come out, he is already in bed, not having bothered to do more than kick off his shoes.

"Luc? Bathroom's free," I say, but he only makes a low noise that suggests he's fine just how he is. Silent, I lock the door and turn off the lights before crawling into bed beside him. He isn't fully asleep, really, but enough that he only says "Mm-hmm," when I tell him good night. I cover him up and take his hand, but tonight, he doesn't squeeze back.

I'm up bright and early, trying to get in some homework before Luc wakes up and we pack to leave. I've been slacking the last few days. Even if I'm close to being done, it's no excuse for letting it pile up.

Luc seems to be more himself for at least the first thirty minutes of our day, but after we've had breakfast and loaded the car, I'm noticing he's sluggish again. Dragging his feet.

"I told you, I'm fine," he grumbles as we get into the car and I ask him if he's okay.

He doesn't sound fine. Maybe I'm not a pro at deciphering Luc's moods, but I can always tell when something is just *off.* "Why don't you let me drive?"

He breathes in, out, looking ready to protest but—
"Yeah. All right."

Definitely something wrong. I don't hesitate to switch spots. "Maybe you ate something bad?" As unlikely as that is. We shared our room service meals and our orders at the diner were pretty similar.

Luc agrees—"Maybe"—as he settles into the passenger seat. "I think I just need to sleep it off."

While Luc closes his eyes, I hook up his iPhone and let it play randomly so he has something enjoyable to soothe him. Maybe he hasn't been sleeping much? Or could be that he's homesick. I really don't want to think it's anything to do with his mystery illness. He plays it off like it doesn't affect him.

Still, I let Luc sleep while I drive. Our destination is Crater Lake, our first stop in Oregon, and I can use his phone to navigate me there. It's a few hours' drive. I'm hoping by the time we arrive, Luc will be awake and feeling better.

wake because it's cold and my chest hurts. How long did I sleep? Where are we? We aren't driving and it's dark outside. I'm alone in the car and that has me sitting straight up and glancing at the dashboard clock.

Oh. Wow. I slept a lot longer than I meant to. I run a hand through my hair and crawl out of the car. I can't say I'm feeling any better, but apparently sleeping isn't helping that, so...

Looks like we've reached Crater Lake. We're the only ones in this section of the parking lot, and I spot Evelyn wrapped in a blanket, seated on the grass near the cliff side overlooking the lake. She turns her head when I shut the door and smiles.

"Hi, sleepyhead. Want to watch the sunset with me?"

Might as well. I shrug and move over to her. She opens the blanket and I sink to the grass beside her, drawing a corner of the fabric around my shoulders.

She asks, "Are you feeling better?"

No point in worrying her with the truth. "I guess."

"Do you want to get some more sleep?"

My eyes drift closed. "Maybe."

She takes a deep breath, and I'm dreading the incoming prodding questions that are, unfortunately, probably justified when I'm looking and feeling this crappy. She surprises me instead by gently coaxing me into lying down with my head in her lap, and I don't feel up to protesting or pulling away. She's warm. She smells nice. The breeze calms the heat I feel pulsating in my veins. Her fingers stroke my hair and her voice is quiet, gentle. "Sleep as long as you want. I'm not going anywhere."

I wish that brought me more comfort than it does. At home when these symptoms would kick in, I would lie in bed and drift in and out, wondering...will this be it? The last time I fall out of consciousness and don't wake up? Sometimes it scared me. Sometimes I found it peaceful. Now, though...it isn't just me I'm worried about. I'm scared for Evelyn, of what she might do, of how she might feel if I were to close my eyes right here, right now, in her lap, and she wouldn't be able to wake me up.

It's that thought that coaxes me into moving when, some time later, Evelyn is telling me, "We should get a hotel room and let you rest."

A room. Yeah. I had planned on sleeping in the car tonight, maybe parked right there by the lake, but I think I need a day to recoup. I've been taking my meds like I'm supposed to, so maybe I just need to get some uninterrupted shut-eye, maybe it'll be okay. I can survive without a doctor's visit.

Evelyn holds my hand the whole way to the car, guiding me, I think. I'm not aware of her driving, of us pulling into a parking lot. I'm not aware of anything until she's opening my car door and telling me to follow her—which I do, without question—into a hotel room. A bed has never looked so inviting. I crawl into it, kicking the blankets down as far to the foot of the bed as I can.

The other side of the mattress dips slightly as Evelyn finds her way beside me. "Luc, we really should take you to a doctor. I'm getting worried."

"No," I say sharply. "No hospitals." I came all this way to get away from them. From their tests and procedures and grim diagnoses. I wanted to be alone. I wanted to reclaim the life I've spent dying and try to live a little before my heart gives out, or before I decide to end it myself. I wanted to show Evelyn some of the sights she's never gotten to see. To let the both of us be…well, *us* away from everything in our lives that drags us down.

Evelyn whispers, "Tell me what I can do."

"You're doing plenty." I reach for her hand, lacing our fingers together because in that exact moment, I think the only thing I really want is for her to stay right where she is to reassure me she'll be there if I open my eyes again.

TEN

Evelyn

Luc is finally resting easily when I drift off to sleep. I'm thinking if, in the morning, he isn't feeling any better, then I'll prod him into stopping by one of the free clinics here in town or something. Just to make sure he's okay.

I wake at midnight to find his shirt drenched in sweat and his forehead scalding to the touch.

"Luc?" When he doesn't respond, I shake him gently and push myself up to sitting, unable to keep the panic from creeping into my voice. "Luc? *Luc.* Wake up!"

He makes a noise. That's it. Just a low, displeased sound and nothing more.

Something is wrong.

Something is wrong and Luc won't wake up and I don't know what to do.

I hit the light switch. Where's my phone? I was so

worried about getting Luc inside earlier that I must have left it in the car, so I grab Luc's bag to look for his. Clothes. Phone charger. Medicines.

Medicines?

I overturn his bag onto the foot of the bed, looking through the plethora of pill bottles all made out to Luc Argent. Medications I've never even heard of. Among them is Luc's phone. I grab it, open the web browser. Several tabs on euthanasia pop up. The word gives me pause, but I don't have time to think about it right now. I type in one of the medication names.

"Diuretic used in the treatment of congestive heart failure and edema."

My heart drops to my stomach.

This is not a flu, not a bug, not something passing. With shaking fingers I exit the web browser and open the dial pad, numbly pressing buttons until a voice on the other end says, *"Hello, what's your emergency?"*

Name: _____

I stare at the question blankly, at a loss for what to write. Even in the fog of the ambulance ride here and the distress of them wheeling Luc away from me, I am eerily calm. Thinking with surprising clarity. If I put Luc's real name, would they call his parents? Luc obviously does not want to be found.

I write *Lucas Smith* because the 911 operator already heard me referring to him as Luc and this seems as good a cover-up as any. Age: 19. Gender: Male. Insurance? I'll leave that blank and say I don't know. Currently prescribed medications. That one I can answer. I took pictures of Luc's medication while waiting for the ambulance to arrive at the hotel. Can't give them the actual bottles but I can write down dosages and names. Names I can't pronounce, names I had to stop searching for online because it was only increasing my desire to cry.

Heart failure. Rejection. Euthanasia. Those words loop over and over in my head.

I put my name down as Emily. Emily and Lucas. Relationship to the patient? If I put *friend*, they aren't going to let me see him, are they? Sister? We don't look anything alike. I press pen to paper. A bubble of ink begins to pool at the tip until I slowly spell out *Spouse*.

A nurse takes the clipboard from me when I'm done. Then I wait, sitting in a small hallway lobby while nurses and patients and family wander back and forth, oblivious to me and the inner turmoil I'm trying to quiet. Two hours pass before a female doctor with a short A-line haircut approaches and asks, "Emily Smith? I'm Doctor Patel."

I start to stand and she beckons me to remain where I am, taking a seat in a chair across from me. My throat is a desert. "Is Luc okay?"

"Lucas is all right for now," she assures. "He's resting. We were reviewing a few tests we did on him and looked at the medication he's prescribed. How long ago was his heart transplant?"

My fingers lace, wringing together painfully tight. Given the medications he's on, I had put things together myself. But a heart transplant? That is far more serious than I ever would have thought. If I had to take a guess... "Just a few years," I say quietly. "I, uh, don't really know much about it. It's a topic Luc doesn't like to discuss."

She nods and the way she's studying my face makes me want to crawl under my chair. Like she doesn't believe me. "Emily…Luc is okay for now, but I want to tell you that it's very, very important we know Luc's *real* full name and any other information you might have so that we can get ahold of his medical records."

I wish I could tell her. Honestly, I don't know how much good Luc's real name would be if I know nothing else. No social security number, not even what hospital he's been treated at. (Though I could take a few guesses.) "What could be wrong with him?"

Dr. Patel leans forward, elbows on her knees and her voice gentle. It's a trained sort of gentleness, but it isn't insincere. "Heart transplants are complicated things. It could be an infection—which we're checking for as we speak—it could be complications from his high blood pressure. Organ rejection. Diabetes. Reappearance of the disease that required him to get a transplant to begin with."

My whole body aches with the weight of this news. Why didn't he tell me? All this time, and never a word? "If you had to take a ballpark guess…"

"Without all the test results back, my guess would be leaning toward rejection."

"I thought that happened, like, right after a surgery." Not that I know anything on this topic beyond what little I've gleaned from TV.

"Risk of rejection goes down with time, yes, but the body never really stops trying to fight off something that doesn't belong there," she explains. "And, sometimes, the body just… keeps attacking the new organ until it's destroyed."

I hope she won't take it personally if I throw up on her feet. "So if it is...if it's what you think it is, what happens now?"

She smiles distantly. "That depends on both of you. Being able to speak with his doctors would be vital to helping Luc."

My head is a mess. The tears are coming, sliding down my cheeks, catching in my lashes. I can't tell her anything. Not without seeing Luc first. "Can I sit with him until he wakes up?"

Luc

fucking hate heart monitors. Their obnoxious beep is a steady reminder that I am, in fact, in a hospital. Again. Sometimes even at home, I would wake with that sound ringing in my ears, as familiar to me as my own pulse. I breathe in and out for a few minutes, waiting for the nurse taking my blood pressure to leave the room before I open my eyes.

Not a familiar hospital. Then where? What happened? My brain is still trying to clear.

I remember...Crater Lake. Evelyn. Petting my hair, lying in bed next to me...and then nothing.

This would be disarming if it hadn't happened multiple times before. The fatigue and the fever, the disorientation... they're all things I've dealt with since my transplant. I've been in hospitals no less than eight times in three years with signs of transplant rejection. The first few visits, my doctor told me it was normal. It was my body trying to adjust and I needed to remember to take my medication, eat right, exercise.

The last few times, they stopped trying to convince me it wasn't something to worry about.

Then, of course, there was my biopsy that confirmed what none of us wanted to hear: that my rejection is chronic. That my body would eventually kill my new heart and me along with it unless another transplant took place.

This is such bullshit. What made me think running away from home would let me leave all that behind? If there was any doubt that this—laying around in a hospital—is not the way I want to go, that I want control over my own death, it's gone now.

"You're awake," Evelyn says.

I close my eyes immediately so I don't have to see her standing in the doorway. "I told you no doctors."

"I probably saved your life." Her voice is unreadable, but there's an edge to it. I can't place it, which is disconcerting considering this is Evelyn and she's normally an open book. I force my eyelids to lift and watch her take a seat at my bedside. She has my phone clutched in her hand.

"I didn't ask you to."

She replies, "I didn't ask to be lied to."

"I never lied to you."

"Lying by omission is still lying, Luc." Her gaze is steely. "Tell me the truth. What have you been keeping from me?"

I can't stand the look she's giving me so I avert my

eyes, uncomfortable. "Get me out of here first and I'll tell you whatever you want."

"Give me one good reason not to call your parents and let them know you're here so the doctors can treat you."

"Because you're not like that," I say. "And you want to hear the truth from *me*. Not a doctor, not my parents. I'll tell these doctors what they need to know to get me back on my feet and then we leave. Deal or no deal?"

I still can't read her. She looks calm. Too calm, really. Not sure if this pisses me off or worries me. A little of column A, a little of column B, I guess. She purses her lips and looks away, which I'm kind of grateful for because I get the feeling she's trying to refrain from throwing herself at me and strangling me with my IV line.

We sit in silence until a doctor comes in. Judging by the look they exchange, I'm willing to bet she and Evelyn have already met. She smiles at me, coming to a halt at the foot of my bed with her hands resting against the foot rail.

"Hello, Mr. Smith. I'm Dr. Patel. How are you feeling?"

Smith? Guess Evelyn thought ahead and gave us fake names. It makes my urgency to get the hell out of here dull a little. If they don't know who I really am, then they won't be calling my parents. I can handle a lot of things, but my mother crying hysterically is not something I want to face. She wouldn't understand that it's better for her and Dad this way.

"Feeling better," I assure her. "I'll feel great when I can get out of here."

Her expression softens. "Well, as I was telling your

wife out in the lobby…"

My what? Oh.

I glance at Evelyn, wondering if they noticed that, you know, she doesn't even have a ring.

"I was hoping you might give us permission to request your medical records from your primary physician and see what we're dealing with to better treat you."

Evelyn says nothing and busies herself staring down at my phone in her hands, smoothing her thumb over the screen. I'm impressed she isn't opening her mouth. I'm sure I'll get an earful later; she's too polite to make a scene in front of a stranger.

"No one knows what we're dealing with better than I do." I force a grim smile. "I can tell you exactly what meds to give me and I should be good to go by morning."

She doesn't give up easily, I'll give her that. She tries a number of tactics to convince me to stay, to let them run tests, but ultimately…my decision, right? I'm grateful when she leaves to deal with other patients who are probably more agreeable than I am. The exhaustion still has ahold of me and since Evelyn is giving me the silent treatment, I sleep.

The nurses wake me throughout the night to check my vitals and administer meds. This is a tired routine I'm all too familiar with, just with different faces than I'm used to. At some point while a male nurse is injecting a round of something-or-other into my IV, I look over to see Evelyn curled up in her chair, head tipped at an uncomfortable angle, arms tucked into her jacket sleeves and sleeping. I ask the nurse to get her a blanket.

With doctors coming and going and making their

morning rounds, I don't see Doctor Patel again until almost noon. By that point, I'm seriously tempted to yank out my IV and monitors and just leave, but I think I've pissed Evelyn off enough. Of course, the good doctor isn't going to let me off the hook so easily.

"I can't legally keep you here, but I really wish you would consider staying. Even just one more night for observation."

I ignore Doctor Patel and sign off on the discharge papers she's brought me. If I never see another set of these in my life, I'll be content. "I appreciate the concern, but no thanks."

She doesn't try again. I'm grateful for this woman who only wants to help, and maybe on some level I feel bad I can't give her any peace of mind that I'm going to be fine. That she did her job to the best of her ability and anything that happens to me from here on out is entirely of my own doing.

Evelyn is deathly silent as we leave the hospital and get into the car. She automatically gets behind the wheel, so I don't question it, seeing as I have no idea where we're going. Our stuff is still at the hotel, it looks like, so...back there? I stare straight ahead, trying to wade my way through the silence with words and speaking only when we've turned onto an empty street. "So, I figure we'll stay at the hotel another night and head out tomorrow."

The car wrenches to one side. Evelyn throws it into park, kills the ignition, and shoves the door open to get out.

Fuck.

I sigh and lean back against the seat, eyes closed. Maybe it was a bad idea to bring her along. No, there's no *maybe* about it—I *know* now it was a bad idea. What had I been thinking? I should have come up with another answer for her, should have—

Should have what? What else was there to do? I couldn't leave her there to go back to Arizona, but I couldn't change my plans, either. (Wouldn't, anyway.) Was there really anything I could have done that would have landed us anywhere but here? No matter how well I took care of myself, something like this was bound to happen sooner or later. I had been taking my medicine as prescribed, avoiding all the things the doctors told me to.

When I realize Evelyn isn't coming back, I sigh again and crawl out of the car to call after her. "Evelyn… I swear, I didn't lie to you."

She whips around to point at me, heat in her voice I'm not used to hearing. "Don't you *dare*. This was *important* and you couldn't be bothered to tell me. That's *still lying.*"

"Evelyn—"

"You left me totally blindsided with no idea what to do or what was happening. What if you had *died* back in that hospital, Luc?" She stalks toward me, fire in her eyes in place of tears. "I'm willing to bet you won't even say *why* you wouldn't tell me?"

"Because it's *my* business," I say, somewhere between irritated—with myself, really, not her—and exhausted. "I told you it was a bad idea for you to hang around me and that I had my reasons for trying to keep my distance."

"Then you could have told me and let me make my own decisions!" she snaps. "Instead of making me feel like I wasn't *good* enough or that you didn't care. Most of this could've been avoided if you'd just been a little more honest. What were you afraid would happen if I found out?"

I'm too tired to deal with this. I want nothing more than to put distance between us, to go to sleep. It isn't that I'm angry with her. Not exactly. More that I'm angry with myself, with life, with circumstance. Angry that I can't tell her what she wants to hear. "I'm not afraid of anything," I say, even though it's far from the truth. I'm afraid of a lot of things, aren't I? This whole fucking trip is based in fear.

She shakes her head. Her hair, which was tied up in a bun, is falling loose, making her look just as disheveled and tired as I feel. She stops a few feet in front of me. "Were you worried I'd look at you differently? That *I'd* make the choice to not want anything to do with you? That I'd pity you? Because I can tell you right now, the only pity I feel is that you were too much of a coward to tell me the truth. I do feel worry and hurt because that's what happens when you care about someone."

"Stop complicating an already complicated situation!"

Her arms spread wide, eyebrows raising. "Oh, *I'm* complicating things?"

I run a hand through my hair. Turn away. Trying to force back words I know I shouldn't say. "Shut up."

"What am I complicating, Luc?"

"Everything!"

"How?"

I throw my hands into the air and whirl around to face her again. "Because I care about you so fucking much and I didn't want to! I didn't want to get in any deeper so that when I inevitably fucking *die*, you're left behind all by yourself!"

My words are cold water on a fire. All the fight immediately floods out of Evelyn, leaving her shoulders slumped, her eyes glassy. It's all too obvious to me that what I feel for Evelyn transcends our insistent label of "best friends." It always has. But it's different to say it out loud, to address it. I wanted these things left unsaid between us because putting a name to it, putting depth and meaning... Evelyn giving a damn about me is only going to hurt her in the end.

I'm in love with this infuriating, frustrating girl, and I'm going to die, and her broken heart is going to be all my fault.

When she speaks, her voice is softer, almost lost to the wind. "If our positions were reversed, would you have done any different than I did?"

In that moment, I try to picture Evelyn in my place and me in hers. I imagine her in a hospital bed with an illness I know nothing about and how out of control, how powerless and afraid I would feel. I try to imagine her telling me to get lost, shoving me away.

And...I don't honestly know how I would react. That's never been how our relationship works. Evelyn is so kind and caring and would offer anyone the shirt off her back without a single complaint. Me? I always feel like I need to take care of her. If she wanted to get away from me, I have a feeling I would blame myself. It would never dawn on me she was doing it for my own good. When I take into consideration Evelyn's lack of confidence in herself, I start to wonder if she's been feeling the same thing. *Unwanted.*

That has never been the case. I just didn't want to hurt anyone.

She doesn't seem to expect an answer from me. She hugs herself, head bowing, as though the weight of this has worn us both into the ground. Yet she doesn't say a word as she walks back to the car and I stay silent, too, resisting the urge to follow after and gather her up into my arms. We've both already said way too much.

Evelyn

Our silence is tired. The hotel room is as we left it, complete with Luc's medications scattered across the floor. A tense look passes over his face as he stoops to gather them up and I automatically move to help, stopping only when he insists, "I got it."

I step back and fold my arms, watching him. I haven't asked for the information he promised me. Whether it's because I don't *really* want to know or I don't want to fight with him again, I'm not sure.

Maybe it isn't even the sickness that has me torn up. It was that word. *Euthanasia.* If Luc is suffering from transplant rejection, why isn't he back home, getting treatment? That single word hangs in the back of my mind, and I can't bring myself to ask him why he was looking it up.

Luc scoops the pill bottles into his bag along with the rest of the discarded contents, then rocks back on his heels. "If you have something to say, then say it."

Oh, now he wants to talk? I'm really not in the mood. I don't even give him a response to that. I simply turn away and sit at the table by the window with a stack of hotel stationery and do what I do best: I fold things. I can feel Luc's eyes on me. He's probably irritated and, frankly, I don't care. I was the one who was lied to, whether he agrees it was lying or not.

I've never kept secrets from Luc. Never. I've always told him anything he wanted to know without him ever having to ask.

Except Arizona. Even then, he knows about it, just not the finer details.

The evening crawls by without a single word exchanged between us. Luc takes a shower. He goes for a walk to a nearby corner store and gets a few bottled waters and some chips and beef jerky. I don't move from the table. I'm running out of paper and have taken to tearing it into fours and making smaller animals with it. Cranes. I wonder if this is a subconscious thing because of everything that's happened.

Fold a thousand paper cranes and Luc won't be sick anymore.

For a while, Luc keeps his distance. Then I hear the television go off and he plops into the chair across from me, watching my hands at work. He asks, "Why do you do that? The animals, I mean."

His voice is sincerely curious, not his usual condescending lilt. It's the only reason I don't ignore him. "I don't know. Something to do with my hands when I'm stressed. Distracts me, I guess."

Luc bobs his head into a nod, picking up one of the cranes and turning it around in his fingers. "Do you really believe the story about the cranes?"

I keep my eyes down, fixated on what I'm doing. The smaller the pieces of paper get, the harder it is to make precise folds. "Does it matter? You said it was stupid."

"I say that about a lot of things." He begins lining the cranes up in a row, from biggest to smallest. There are fourteen of them now. "You haven't asked me anything since we left the hospital."

"I'm tired of asking. You're aware that I want to know, and I'm not going to beg."

"Fair enough." He holds out his hand as I finish another crane. I place it in his palm and finally lift my eyes to his face as he tells me, "Three days after you left, I had a heart transplant."

"Okay."

"I'd been on the transplant list for a few years already but, you know, wait times are killer. Literally. Guess you could say I lucked out with the heart I got."

There's a touch of sadness and bitterness in his voice, but I don't push. I keep my mouth shut and listen.

"So things were cool for a while. I had a few rejection scares but that isn't really abnormal. You go into the hospital, they run a few tests, give you some medication, then send you home."

"Is that what this is?" I ask quietly. "One of those normal scares?"

Luc sets the paper crane down. "It's chronic."

"And that means…"

"It means I got a heart because some girl died in a car crash and happened to be a match, and now my body is killing it. It means medicine isn't going to fix me."

I allow the weight of this to settle over me. It brings everything into such startling clarity. Luc's bitterness, his anger, his fear. His panic at the mere mention of going to a doctor. His fatigue and his need to get away from his parents, even if just for a short time. Which leads me to ask, "What's in Oregon, Luc? What brought you here, of all places?"

He opens his mouth and his throat seems to constrict, like he can't force out the thoughts. He looks at me, wordless. Maybe there're some things I don't need to know just yet. Maybe I'm not ready to know. I can't even bring myself to form the questions: *Are you dying? Do you want to die? Did you come here with the intention of never going home again?* because I'm certain the weight of the answers would crush us both.

But that's what this is, isn't it? This is the truth he's been hiding.

Luc is dying. And maybe he's looking at ending things on his own terms.

I'm such a coward that I can't bring myself to ask. Would I be able to change his mind, if the answer were yes?

He inhales and exhales heavily through his nose. "All right. Show me."

"Show you what?"

He draws a piece of paper over to himself with a small smile. "Show me how to make one of these stupid things."

ELEVEN

Evelyn

We allow ourselves three days of rest. Luc sleeps every night like the dead—which is unnerving, given the circumstances—but he stays close to me when he's awake.

Something has changed.

Not just with me and not just with him, but with *us*. The first night he lies at my back and I pull his arm around my waist and he stays there, spooned around me, breath soft like feathers on my neck. It's the only way I can sleep, being able to hear or feel him breathing, being able to feel the rise and fall of his chest.

I let him rest as much as he wants. Sometimes he sends me out to grab food and I think it's more to give himself some alone time than anything else. I'm okay with that. Or at least, I'm trying to be. And I'm trying not to think about what I saw on his phone that night. *Euthanasia*. It could have meant anything; it could have been nothing more than simple curiosity.

It doesn't matter, I think, because I'm going to show Luc all the reasons why he should live, and how much fun we're going to make the rest of this trip. I want him to see that it's worth it. That *life* is worth it.

The day we pack up our things to leave is the day before my eighteenth birthday, and I dare to call Mom again. There're twenty-three missed calls and enough voicemails to fill my inbox. I delete them all without listening, not wanting to be jaded by whatever she might have said before I actually hear her voice on the phone.

I say, "Hey, Mom."

"Please tell me you're coming home."

"Not yet." I lean against the side of the car. Luc is in the lobby, turning in our keys. "I'm fine. I'm safe. You aren't doing something dumb like sending the cops after me, are you?"

She snorts and says sullenly, "They weren't willing to do it. Especially after tomorrow. If you had gone a few more days without calling, I probably could have gotten them after you as a missing person."

I roll my eyes to the sky. "Sorry to disappoint you."

"You aren't in San Diego, are you?"

"Does it really matter?"

"I'm your *mother*. Of course it matters!"

I scuff my heel against the ground. It was too much to hope for that she would be someone I could talk to about all this. "Is that what Grandma Jane said when you ran away with Dad?"

Mom falls silent.

I don't know much about my father. What little I've gathered from Grandma is that he was a trucker. Handsome, friendly, but not the sort to stick around. He picked up my sixteen-year-old mother and they drove clear across the country. When she showed up back on Grandma's front porch, she had a suitcase in her hand and a baby eight months along in her belly.

"I don't want you to make the same mistake I did," Mom finally says.

"Oh, I was a mistake?"

"*You* weren't a mistake. My decision to drop out of high school and run away from home with a man I'd just met was."

"Nice save. But there's a difference, Mom. I've known Luc for years and I didn't drop out of school. I'm still doing my work." I don't tell her that I am, honestly, starting to fall a little behind with school. I don't tell her I ran away because the idea of seeing Robert again makes me sick. "I can't go back to Arizona. Go without me. I'll be fine, okay?"

Mom lets out a shuddering breath. "Baby, please come home. I don't want to see you get hurt."

Luc emerges from the hotel and approaches the car, looking normal and energized. Deceptively well considering he's dying. I think, *too late*, because I've already been hurt and I know it will continue to hurt, and yet I have no inclination of turning back now. I'm with Luc until the end, whatever and wherever that end may be. "I'll call you in a few days, Mom. I love you."

...

Luc

Straight through, driving from Crater Lake to the Oregon Coast Aquarium would take us around four hours. The route is pretty and I'm not in a particular hurry, so I take us through a few scenic back roads along the way. With the windows down and the music up and Evelyn watching the roads go by, the wind making a mess of her wavy hair, we could be two regular people going on a regular road trip.

Regular. As though I didn't spend any alone time I got the last three days re-reading through Marilyn's blog and emailing back and forth with her about her husband and his story. Getting her familiar and comfortable with me until I was able to ask her what she did with her husband's medication that he chose not to take to end his own life.

To everyone else, it's probably going to seem like overkill. (Ha. Funny.) It wouldn't have been that hard to off myself back home. I could have overdosed on my medication, driven my car off a bridge, gotten Dad's keys for his gun lockbox. But dying was never the purpose of this trip.

The purpose was *living*.

I wanted to be a normal guy, just for a few weeks. I wanted to experience things without a leash connecting me to my parents and the nearest hospital. Sure, maybe all those other ways of committing suicide terrify the hell out of me because so much can go wrong, but that wasn't all. More than that, I didn't want my parents to ever, *ever* think this was their fault. *If we hadn't let him drive, if we had just monitored his medication, if I had kept hold of those keys...* A million and one ways I know they would blame themselves, and I can't have that. I didn't want them to be a part of it and I didn't want them to find me after the fact.

Even if, on the off-chance Marilyn had the medication and chose to give it to me, would I take it? I don't know what I'm going to do. Coming to Oregon, I'd intended to look into dying on my own terms, but I'd never *really* given weight to it until now.

We sleep in the car that night despite Evelyn protesting that I need a bed and me really wanting just a few more nights of sleeping close to her. Just because I have a savings account and a few cards doesn't mean I want to completely drain them. Whether I die here or back home in a hospital bed, my goal is to leave as much in there as possible to go toward bills and funeral costs. I'm lucky Mom hasn't been able to—or hasn't tried, not sure which—get my name off the account and shut off my debit card and credit cards.

Evelyn lays her seat back as far as it will go and rolls onto her side to watch me until I turn my head to ask, "What?"

She says, "Nothing," but smiles in a way that means it's something. "I like watching you."

I snort and roll my gaze to the roof. "Mm. Why is that?"

"I don't know. Because you look like home."

That gets me to stare at her, blinking. "That sentence doesn't make sense."

"Doesn't it?" Her lashes lower and she rubs at her eyes like she's fighting sleep.

I'm trying not to smile because I don't feel like I deserve this kindness from her right now. I'm aware I've been an asshole, and that the things I'm thinking about doing would only make her angry with me all over again. "You're entirely too nice for your own good, you know that?"

"So you've told me." She snakes her hand beneath the blankets, searching for mine. Her fingertips brush the curve of my elbow in their journey, slide down my forearm and wrist and palm; it makes me shiver, sends tiny little pleasant jolts of electricity through every nerve. "Maybe I am, but someone has to balance out your ability to be a complete dick."

A soft laugh escapes my lips. "Thanks."

"Just telling it like it is." Her eyes fall shut again, emphasized by a yawn. This time, she doesn't open them and her breathing evens out, while her fingers are still resting against the palm of my hand.

Lying there watching her, I'm struck by an odd sense of melancholy. After our blowup, I can't say whether things between us are strained, or if they've improved. She asked me if I was afraid she'd choose to leave if she knew the truth…and I'm not entirely sure I've ever been afraid of that.

I was afraid she would stay.

Because that's the kind of person Evelyn is. She would never walk out on someone she cared about just because things got difficult. Chalk it up to years of dealing with a mother who was constantly uprooting her both physically and emotionally with her rapid-fire relationship switches. I'm honestly a little surprised she hasn't shown any signs of becoming the same way. Sure, she ran away with a guy, but I don't think it's the same. It's not like I swept her off her feet and across the country only to send her back home a few months later when the magic wore off.

I reach my free hand out to give in to the stupid temptation of brushing the hair from Evelyn's face. No, her mother couldn't understand. Our magic is the kind that doesn't go away.

Morning comes too early, and with it the aches and pains of sleeping in a car. I should've rented a van or something. Might've been a smarter choice and we would have saved on a hotel room. Evelyn is still asleep, so I leave her where she's at while I get out and head for the grocery store we're parked in front of to use the bathroom.

On my way back out, I give in and call Mom again. I'm window shopping down the rest of the strip with the cell to my ear, and Mom answers on the first ring, which makes me think she's probably been waiting by the phone. Ugh, guilt.

"Luc?"

"Just checking in. Wanted you to hear my voice so you knew I wasn't snorting coke and prostituting myself out in Vegas or something."

For a few moments, Mom is silent. Never a good sign. It means she has something big to say and she's calculating how to say it. Subtlety and beating around the bush have never been her thing; maybe that's where I get it from. "I talked to Dr. Nadeen. She told us about your test results."

"Whatever happened to doctor-patient confidentiality?"

"She's concerned about you, sweetheart. You need to come home. If a donor were to become available again like last time—"

"I don't want it to be like last time," I blurt, inwardly cringing at the silence on the other end of the line. "Mom. I love you both, you *know* I do. But I don't know—I don't think I can…"

"You're young and you're strong," she says firmly. "Don't give up your future just like that. What were you hoping to accomplish in Oregon? That's where you are now, right?"

"I've got to go, Mom," I murmur. I'm sure to say, "Love you," before I hang up and switch off my phone.

My stomach twists. What future does she think I have waiting for me? A future of hospitals and tests and possibly another rejected heart that could save someone else? I got my one shot, and my body failed. I shouldn't be allowed another chance. I don't want another heart of a dead girl.

Without realizing it, I've stopped in front of a boutique store window and am staring at the jewelry lined up on display pieces, silver and gold and stones catching the light. It's November twenty-third. Evelyn's birthday. I should get her something.

If I were normal, if my body had taken the first heart like it should have, I would be in college right now. I might even be in my own place instead of living at home. Maybe I would've chosen to study abroad. Maybe I'd have found out Evelyn was back in town and done everything right. Swept her off her feet. Brought her home with me to give her a safe place to stay instead of going back to Arizona. Not whatever it is I'm doing here and now.

I've had dreams about that. About life, if I could've done everything I wanted to do. I don't know if it's too late to fix any of that now, but I know I'm going to have a thousand regrets when I die. Like my parents. I'm going to disappoint them, I'm going to hurt them, and there's no way to get around that. I'm doing a necessary evil to spare them financial pain on top of the emotional agony they're going to suffer down the line anyway.

Maybe I should write each of my one thousand regrets on a thousand paper cranes to see if it really does make me better.

I have a thousand regrets, but I don't want everything with Evelyn to be one of them.

I've been to aquariums before. Monterey Bay, San Francisco, San Diego. Maybe Mom and Dad thought they were safe vacation spots because they didn't involve a lot of physical exertion or something. Not that I minded. There's something calming about the blue-green hues and soft lights and reflections, watching the graceful swimming of fish and dolphins, the rhythmic, almost trancelike movements of jellyfish. I want to see it all one more time.

Evelyn looks on in amazement as we step inside and pay for our tickets. She immediately gets a brochure and a map, eyes big and mouth pinned into a permanent smile.

"Otters! Luc, they have otters."

"Yeah, no surprise there."

I have to coax her out of the lobby and into the aquarium itself, where the first long hall is surrounded by one big tank, full of tuna swimming in sync around and around. I nudge Evelyn until she lifts her head, and her breath catches. "Oh…"

"Cool, huh?" I have a feeling seeing her reaction to everything will be the best part of this trip. Hell, maybe that's been the best part all along. Even if this was a bad idea, even if it went against every inch of distance I've tried to put between us and the world, I can no longer imagine what this trip would have been like without her.

Evelyn takes my hand—an act I no longer even blink at, it seems so natural—and leads me through the halls from exhibit to exhibit. "We need to make sure we don't miss anything," she insists.

The jellyfish are some of my favorites. Evelyn locates the moon jellies, which are nearly invisible in regular lighting. The display has a button that triggers a light, which illuminates the jellies in a bright, beautiful glow. Evelyn has fun pressing this button on and off, as amazed as I remember being the first time my parents took me to the Monterey aquarium years ago.

"Do you think they're unhappy here?" she asks. "Being in tanks, I mean."

"Fish don't really have the thinking capacity mammals do." I shrug. "And they're small. Their habitats can be simulated pretty well."

"What about the sharks?"

"I don't know. Same concept, I guess."

"But sharks migrate. You can't really reproduce conditions for that."

I watch a hammerhead swimming slowly near the bottom of the massive enclosure. "Huh. Didn't know that."

"I mean, they're different than orcas or dolphins, which are really big on socialization and family, but still…" She trails off and we watch the sharks in silence. Do they feel trapped, I wonder? I always thought keeping killer whales and dolphins in captivity was shitty, but I hadn't thought about things like sharks. On the one hand, they get the perfect diet and water temperatures and no threats…but does that substitute the feeling of being free?

I was always watched over by my parents. Never wanted for anything. Yet I always felt trapped and a little smothered, and the taste of freedom that being out on my own has given me is better than anything else in the world. Maybe the sharks feel the same way?

"Come on," I finally say. "I think I saw the otters over here."

Evelyn's expression brightens from pensive to excited. The otters we saved for last, because she thought nothing else would compare to them. Judging by her expression as the tank comes into view, I'd say she was right. For her, anyway. Her dark eyes grow large and she's instantly gone from my side, standing with her nose nearly to the glass and watching the playful, graceful swimming of sleek otters in the water. Toward the top, where the water ends, other otters are sunning themselves on rocks or floating on the surface, paws tucked against their chests.

An otter swirls around in front of Evelyn and she laughs, delighted, and presses her palm against the glass. "They're so cute. Look, are the two up there holding hands?"

"Seems like it." I'm not honestly paying attention. Watching Evelyn is way more interesting. There's a swelling of pride in my chest, knowing I was able to bring her to a place like this and show her things she hasn't gotten to see. I would take her all across the world, show her everything she's ever wanted to see, if only I could. It would be something worth living for.

The thought makes my chest hurt. Something worth living for, huh?

She looks over her shoulder with a smile that could light up the room. It fades a little when she sees me. "What's wrong?"

Damn, was it showing on my face? I shake my head and glance away. I've been carting a gift around for her in my pocket ever since I saw it in the boutique store window, debating whether or not to give it to her. Now might be as good a time as any, right? "I got you something."

"A present?" That is apparently more interesting to her than the otters. She turns to face me completely, frowning. "Why?"

"Am I not allowed to get you something for your birthday?" I remove the jewelry box from my jacket pocket and hold it out in her direction until she takes and opens it. It's nothing special. I saw it and thought of her and it was there and maybe some stupid part of my brain thought: *I want her to look at it and remember me when I'm gone.* Which is dumb, because I can't take her all around the world to see everything, because I won't live that long, because she's going to hate me someday and not want to remember anything about me. It's my selfishness shining through. Wanting to be remembered, to be missed.

"We'll find you a better chain for it," I say awkwardly as she takes the necklace from its box and admires the blue butterfly pendant. "If you like it. I mean, you don't have to wear it or anything. I know you aren't big on jewelry." At least I think she isn't? I've never seen her wear anything. I don't even think her ears are pierced.

"It's beautiful." She smiles so widely that it encourages my shoulders to relax. I watch her unclasp the gunmetal chain and fasten it around her neck. The butterfly rests just below her collarbone, bright against her olive-toned skin. "I'll wear it always."

I kind of like the sound of that. No one else has to know I gave it to her; I don't care about that. I want *her* to know I think about her when she isn't around. That ever since meeting her, I've never been able to look at a butterfly without thinking about her folding them out of paper and napkins. Not to mention, I want her to know that I didn't forget what today is, even after all this time. "Happy birthday."

"I'll admit, I'm pretty surprised you remembered." Evelyn tucks the empty box into her coat pocket and wraps her arms around my shoulders in a brief but tight hug. I let my hand linger on the small of her back for just a moment, swallowing hard. When she pulls away, there's only a little bit of space separating us. The glow from the otter exhibit lights up her face and makes her eyes shine.

For a while, we stand like that, our eyes locked, watching each other like we aren't standing in the middle of an aquarium with otters swimming by and peering at us through the plexi-glass. It would be ridiculously easy to close the distance between us, to pull her right up against me, her mouth against mine.

As though she's reading my mind, Evelyn asks, "Are you going to kiss me or do I have to kiss you?"

I fight back a smile and groan instead. "Way to ruin the moment."

"What moment?"

"You aren't supposed to plan out a first kiss, Evelyn. It's supposed to just…happen."

She huffs, and I know she's going to protest and it's going to make this really awkward. Besides that, she's ridiculously cute when she's indignant and I think of every night we've slept next to each other and how badly I've wanted to kiss her up until now, and every stupid excuse I've used to keep myself from doing it.

To hell with restraint.

I catch her face gently between my palms and kiss her. It silences any complaints on her lips and this…this is *good* and *right* and maybe the only thing in the world that has made sense to me in a very, very long time. It's a dumb, bad idea and it doesn't matter because I'm kissing Evelyn and she makes it okay, because it makes me think about everything that could be. I don't think about transplants and being sick.

Instead her lips make me think of Paris, Australia,

Peru, Brazil. I'm picturing holding Evelyn's hand while we walk into a home all our own, of traveling with her, of *living*. That makes kissing her the single most beautiful and painful thing all at once, and I don't want to stop.

I don't know why I didn't do this sooner. I don't know why I'm doing it at all. It's a great idea, it's a terrible idea.

Fuck.

Evelyn pulls away first. I can't see in the dim lighting, but when I brush my thumb across her cheek it feels flushed, warm to the touch. She smiles and ducks her head with a soft laugh, burying her face against my chest.

"What?" I ask. "Was that bad?"

She shakes her head, arms looping around my middle and squeezing. "No. I feel like I've been waiting for years to do that. Was that some kind of one-time thing?"

So have I, I think. I'm just more aware of the flood-gates I've opened than she is, and it's getting harder and harder to care. "No, I don't think it was."

Evelyn

My feet have not touched the floor. I could float away if it weren't for Luc's hand holding on to mine.

When I met him as a freshman, I thought of kissing him all the time. I remember it pouring outside and everyone else at school stayed indoors, hidden in classrooms or the cafeteria, while Luc and I snuck out past the gym and huddled beneath a narrow awning of the library while we watched the raindrops come down in torrents. Luc had been so warm, and I'd nestled myself up against his side and got as close as I could to leach the heat from him while we talked about anything and everything.

At one point, Luc had turned his head toward me and I could feel his breath against my ear and cheek when he spoke, feeling the words as much as I could hear them. I don't remember what he said, because what he said wasn't important. The important part was that I had been so fascinated by his mouth and how inviting it looked.

Now, all these years later, and I finally got my kiss.

I don't know what it means or what will change between us, but something has. Something major has shifted between Luc and me.

He doesn't let go of my hand the rest of our time at the aquarium, or for the return walk to the car. Where he would normally shift away and slide his grip nonchalantly from mine, he keeps his fingers wrapped tight, like he's afraid I'm going to slip away into the ether if he doesn't hang on.

That's it, though. Just hand-holding. Up until we get back into the car and I start to ask, "Where next?" and there's just…something in how Luc is watching me, gentle and soft in a way I'm not used to having Luc ever look at anyone—least of all me.

"The next place is all mine." Luc starts up the car and takes the nearest on-ramp to the freeway. The drive from the aquarium up the coast is only an hour or so, and during that hour, I find myself stealing glances at Luc more than usual.

I'm watching his mouth because I really, really want to kiss him again.

Did he mean what he said about it not being a one-time thing? I guess we'll find out.

We stop at a grocery store to grab some deli sandwiches for dinner. While chowing down on them in the car, Luc turns on his phone—I see him quickly swiping aside the notifications for missed calls and texts from his parents—and he searches online for a number and calls it, putting it on speakerphone.

"Thank you for calling the Butterfly Emporium! For directions, press one. For hours of operation, please press two."

Luc presses two.

That's what he meant by this next stop being all his. Even so, I can't help but grin. To get to see Luc surrounded by something he cares so much about is as much a treat for me as it is for him.

His smile quickly fades.

"We regret to inform you that at this time, the Butterfly Emporium is closed for renovations. We'll be reopening this spring. Come see us again soon!"

He hangs up abruptly, brows knitting together.

"Sorry," I murmur. "But, you know, maybe when they're open again, you and I can take a road trip up here and see it?" It's only a few months away. Maybe it's a subtle, passive-aggressive way of insinuating that he needs to be here in a few months.

Luc opens his mouth as though to say something, but stops himself. He doesn't smile, but I can tell by the strain in his voice he doesn't want to take out his disappointment on me. "Finish your sandwich. Let's get a hotel tonight."

I don't object to that.

By the time we've found a place, darkness has settled in and I'm worn out from the day's events. The closest motel isn't exactly top of the line, but they're advertising a low weekly rate, to which Luc pauses and looks at me to ask, "What do you think?"

"About?"

"Hanging out here for a week. We can always leave early if we get bored. The ocean is nearby and all that."

Staying in one place doesn't sound like such a bad idea. At least this time it won't be because of Luc's health, unless he's feeling crappy again and doesn't want to tell me. "Sounds like a plan."

The motel room smells vaguely of ammonia, but I'm hoping that's a sign that it's clean…ish. Just in case, the first thing I do after setting my bag down is to pull back the blankets to make sure the sheets are stain- and bedbug-free. Luc waits patiently for me to finish my examination and when I turn to look at him, he's standing there, right behind me, so close that I startle.

"What is it?"

Luc doesn't answer. He catches the back of my head in his hand and draws me to him, bowing down to press his mouth to mine. Unlike at the aquarium, I'm not caught quite as off-guard. It only takes me a moment before I'm rising up on tiptoe, lips parting, coaxing him along to assure him this is all right.

It's *more* than all right. It's everything I've wanted for such a long time.

He pulls away and it leaves me lightheaded, grasping

hold of his shirt. I'm vaguely aware that I have a really stupid smile on my face. "What was that for?"

"I don't know." Luc touches his fingers to his mouth as though he's surprised he did it. "You were standing there and I realized I could kiss you, so I did."

It's such an honest admission coming from him that I have to laugh. "Well, you can do it whenever you want. Except…"

"Except?"

I duck my head and turn away from him to start unpacking my bag, since we're going to be here for a while. "You haven't taken me out on a date yet. Shouldn't you do that before we start randomly making out? Make it official or something?"

Luc snorts. "We've spent all this time stopping places."

"Those weren't dates."

"No?"

"Dates aren't retroactive," I say mildly, aware that I'm being a pain, and also aware that he's amused by this discussion more than anything. "A *real* date. Then as much kissing as you'd like."

"A real date, huh," he muses. "Okay, fine. Tomorrow will be our date day."

That's more than enough to placate me. And because I'm still sad for him that he doesn't get to see the butterfly house, I spend the evening making him a dozen origami butterflies out of cheap motel stationary to accompany all the butterflies in my stomach.

TWELVE

Luc

I leave Evelyn to sleep in the morning with a note that promises I'll be back soon, and with breakfast. In truth, I had wanted nothing more than to keep lying next to her, watching her sleep, but—

Marilyn, the woman from the blog, has been emailing back and forth with me ever since I initially contacted her. It was casual conversation at first, asking questions about her husband, about the route they had chosen to take to end his life—even if he ultimately changed his mind. I told her about myself, about my failing heart. That I didn't think I'd get another transplant and even if I did, it wasn't worth it to me to keep doing this.

I finally asked her if she still had the Nembutal, and if she would consider selling it to me.

She got back to me in the middle of the night. "Lou's

Café, 8:30" was all it said. No address, no information, no nothing, though at least an internet search only brings up one Lou's and it's thirty minutes from the hotel. She was the reason I suggested hanging out in town for the week. It had nothing to do with me needing a break, but rather me wanting to be on hand in case Marilyn agreed to meet up with me. Guilt gnaws away at me for having to lie to Evelyn just to get here.

As I sit down and order a glass of water, I don't entirely know who I'm looking for. There was a single photograph on her blog of herself and her dying husband. She's an older woman, maybe my mom's age. The only woman who comes into the café looking anything like the photo is significantly thinner and more worn than the lady in the picture, but it has to be her. She clutches her large purse to her chest, glancing around before taking a seat near the window.

I take my water and approach her table, uncertain how this entire thing is going to progress. If it's going to progress at all. "Marilyn?" She lifts her chin and her eyes grow large at the sight of me. Obviously I have the right person, so I slide into the seat across from her and offer my free hand. "I'm Luc."

Marilyn takes my hand and shakes it, but reluctantly. "You're…much younger than I thought you'd be."

God, this feels like some bad movie where a guy is whoring himself out to an older woman or something. That's the impression people around us would get if they were watching. "I'm sorry; maybe I should've mentioned my age in the email." No, I shouldn't have. I intentionally didn't. No one wants to believe a guy my age has reason to kill himself.

I feel her eyes raking over me as I sip my drink. To an outsider, I don't *look* sick. I mean, I'm on the too-skinny side, but that doesn't have to signify *death*.

"I'm sorry about your husband," I offer, figuring small talk might be better to get her to warm up to me. "Are you holding up all right?"

Shrugging, Marilyn leans back in her seat and turns her gaze out the window. "As best as I can, I suppose. You spend twenty years with a man and then he's gone, and you don't really know what to do with yourself."

The details of her husband's death were covered in her blog, and further in the emails we exchanged. ALS. No cure for it, of course, but he tried every treatment he could find anyway. Carl Baxter was a fighter to the end, even deciding not to take the prescribed meds to end his own life. *Why* he chose that, though, I don't know. "Do you want to talk about it?"

"Not really," she admits. The waitress wanders over. Marilyn orders a cup of coffee and is silent until the waitress brings it back. She adds in creamer like an afterthought. "I'd rather hear about you. I never thought someone would contact me asking for my husband's medication."

I shift in my seat. Truthfully, the only way for her to know I'm being honest is to show her. I hook a finger into the collar of my shirt and tug it down a ways, enough that she can see the top of the scarring on my chest from my transplant. Proof of everything I've explained to her in writing.

"You're so young," she murmurs, gaze returning to my face. "I would think you'd be a prime candidate for a transplant, even a second one."

"It would have to be a miracle. I've got a couple of months left at most, assuming this sucker doesn't clock out early." From stress. From a weakened immune system. From me not taking care of myself. I know all this road trip stuff has been taking a lot out of me, probably shortening what time I do have left, but it needed to be done. "I can't move to Oregon and qualify for the Death with Dignity Act on my own, which is why I'm trying this."

She sips her coffee slowly. "Then what's the point? If you wanted to kill yourself, there are a hundred other ways it could be done that didn't involve coming here."

Everyone will wonder about that when I'm gone, and I'm ashamed of my reasoning. But I probably kind of owe it to this lady, though I can't meet her eyes as I say it. "I guess…I'm afraid. Too easy to mess up—and let me tell you, I'm *good* at messing things up—and I've always had nightmares about trying to kill myself some other way and someone finding me, someone saving me. I've researched the Nembutal. It would be peaceful, painless. That's all I want." And I can't help but ask— "Why didn't your husband take it? What made him change his mind?"

Her fingers tighten briefly around her mug, then loosen, and she strokes her thumb absently over the porcelain handle. "He said he felt it was against his personal morals if he died without spending every moment he could with me and our children."

"At the end, was he…"

"Suffering? Oh yes. Dying was painful. It was ugly."

I swallow hard and take a drink to soothe my dry throat. "Do you wish he'd done it?"

Marilyn seems years away from me now, staring off at nothing as though watching the memories in her head play out right before her eyes. "That's a difficult question. I wanted him to do whatever he wanted to do. To see someone you love in pain…it's a terrible thing. But at the same time, you want to hold on to every hour, every second you possibly can, telling them all the things you never could before. How much they changed your life, how beautiful they are. I don't regret his choice, and up until his very last day, he said that he didn't, either."

He's a braver man than I am. And he's someone whose parents weren't being made to carry the burden of his medical bills. Frankly, Carl and Marilyn's case is different from mine, so I shouldn't try to compare it.

Marilyn swipes at the tears dotting her lashes and sets down her coffee. When she reaches for her purse, my stomach flip-flops. She's really going to give me the Nembutal, isn't she?

Except what Marilyn slides across the table to me is a business card with a name and a website. Nothing more. I stare at it, equal parts frustrated and disappointed. Why call me here to meet with her if she had no intention of selling me the medicine? "What's this?"

"I cannot, in good conscience, hand over something to let anyone kill himself." Marilyn picks her coffee back up. "But I won't deny someone the choice that we had. Carl didn't qualify to get the Nembutal legally due to his mental health—I didn't want to mention that on my site—so we had to go about getting it through other means."

Illegally. The initial unease I feel about doing that is immediately quashed down. Getting it from Marilyn would've been just as illegal. Maybe even more so because I'd be asking her to be an accomplice to my potential death.

"Thank you, Marilyn." I pull some money from my pocket to try to leave it on the table to pay for her coffee and a meal. I know it isn't much, but I feel like I should offer *some*thing in exchange for this information. "Please, grab yourself some breakfast. My treat."

Marilyn only scoffs and waves my hand away. "I don't want it. I have enough money from Carl's insurance policy to last me the rest of my life."

"Does that bring some comfort?"

"Frankly? No." She gives me a thin smile. "Because it's an everyday reminder. I'd trade it all to have him back. What would bring me comfort is if you make the same decision my husband did, and choose to live as long as you can."

Marilyn understood why her husband wanted to end his own life. Would Evelyn feel the same?

Evelyn

I don't own a lot of dresses.

Okay, that's an understatement: I don't think I own *any* dresses. Most of my wardrobe consists of jeans or leggings, sweaters, and T-shirts.

So to be staring at myself in the mirror at a mall store, wearing a dress I only ever would have glanced at longingly before, seems a bit surreal. Not because I dislike dresses, but because I dislike dresses on *me*. Always thought my legs looked funny or too pale or too chubby… something, and I didn't want to draw attention to myself.

But actually putting it on and looking in the mirror, it's kind of nice. I'm glad Luc not only brought me here, but encouraged me to pick something out to try on for our date tonight.

Speaking of Luc, he's waiting outside the dressing room patiently. I open the door and step out, adjusting the dress straps. "Well?"

Luc's gaze sweeps over me and he tilts his head. Maybe there's a slight twinkle to his eyes that wasn't there before, and I take that to be a good sign. "What do you think?"

"Aren't I supposed to be asking you that?"

"My opinion doesn't matter, Evelyn. What's important is that *you* like it. Do you?"

I turn to one of the full-length mirrors to look at myself again. "You know, I think I do."

Behind my reflection, I see one corner of Luc's mouth twist up. "Let's get it, then."

"Are you sure?"

"Why not?" He shrugs, rising to his feet. "You like it; it looks good on you."

I glance at the price tag dangling from the left strap and cringe. That's why. Luc doesn't seem fazed. Rather than have me change, he has me gather my things from the dressing room and when we get to the register, he tears off the price tag to hand it to the clerk. "She'll wear this out."

My shoes really don't match the dress, but I have a pair of flip-flops in my bag that I can slip into. I'm trying not to feel self-conscious, but that sensation dissipates when we've left the mall and return to the car.

It isn't Luc I'm self-conscious around, I realize. It's the rest of the world. Around Luc, I feel perfectly at ease. Comfortable with myself. What a wonderful feeling.

Next stop: the beach. Even though we've gone to the ocean a few times already, it never gets old for me. The air is chilly, sweeping up under my dress and making me shiver and leaving my toes numb when I discard my shoes to venture into the sand barefoot. Rather than sit back a ways, Luc comes with me this time, hands in his pockets and watching the water rush up to lap at his feet.

I twirl once, liking the feel and look of the fabric as it swirls with my movements. I stop only when Luc says, "Hey, look!"

Together we gaze out over the water where he's pointing, and it takes me a moment to see what he sees. Fins, peeking up from the water. Dipping out of view and reappearing again. I clamp a hand to my mouth.

"Dolphins?" he whispers, like they can somehow hear us all the way on shore.

"Too big," I whisper back. "Whales, I bet." No idea what kind of whales would be coming anywhere near the Oregon coastline, but they're beautiful. A whole pod of them, their dorsal fins slicing through the surface of the ocean. Only once or twice do we get to see one breach up out of the water, but it's an incredible sight. I only wish we could be closer so that it isn't so short-lived, because before long, the pod has gone too far out for us to see anymore.

We stay on the beach for hours, collecting shells, following a crab down the shore, keeping an eye out for the whales, although we don't see them again. When we finally do leave, it's because I'm freezing and we're both starving from having skipped lunch.

Luc humors my pizza craving, insisting a little bit of greasy food isn't going to be the end of the world, since he typically sticks to his diet. So it's with a pizza we return to the hotel room and order a movie, lounging around in bed for the rest of the night. It really is like a date, though it isn't entirely unlike any other night we've spent together. Giving it a label makes it feel different, and I'm somehow aware that Luc is a little calmer, less snappy than he'd normally be. I am, too. Maybe it's that all the tension built up between us has been let loose with that first kiss in the aquarium. Whatever it is, I'm not complaining.

Though I also find myself a lot more aware of him physically. The way he feels when I lean into him, the shift of his arm around my shoulders, the rise and fall of his chest as he breathes. Long after the pizza has been devoured and we've settled into a food coma, all I can think about is how comfortable Luc is, and how much I want to kiss him.

Technically I can, can't I? We had our date and now here we are. This would almost be the equivalent of him taking me home and me inviting him in or something, if I wanted to be so cliché.

When I lift my head, Luc's eyes are closed, like he might be drifting off. I take the opportunity to twist around a little and lean up, ghosting my lips across his jaw in a way that makes him shiver and open his eyes to look at me. I cup a hand to his cheek and kiss him on the mouth. Just once. Just enough that it makes the corners of his lips tick up into a not-quite-smile before he leans in to kiss me back.

Luc's kisses are my new favorite thing in the world. His mouth is warm and soft and inviting, and the way his arms tighten, the way he shifts his body forward until my back is against the mattress and he's over me, all around me, like he can shield me from anything and everything, all without breaking the kiss.

My entire body tingles. The weight of him on top of me, his hips settled between my thighs, makes my insides twist in nervous anticipation, and I'm embarrassed by my own thoughts of getting Luc out of his clothes, of getting out of *my* clothes, of having his hands all over me.

He splays his fingers out on one of my thighs. When it slides north, he pushes the bottom of my dress with it and my breath hitches. This might really be happening. I *want* it to happen, there's no doubt about it.

But the second my eyes close and I try to lose myself to the feeling of Luc's hands against my skin, I can't breathe.

Suddenly it's Robert, leaning into me, telling me that I'm pretty.

Hugging me for no reason, his body pressed against mine and holding on to me until I could feel him through his pants.

Watching me walk through the house in shorts and a tanktop because it was too hot for anything else and the look in his eyes making me feel naked and open and I just—

I plant a hand against Luc's chest to push him back, sucking in a sharp breath. My heart is racing. Not in the good way. With my vision swimming, I roll to the side and will the anxiety attack to pass.

Luc doesn't say a word. He sits beside me, perfectly silent, and only tentatively touches a hand to my back. "Evelyn?"

As the minutes tick by and I can breathe again, the guilt and embarrassment settles in. I squeeze my eyes shut. "Sorry, I'm sorry—it wasn't you…"

I can feel his eyes on me, and his voice is achingly gentle; surprising coming from Luc. "What happened in Arizona?"

I blink my eyes back open because I'm unable to scrub the image of Robert's gaze burning into me from the back of my eyelids.

"If you don't want to talk about it," Luc murmurs.

I don't, really.

But maybe I should. If anyone could give me insight into what happened, if anyone could tell me if it was all in my head and I would believe them, it would be Luc.

I focus hard on the opposite wall. "Robert. Things with him got…weird."

"Weird how?"

Trying to think of how to put it into words makes my head hurt. It isn't simple. To explain to Luc what happened is to relive the moment, and my insides are already screaming in panic at the thought. "Little things. The way he looked at me, starting out, just…*leering*. Then sometimes he'd touch me, like…putting a hand on my waist or the small of my back. It felt…intimate. Not how a guy should be touching his sort-of stepdaughter."

I glance at him and he's watching me intently, although I can't read his expression.

"There was this one time... I turned on the shower and realized I'd forgotten a towel in my room, so I left the water running while I went to get it. When I stepped back into the hall, Robert was at the bathroom door, looking inside like he thought I was in there. And I just..."

I don't realize I'm crying until Luc is touching his fingers to my cheek. He doesn't say anything. Simply pulls me into his arms and holds me tight to his chest, and there might be a slight tremor in his touch. Anger. I keep speaking because now that I've started, it all wants to come pouring out; I was afraid of this. "I kept trying to make excuses for him. Kept trying to explain it away. Like, maybe I encouraged it somehow? I'm so stupid..."

"You're not stupid," Luc says quietly. "It was wrong. *He* was wrong."

My eyes squeeze shut. I burrow my face against his shirt; it smells like seawater, chilly and salty. "I'm sorry."

"For *what*?"

"I don't know. Because I can't help but think that I did something, that maybe I gave the wrong impression... Someone wouldn't have done those weird things without prompting, right?" And because this was supposed to be a first date with Luc, not a date for me to be spilling my secrets all over him.

Luc smooths his hands across my back. I feel him press a kiss to the top of my head. "Evelyn. *It wasn't your fault.* Got it?"

Those are the words I think I've been waiting for. I

slide my arms around Luc's shoulders, wanting to hold on to him for dear life. For a few minutes, we simply sit like that until he asks, "Why not tell your mom? You said you wanted her to be able to be happy with him, but what kind of answer is that?"

The only answer I could think of at the time, really. Why *didn't* I tell Mom about Robert? "I don't know. Maybe a part of me was worried she wouldn't believe me. Or she'd make it out to seem like I was overreacting."

Luc pulls back enough to look down at me. "She's your mom. Why wouldn't she believe you? You aren't exactly someone who makes shit up."

That's the real question, isn't it? The question whose answer makes my throat close up and the tears spring to my eyes.

"Evelyn?" he asks when I've been quiet too long.

I toy with the collar of his shirt. "Because I'm not a necessity for her happiness."

Luc frowns. "What?"

My toes dig into the carpet, my fingers twisting into his T-shirt. "Mom doesn't *need* me to be happy. She *needs* a relationship. When she isn't in love, she's miserable all the time. That's how it's always been. And that's okay, I've come to terms with the fact that I'm second place in her life, but I guess I couldn't stand the possibility of hearing her say that she didn't believe me because Robert was more important to her."

I spent so many years trying to make Mom happy when it was just me and her. I wanted to make her proud. I wanted her to smile and laugh. To make her realize even if her relationships were short-lived, the love of her daughter was unconditional.

None of my efforts mattered. I was second choice to Mom in the way that I'm second choice to everything and everyone in life. It's also why I worry Grandma Jane won't let me stay with her, because Mom won't want me to, and Mom is Grandma's number one. Evelyn is runner-up.

Luc doesn't say anything. He doesn't try to argue my point. He just pulls me to him again. And I find the magic of the moment hasn't been entirely lost, because I feel better. Communication is what I've always wanted from Luc, to be able to tell him everything I'm afraid to tell anyone else. To know that he won't laugh or judge me, or say that I'm overreacting.

Maybe that in and of itself is magic.

THIRTEEN

Evelyn

The last few days have been more than perfect. Luc's been in a good mood, I've been happy, and we've been ignoring our parents and the outside world to enjoy each other. I caught up on the homework I let lapse when Luc went into the hospital. Our routine is starting to feel natural, normal. Familiar.

We went to the beach this morning like we did most mornings during the last week. We have a collection of shells and beach glass, and enough sand around the hotel room to last us a lifetime. I feel bad for the housekeepers who have to come in and vacuum when we leave.

Our beach trips always result in me needing a shower because I can't stand the feel of sand and salt on my skin. As I leave the bathroom, freshly washed and towel drying my hair, Luc is playing on his phone from his place on the bed.

He doesn't look up as he asks, "What do you think about staying here for a few more days?"

It's not like we're on any kind of a strict schedule; I'm not even sure what our next stop is supposed to be. "I don't mind. Any particular reason?"

He shrugs, finally glancing my way. I notice how his gaze lingers on me, and unlike how disgusting it made me feel when Robert would leer at me or brush his hands against me when we passed in the hall, I don't mind it. Because it's Luc. And because ever since that night where I freaked out, Luc has been a complete gentleman and done his best about being careful where his hands travel when we get carried away making out.

It isn't that I don't *want* it to go further than that. And it isn't that I don't think I could do it, so long as I was prepared and reminded myself that this is *Luc* and Luc would never hurt me, never make me feel uncomfortable, but... I don't know. Maybe I haven't been sure how to bring it up yet. Every time I think I might, my chest starts to fill with nervous giggles and I get too embarrassed.

"Not really." Luc scoots over so I can join him on the bed, folding myself neatly up against his side. "Just thought we were enjoying ourselves here."

He slips an arm around my shoulders while I sneak my hand up beneath his shirt, fingers splaying out against his stomach. Luc turns his head to press his face against my wet hair and breathes in deep, and it makes me smile. "We are. This has been my favorite part of the trip."

"Yeah? Even more than the otters?"

"Even more than the otters." I grin and tip my head

back in order to kiss him. My favorite thing is kissing Luc, but more than that, I like how he reacts. The way his arm tightens around me, wanting to draw me closer, the hitch of his breath and the soft sigh that escapes his lips when I finally pull away.

He opens his eyes halfway, almost smiling. "Well, if you'll excuse me...I'm gonna take a cold shower."

Laughing, I let him go and watch him slide off the bed and shuffle to the bathroom. Once I hear the water going, I start picking up around the room. I gather our clothes and carry them down the hall to the on-site laundry room, which is damp and smells musty and old, but it does the job well enough. It's not like we have a lot to wash.

Habit has me checking all the pockets before tossing pants and shorts into the washing machine. I retrieve a few crumpled dollars, a receipt, Luc's driver's license, and a business card, which I stop to look at curiously.

Just a name and a web address. Weird. No company, no phone number.

I set it aside with the other pocket stuff. Once the laundry is going, I return to the room and lay the items on the table.

But the card is bothering me. A niggling sensation in the back of my brain because who has a business card with no company name or even a title? I glance at the bathroom door. Shower is still going. Taking out my phone, I type in the URL on the card.

PURCHASE NEMBUTAL ONLINE
Nembutal Sodium III Oral

Nembutal Sodium III injectable
Nembutal Sodium III 50mg (30 capsules in 1 pack)
Order now

Nembutal isn't a name I recognize. One of Luc's medications? Something he wanted to try that he couldn't get here? He didn't tell me anything about it. I Google the name and get an array of results: *Nembutal (pentobarbital), sedative and anticonvulsant. Used to treat tension, anxiety, nervousness, and epilepsy. Pentobarbital may induce death in high dosages and is used for euthanasia in both humans and animals.*

My legs nearly give out.

The night Luc went to the hospital, I saw webpages open on his phone on euthanasia in Oregon. It hadn't seemed right, and I hadn't been able to wrap my head around it at the time, and so I'd shrugged it off and never even broached the subject with Luc. He could have been looking it up for any number of reasons. Curiosity brought about by temporary desperation.

This, though? This is a step further. This makes me feel cold all over.

The bathroom door swings open and Luc steps out. I hadn't even heard the shower turn off. He's dressed in jeans and a T-shirt, towel around his shoulders, and he pauses when he sees me. "Evelyn?"

I could ignore it. I'm overreacting. I have to be…right? Yet I find myself turning to stare at him, holding up the business card and trying to keep my voice level. "What's this?"

There's a hitch in Luc's step as he crosses the room to take it from me, and he won't meet my eyes. "Just something someone gave me the other day. I don't know."

Any hope I had that this was some dumb misunderstanding is quickly fading. "Don't lie to me."

"It's nothing," Luc insists, pushing a hand back through his wet hair and turning away. "Just…don't. I don't want to—it's not…"

"It's not *what*? Not what I think it is?" My voice cracks near the end, and Luc goes still, as though he knows this entire conversation is about to hit the roof. I snatch my phone back up and read to him aloud: "Pentobarbital is contained in a group of drugs called barbiturates."

"Evelyn…"

"Used to treat insomnia and seizures—"

"*Evelyn.*"

"—and for human euthanasia. *Death in a bottle.*" I lower the screen and stare at him, fighting back the overwhelming flood of tears threatening to reduce me to a complete mess. "Is that not what I think it is?"

Slowly, Luc turns to me, his expression one of guilt and grief and frustration. "I'm dying. You know that."

I twist my fingers around my phone so tightly it hurts. "We're all dying, Luc."

"Some of us faster than others."

"So…what, you figured killing yourself was a better alternative than any other option presented to you?"

"I hadn't exactly…" He grits his teeth, pulling the towel from around his neck. "It's not like I've completely made up my mind—"

"Did you buy it?"

"What?"

I drag in a slow, deep breath, each word trembling.

"Did. You. Buy. It?"

Luc doesn't answer, just stands there with that deer in the headlights look in his wide blue eyes. His silence is all the answer I need.

"Do you have it yet?"

"No," he responds quietly. "I ordered it the day before yesterday."

I nod slowly and turn away, forcing myself to set the phone on the table before impulse has me throwing it at the wall. Or at Luc.

"Evelyn." Luc dares to advance toward me, cautiously reaching to touch my shoulders. "I don't want to—I *can't* go through another transplant. I just can't do it. I've been living with a dead girl's heart inside me and it's never felt *right*, okay? My parents will forever be in debt for my medical bills. What happens if my body rejects another one? Survival rates for second transplants drop significantly."

I shove his hands away, not wanting any part of him touching me. "Was this the plan from the beginning? Is that why you came here?"

"*No,*" Luc says with such intensity that I'm inclined to believe him. "This wasn't the plan. I mean, I'd thought about it, but I never would have brought you with me if I'd been completely sold on the idea to begin with."

"Gosh, that's a comfort!" I pull back again when he tries to reach for me a second time. "You are the world's *biggest asshole*. You think *dying* is going to solve everyone's problems? You think your parents are going to say, 'Oh, we're glad he's dead. One less bill to pay!' Do you think any of us who love you and have fought for you would be okay with it? You aren't helping anyone by checking out early. You're so *selfish.*"

Luc's arms drop to his sides. "I was trying to make an executive decision on what's best for everyone."

"*You don't get to do that!*"

He startles into silence, sinking onto the edge of the bed. "I warned you this trip wasn't necessarily going to be what you thought it was."

The disappointment and anger boils over. I'm sobbing openly, hysterical and lost and this is all so *stupid.* "Oh, *fuck you,* Luc."

I storm out of the room, slamming the door hard enough that the gust of air knocks every paper animal off the table.

Luc

A paper crane lands at my feet.

I stare at it for a while, feeling… I don't even know what I'm feeling. Can't seem to sort out the guilt from the anger and sadness.

I've let Evelyn down. It was something I knew was coming, because I would have to tell her eventually, I had just hoped…*eventually* would be a ways off. Maybe I'd even deluded myself into thinking she'd understand. I can't be disappointed by that. If our situations were reversed, if I didn't know what it was like to be sick and dying every day of her life, I think I would also be angry with her for keeping that sort of information from me.

Slowly I pluck the crane from the floor and cradle it in my palm. Where did she storm off to, and should I try to follow her? What would I say if she wanted to listen to me? If there's anything I want to apologize for, it's that I started this relationship when I knew what a horrible, selfish idea it really was. If I'd never kissed her that day at the aquarium, maybe we'd still be going as we had been. Friends. Awkward friends, but friends.

Or maybe that idea is stupid. We've been *just friends* for years, but that was only because I kept her at arm's length, wasn't it? It didn't mean the feelings weren't there, just that I refused to give them a voice.

I leave the bed and mechanically begin to gather the origami animals from the floor, placing each one back on the table. There are forty-two total. She could have kept going if she hadn't run out of paper. I could have sat and watched her for hours.

Two days ago, I spent four hundred dollars ordering two bottles of Nembutal from that website. I'd planned on getting a PO Box at a nearby post office, but the lady at the hotel's front desk said they could accept a package for me, and so I had it sent here. In a few days, I'll have my very own death in my hands, pretty literally.

My choice now is *when* to take that final step.

And whether or not Evelyn will stick by me until then.

· · ·

Evelyn

The laundry room is unbearably humid after the first fifteen minutes and my shirt is clinging to my back. I could take a walk, but I don't want to be around anyone. Don't want anyone to see me and risk them asking why there're tears staining my face, why my eyes are red. Why I can't seem to stop crying for the better part of an hour.

I thought…after all these years, we were finally, really together and that meant a *future*. It meant if I could make him take it easy for the next few weeks, that I might be able to talk him into going home and getting the treatment he needs to prolong his life. Whether that meant he'd live a few months or a few years, I don't know, but I would have been there with him every step of the way to show him it was worth it.

I love him so much, and I hate that it's all going to end. I hate that he won't fight. I hate that I know when it comes down to it, I don't truly understand the struggle Luc's endured. I don't know what I would do in his place, if I would think dying would be what was best for everyone around me even if they didn't agree.

I hate that I'm not worth living for. Second best, runner-up, just like with Mom.

Stupid me, thinking our relationship, *me*, was worth him sticking around.

I press the heels of my palms against my eyes, so exhausted from crying. A sharp ache has worked its way into my shoulders, neck, and back and won't go away.

The buzzing of the dryer has me jerking upright, jarring me out of my self-pity.

Luc wants to kill himself.

What am I going to do about that? What *can* I do? What are my options?

I could leave. Use my own savings to get on the next bus home. If that meant telling Mom I refuse to go back to Arizona, I think…maybe I could do that. Maybe this trip has taught me something about myself, in that Mom isn't faultless and that what happened with Robert wasn't my fault.

I could carry on like nothing happened. Pretend our argument is done and over with, be supportive of his decision. As much as I've always wanted to support Luc in anything he truly wanted to do, as much as I've kept my mouth shut about him even *being here* when he should be home seeking medical care…I can't envision myself doing it this time.

I could push him to change his mind. With all the beauty in this world, even just the fraction we've seen on this trip… The fun we've had together… Surely Luc has to think, at least a little, that there're things worth living for?

Even if I'm not one of them.

A flicker of hope ignites in the back of my heart, spreading until I'm wiping the tears from my face and standing with newfound energy. That's what needs to happen. Me and Luc, enjoying our time, my showing him what living truly is and why this can't be the end of things.

I've been gone for close to three hours, given the number of times I had to restart the dryer because it wasn't fully drying our clothes. They're done now, and I take the time to fold them up before carrying them back to the room.

Luc is seated at the table when I come in. He's picked up all the origami animals from the floor. As soon as I step inside, he jerks to attention, pushing his chair back and standing like he's ready for me to resume yelling.

I've resolved not to do that. It isn't going to fix anything.

Instead I set the folded laundry on the bed and take a deep breath before turning to face him. "When were you planning on doing this?"

Luc shifts his weight from one foot to the other, glancing side to side like he's half expecting this to be some kind of joke, a trick question. "I don't know. Like I said, it wasn't something I'd planned out…"

Good. That's good, right? There's still time.

I put my hands on my hips. "Until then, what's supposed to happen with us?"

Immediately his gaze flicks away, a guilt-ridden frown pulling at his face. "I understand if you want to go home."

"I'm not going home, Luc. We've come this far together; it seems stupid for me to turn around and run away now."

"I figured it would've been the smarter move," he mumbles.

"Not your decision."

Sighing, he runs a hand through his hair and bows his head. "Okay, then what do you want to do?"

What do I want? I want…Luc to be okay. I want us

to go home, to be happy together. We could get our own small place, just the two of us. I would find a job, and I would take care of him if he had to go through another transplant. I would watch him pin butterflies and he would watch me make paper cranes and every night, I'd fall asleep next to him.

And I need to do everything within my power to make that happen.

"I want to enjoy the rest of our vacation," I say quietly. "However it might end."

My answer must catch him off-guard because he's silent for a long time before letting out a heavy breath. Maybe he expected me to ask him for more. "Okay," he says slowly. "We can do that."

I force a small smile. "We still have a few places on your list to go, don't we? I just want to see them with you." I cross the distance between us and lift my hands to his face, sliding my thumbs along his cheekbones.

"I'd like that." His expression softens when he finally lets himself make eye contact with me again.

It's all I can ask for from him. I have to show him how great this can be. If I fail, if he still chooses death over life… I will be angry. I know that. I will be resentful and so heartbroken I can't stand to think of it. For now, though? I can lean in and kiss him and know that I have this, right here and now.

I pray it's not too late to show him that he should keep fighting.

FOURTEEN

Luc

The remaining days we spend just outside of Newport, Evelyn seems intent on cramming as much as humanly possible into our schedule. We've explored Newport from top to bottom, from South Beach State Park to a fish market, to the Hatfield Marine Science Center and Ripley's. But every night we return to our little hotel off US-101, with me absolutely exhausted and Evelyn in high spirits. It's worth it.

The evening before we're scheduled to check out of the hotel, I stop by the front office and find a package waiting for me from Mexico. My heart promptly lodges itself into my throat and for a long while, I simply stand there and stare at the box, at a loss for what to do with it.

I take it to the car to unwrap it. Inside are two small bottles, largely in Spanish, but the important stuff is in English. *NEMBUTAL Sodium Solution.* Everything I've read states that one bottle should be enough, but it's not unheard of for people to survive after drinking just one. I bought two bottles, just in case. I could've gone the injection route, but I wasn't sure I could handle it.

If I do this, it needs to work. Not land me in another hospital suffering from severe side effects.

As delicately as I can, I wrap the glass bottles in a spare blanket and tuck them into the trunk. The weather is cold enough that they should be all right, and I don't want to risk Evelyn stumbling across them in the hotel room. We'll be leaving tomorrow anyway, though I don't know where we're going yet.

Heading back inside, I find Evelyn seated on the bed, finishing her homework for the week. Her head snaps up at me, and the intensity in how she says "Luc!" almost makes me terrified that she knows what I was doing. Except then she's making grabby-hands at me, a smile lighting up her face. "Let's go see the butterflies."

I frown but go to her, sinking onto the bed as she catches hold of my hands. "Did you miss the memo that they're closed?"

She stares at me, eyebrows arching. "So?"

"So…" I pause. "Are you suggesting what I think you're suggesting?"

"You only live once."

I bite back a laugh. This sounds like a terrible plan that is going to result in both of us getting arrested, and yet… "Okay, let's hear your plan."

Evelyn releases me and hops off the bed. "Come on. I was reading up and looking at Street View on Google Maps. I think I know where we can sneak in, and it's pretty much in the middle of nowhere."

"Oh, do you?"

"It's not like we're breaking into a bank." She begins pulling on her jacket and slipping into her shoes.

I can't help the amusement in my voice. "Guess we could do that, too."

Evelyn wrinkles her nose and throws my jacket at me. "I want you to see the butterflies."

She's so insistent on this that it's almost confusing, and I have a sinking sensation that maybe she's doing it as a means of talking me out of killing myself. As though it'll somehow make me decide to go home and get treatment. I can't stand the thought of asking her, because that last argument took a lot out of me. I just want to enjoy our time together.

Evelyn leads me to the car so we can drive the forty-five minutes to the Butterfly Emporium. It's pitch-black, of course, and there really isn't anything around. Grass and open road with the ocean in the distance. Construction equipment sits still and silent in the parking lot where the concrete is all torn up. The sign hanging above the front glass double doors is, unoriginally, of block lettering—THE BUTTERFLY EMPORIUM—with a silhouette of a butterfly rising from the B. We park across the road and sneak around to the rear of the building. I eye the back door, an employee-only entrance, with some skepticism.

"What's the worst that will happen if we're caught?" Evelyn whispers, *now* sounding a little nervous.

"Uh, aside from getting arrested?"

"Worth it?"

I shrug. Why the hell not? "Let's do it."

This isn't the Museum of Natural History we're breaking into. It's a rundown little place that looks like it might have been a small set of offices at some point in time and was later converted. Which means the windows in back are rickety and Evelyn seems to have counted on that. She pulls her driver's license from her pocket, wedging it between the frame and the windowsill, wiggling it back and forth until it catches on the latch and she's able to unlock it.

She casts a triumphant smile and pockets her ID. "Voilà."

"I'm not sure I want to know where you learned that."

"A lot of TV." Evelyn hoists herself through the window and I follow after, glancing around for any sign of cameras. Given their crappy security, I'm not surprised to not see any. We ease the window shut behind us.

We're standing in the middle of a dark break room slash storage room. A counter and a two-person table, along with a plastic shelf of cleaning supplies. Not exactly state-of-the-art technology. "Kind of…old, huh?" Evelyn whispers.

"Well, this place was started by a personal collector who opened his doors to the public, so I'm guessing upgrades aren't really in the budget." Even stepping into the hallway, I'm thinking the renovations are limited to the parking lot. I don't see any signs that anything in here is being worked on.

"Oh. It was?"

"Yeah." We follow the hallway down past a door labeled as a restroom and into a modest lobby adorned with butterfly paraphernalia: posters, pamphlets, photographs, display cases similar to the ones I have back home. "Stephan McAllister, if I remember right. He's like in his seventies and he's been breeding and collecting butterflies since he was our age."

Evelyn stops at the front desk, examining the home-printed pamphlets before taking a few for later reading. "Maybe we should leave some money? Like...the admission fee. Doesn't seem like this place would get a lot of business."

I step up beside her, already fishing in my pockets to toss forty bucks onto the counter. "How did I know you were going to suggest that?"

Evelyn's response is a smile. She tucks the pamphlets into her back pocket, reaches for my hand, and leads me toward another hall labeled BUTTERFLY EMPORIUM ENTRANCE. A set of glass doors open into a large greenhouse, and glass walls and ceilings surround us with a single paved pathway curving gently ahead of us. The foliage has been freshly watered and smells slightly musty, but it's a smell I attribute to forests and nature in the early morning, and it's calming.

For a moment, I forget about Evelyn and everything else. I walk ahead, squinting in the darkness. There're a few solar-powered light stakes in the ground lining the walkway, at least, but visibility is definitely limited.

I'm not deterred in the slightest. I venture down the path a ways and crouch beside a cluster of rocks and logs, pulling out my phone to turn on the flashlight app. A moment later, I can feel my face lighting up. "Hey, come here."

Obediently she moves to my side and kneels, leaning

in to peer at what I'm looking at. Inside one of the logs are at least half a dozen butterflies, all still and beautiful. Purple, orange, green. Every color of the rainbow. I reach in very slowly and withdraw my hand with one perched upside down on my finger. Evelyn covers her mouth to hide a giggle.

"When it's night or when the temperature drops, they sleep," I murmur. "Well, sort of. It isn't really sleeping, but their equivalent of sleep."

"It's so pretty," Evelyn whispers. "What kind is it?"

I slowly sit back, equal parts in awe and at peace. "A Banded Orange, I think."

"I like them a lot better when they're alive."

"Most things are better alive."

Evelyn seems to go very still for a few seconds, shoulders sagging, and I think I probably could have refrained from saying something like that. The look is gone quickly and she braves sticking her hand into the log. When she pulls it back out, her eyes grow impossibly wide. She has two white and gray ones that stretch their wings out as though stirring sleepily. "I caught some!"

"Be careful. Don't startle them. That's a Mottled Swallowtail. The other one…not sure. Mother of Pearl, maybe?" I'm aware I'm muttering more to myself than to her as I admire the butterflies on her hand. Delicately, Evelyn transfers them from her fingers to my arm, where they settle and don't move again.

After a while, some of the butterflies flutter away and we return the remaining ones to their log and continue down the path. There are placards describing the different types of butterflies, their diet, their lifespan… From birth to death, most of them live less than a year. In their actual adult butterfly stage, many less than a month. How fleeting, how sad, that something so beautiful can only survive such a short time.

Evelyn follows my lead and we begin searching under large leaves and logs, finding butterflies in all sorts of places. A few flutter away but most remain dormant and allow us to pick them up, tolerating my intense staring until I move on to the next one.

The path is paved in cream-colored stone, adorned with the occasional wooden bench here and there. In the very center it opens up into a circle with a small fountain—which is turned off at the moment—and butterflies have made their homes here, hanging upside down under the stone overhangs close to the water.

I take a seat on the edge of the fountain, admiring a large Luna Moth fluttering around one of the trees while Evelyn wanders. She returns to me a good fifteen minutes later, positively beaming with pride as she holds out her hands, a blue and black butterfly cupped gently in her palms. "It's a Blue Morpho, right? The one I liked?"

My back straightens. I reach out to take it carefully from her and lift it close to my face to get a good look. Evelyn takes a seat beside me, lifting her phone and—I assume—taking a picture of the butterfly and me. "It's a Blue Morpho," I agree, admiring the deep color of its wings. Despite being as still as I can, the Morpho eventually spreads its wings and takes flight. Evelyn lowers her phone and mournfully watches it go, distracted only when I reach for her and say, "Come on."

Hand in hand, we walk the length of the emporium. Which isn't huge by any means, but it's not hard to spend time finding and identifying as many moths and butterflies as I can. When we find ones I don't know, we sit and look it up on our phones until we can figure it out.

It's close to five by the time we return to the fountain circle and I just...lie down. Evelyn lies beside me and we stare up through the glass rooftop overhead, watching the sky in silence. Eventually she asks, "Was it worth potential arrest for breaking and entering?"

"Worth it," I agree with a grin.

"We should do this every night."

"That'd be nice."

"We could, you know." Evelyn looks over at me. "We could stay in town longer and come every night, if you wanted to."

I don't look at her. As appealing as the idea is, it'd only be a matter of time before we got caught, and I don't want Evelyn having an arrest on her record because of me. "What are you going to do? After, I mean."

Evelyn's expression falls. She looks skyward again. "After what?"

"After I'm gone."

Her fingers wrapped around mine squeeze involuntarily at those words. "I don't know. Try to get a job. Beg Grandma Jane to let me stay with her. Whatever I have to do to not go back to Robert's."

If it were that simple, I think she would have done that already. She wouldn't have upset her mother and grandmother by running off with me. But that's Evelyn; she doesn't want me to worry. She's been so damned focused on me since she found out about the Nembutal that I wouldn't be surprised if she has no concern for herself right now, and that bothers me. *I* worry about what she'll do when I'm gone. This trip won't last forever.

I sigh heavily. Evelyn rolls onto her side, resting her head against my shoulder. A frown creases my brow. How do I protect someone, give something to them, when I'm dead? The only answer that comes to mind is a ridiculous one and she'll probably laugh at me. Maybe the idea started back in the hospital, when the doctor thought Evelyn was my wife. Maybe it's yet another selfish move on my part, too, but—

"Marry me."

Evelyn goes so still and quiet that I almost wonder if she didn't hear me. But then she's sitting up abruptly, startling a butterfly she hadn't noticed was perched on her hair. *"What?"*

What an idiotic thing for me to blurt out, but I've said it and it's not like I haven't thought about it before in passing, so no taking it back now. "I mean it," I say, staring up at her. "I have a life insurance policy. I'm nineteen so I can change who my beneficiary is. I'll leave enough of it to Mom and Dad to help with my medical bills and the rest will go to you. You wouldn't have to go back to Arizona." The words come out of me in such a rush that it doesn't dawn on me that it's probably a poor choice to say to a girl like her.

She scowls. "I'm not marrying you for your *money*."

"Evelyn, don't be difficult."

"*I* should't be difficult? No. Just…no. I don't want it, and I don't need it. Besides, life insurance companies aren't going to pay anything if you kill yourself."

I can't help but flinch at the slight venom in her voice when she says that. "Most policies have an exclusionary period," I say patiently. "I've had mine since I was thirteen. I'm well past that period. It'll be covered. I've looked into it."

She sits up and turns her back to me, knees drawn to her chest and arms hugging herself tightly. I'm guessing she's trying not to cry, and…okay, maybe I didn't word it the greatest, but is the idea *that* bad?

"Evelyn?"

Evelyn swallows hard, desperately trying to level her voice. "I don't want to be a widow at eighteen just for money."

I close my eyes, willing away the sting of those words, along with the images they produce. Evelyn in a wedding dress. Evelyn in a funeral dress. Evelyn standing by my graveside with my parents, having to explain to them why she was with me when I died and why she didn't do something to stop me.

God, I'm a terrible human being.

Taking a deep breath, I sit up. "Then do it because you love me. Do it because I want to take care of you, and this is the only way I know how. If it's the last thing I do in my life, I want to know you'll be okay when I'm gone."

Evelyn sniffs quietly. When she looks over her shoulder, her eyes are glassy and red, but she isn't crying. Yet. The internal debate she's fighting is scrawled across her face, as her emotions always are. She's such an open book, written in every language for everyone to see. It's a weakness, I think, but I would never change it about her.

She says, "Okay."

I blink once, waiting for her to say *just kidding* or to get angry with me. For there to be some amendment to that statement. "Okay?"

She doesn't smile, but the anger is gone from her voice. "If it weren't for…all this, would you still have wanted to marry me?"

That's an easy question to answer and I don't skip a beat: "If I were normal, I would have done so many things differently. I would've…" I struggle for words, not wanting to excuse my actions. "Not exactly like this, and not so abruptly, but yeah. I would have asked you. I would've given you whatever wedding you wanted."

But that's a big *if. If* I didn't have these problems, *if* I weren't dying, then so much would've been different. I never would have stopped fighting for Evelyn when she moved away. I would have visited, I would have written and called every day. Maybe it's stupid for me to think in terms like that, but I can't help it. I'd be in college right now while she finished up high school and afterward, I would have moved her in with me. She could go to school to do whatever she wanted and, maybe by the time we were both done, we'd be walking down an aisle with both our families there.

As it is…all I can offer her is the paperwork, and I'm not sure that's something I can forgive myself for. She deserves so much better.

"Your parents will hate me," she murmurs. Yet she's slowly uncurling from herself and twisting around to face me. "My mom will, too."

"I'll explain everything to them. I'll make them

understand." I reach out to cup her face in my hands. "I promise I will."

Her eyes fall shut and she leans into my hands. I brush my thumbs across her cheeks, wiping away some of the tears that've finally started to fall. She sniffs again and moves forward, crawling into my lap and wrapping her arms around me tightly.

It's sudden, it's drastic, but if it's all I can do to take care of Evelyn, I'll do whatever it takes.

FIFTEEN

Evelyn

Marriage.

I'm barely eighteen years old, I've been traveling with Luc for a few weeks, and…he wants to marry me.

Okay, so maybe it isn't as simple as all that. We've known each other for years, even if our relationship has been strange and strained at times. I'd be lying if I said my saying yes didn't have something to do with his sickness, of being afraid if I don't do this now and something happens to him, if I can't convince him to keep fighting, I'll never have the chance to marry the boy I love.

It isn't about the money. I couldn't care less, and in fact, if I ended up with any of it, I'd be more inclined to beg his parents to take it because I wouldn't want anyone ever thinking that any part of my feelings for Luc involved his money.

What it *is* about is life. Changing Luc's mind. Making him want to live.

We stay one more night at the hotel before packing up. A farewell trip to the beach is in order, too. The Oregon coast looks so much different than California; maybe it's just the weather and the chilliness, but it doesn't stop me from rolling up my jeans and discarding my shoes to trot out to the water's edge while Luc sits a safe distance away and watches the waves chase me up and down the beach.

When I finally return to him, my face is warm and flushed, and my hair is struggling to come loose from its bun. I stop in front of where he's seated. He's been quiet today. "Are you feeling all right? We can head back to the car if you need to rest."

"I am resting," he drawls. "The fresh air is good for me. Besides, I was having fun watching you."

My nose wrinkles. I plop down onto the sand beside him. "You still haven't told me where we're going next."

"I guess I haven't."

"So…tell me."

"You're so impatient," he teases mildly, stretching his legs out to lie back in the sand with his arms behind his head. "I was thinking we'd head to Vegas."

That makes me pause and my eyebrows lift. "Vegas?"

"Vegas. Las Vegas. Nevada? You know, casinos, prostitutes, Elvis?"

"Yeah, I got that. But why?" It's not like either of us is old enough to gamble, and I doubt we'll be making a night of visiting a brothel.

Luc looks over at me, expression guarded but…maybe a

little hopeful. "Wedding capital of the United States, isn't it?"

The image that immediately brings to mind makes me cover my mouth to hide a smile. "Do you want an Elvis wedding, Luc? That's so cute."

He rolls his eyes. "Ha. Anyway, I'm sure we could find a place you'd like, and I have a cousin who lives about thirty minutes outside the city where we might be able to crash."

I wiggle my toes into the sand. "Are you going to call him to ask first?"

"I don't have his number, just an address."

"Dropping in on someone unexpectedly is pretty rude."

"Eh...when you meet him, you'll understand. Max isn't the kind of guy who cares about that."

I give this some consideration. Vegas is a long ways away, but it's out of Oregon and it's doing the job of keeping Luc motivated and moving. Part of me wants to ask him about the Nembutal, if he has it—I'm sure he does by now—and when he plans on using it. Am I going to be married for a week, a month, a year, before he wants to end his life?

The thought has to be shoved down or else I'm going to start crying. "Vegas. Okay, we can do that."

I'm actually going to get married in Vegas. I don't know if I've lost my mind or if this is the best decision I've ever made.

The fifteen-hour drive to Las Vegas is the biggest stretch of time that Luc and I are stuck in the car, and I don't complain once. The farther we get from Oregon, the farther it feels like we're getting away from death, because that was the whole point of going, wasn't it? For Luc to die. I want to feel confident about this, and yet…

Obviously not confident enough to ask him.

For now, I want to enjoy Luc's presence. I want to enjoy reaching for his hand and lacing our fingers together while he drives. I want to enjoy the way he nuzzles his face into the back of my neck when we lay together, or how he slides his thumb up the length of my spine. All these little, perhaps insignificant, things that I want to capture in my palms and hide away for safekeeping.

I've never experienced anything quite like Las Vegas. Sure, you see it on TV, but it isn't the same. The lights make me forget it's two o'clock in the morning when we roll into town, and it's obvious this place never sleeps because the streets are full of people.

But Luc's cousin doesn't live in Vegas itself, so he keeps driving until we reach the outskirts, following directions on his phone's GPS. It takes us to a kind of dumpy apartment complex that looks more like a motel, and even here, people are loitering around this late at night. It doesn't feel safe. Luc must share this feeling because he takes my hand and keeps me close to his side as we scale up to the third floor and locate the unit number.

"What if he doesn't live here anymore?" I ask as Luc knocks. "Then we're waking someone up in the middle of the night for nothing."

"I really doubt he's moved." Luc gives my fingers a squeeze. A moment later, a light through the window flicks on before we hear the sound of someone unlocking the door.

The man who answers isn't as old as I thought he'd be. He's—surprisingly—taller than Luc, with the same dark hair, though his is well past his shoulders and tied back into a ponytail. He's thin and not nearly as nicely complexioned as Luc or…well, attractive in the way that Luc is. (That could be my bias speaking.) He blinks at us over the tops of his glasses and breaks out into a broad, lazy grin.

"Luc? Is that you?"

"Hey, Max." Luc grins back at him, offering his free hand, which Max takes and shakes fervently. "Sorry to drop by out of nowhere."

"Nah, nah! Come on in!" Max steps back and gestures. "Welcome to my humble abode."

Max's "humble abode" consists of a lot of worn furniture that smells like pot, a tower of soda cans in one corner, and various fast food containers and TV dinner trays lying around. Honestly, I don't want to sit down when Max sweeps some of the trash from the couch to the floor and offers us a seat, but Luc is raising an eyebrow at me, and I realize it would be rude not to. The couch cushions sag beneath our weight, and I try to focus on Max rather than look around his apartment. Luc doesn't seem fazed by the mess, or concerned about the prospect of cockroaches running across our feet.

Max is busy moving around the room with a lit joint between his fingers, tossing some stuff into a closet and nudging some of the garbage and dirty dishes to one side as though it makes a difference. "This is totally cool. What's up, man? I haven't seen you in, like, six years?"

"Something like that," Luc agrees. "So Evelyn, this is my

cousin Max. Max, this is Evelyn. My fiancée."

There has been nothing normal about the idea of Luc and me getting married. No wedding announcements, no proper dating for that matter…so to be introduced like that, not as just *Evelyn* but as *Luc's fiancée* leaves my insides fluttering so much that I don't even mind it when Max stops what he's doing in order to gather me up off the couch in a bear hug. "Fiancée? Holy shit, that's awesome, that's great! Congrats. Welcome to the family, Evelyn!"

"Um… Thank you." I pat his back awkwardly until he releases me so I can sit back down next to Luc, who looks vaguely amused by the whole thing.

Max plops onto the carpet in front of us, taking a long drag from his joint. "That's just…so awesome. I can't believe it. You're all grown up and shit, that's so cool. Did you guys need a place to crash or something?"

Luc rubs the back of his neck. "How'd you know?"

He grins. "Dude, people come to Vegas to get hitched. There's this awesome chapel I used to work at that does celebrity impersonator weddings—"

"No thanks," we say in unison.

Luc continues. "We're going to look up a few places online and check them out. If we could just crash on your couch for a couple of nights, that'd be great."

Max spreads his hands wide. "Yeah! Of course! *Mi casa es su casa.*"

I can't envision myself sleeping here. I'm pretty sure there are mice droppings on the floor, and the smell isn't making me feel great, but looking at Max's sincerely happy, warm face, I start to feel guilty for being such a brat. Luc was right about him. It takes a special kind of person to not see a family member for years and yet open his home in the middle of the night, so I should just deal with it. Besides, Luc obviously likes this guy, and it would be good for him to be around family.

Then I realize Max likely has no idea that Luc is dying, and my guilt multiplies tenfold.

We spend the next two hours sitting in Max's living room and talking. Or rather, Luc and Max talk while I listen quietly. Luc orders us a pizza from an all-night place up the street, and Max eats most of it because Luc doesn't really eat greasy foods and I feel horribly out of place and my nerves have made all food sound disgusting.

Which isn't to say it isn't nice to observe Luc having a conversation with someone who isn't me. Despite being stoned out of his mind and living in filth, Max has an easy, friendly demeanor, and you'd think he'd seen Luc and me every day for the last several years with how familiar he acts toward us. He tells us about his ever-changing jobs—from the casinos to the chapels to working as a maintenance guy at one of the brothels— and the band he played in for a while until they all decided to part ways to *pursue individual projects*. Luc takes these stories with a faint smile and an amused sparkle to his eyes, and I'll admit, I kind of admire how Max doesn't care about much of anything except the here and now.

It's close to five in the morning by the time Luc insists we call it a night. Max doesn't have much in the way of spare bedding, but thankfully we have the extra blankets and pillows in the car. I slip into the bathroom long enough to change, cringing at the unsightliness of the toilet and tub, not to mention the shavings in the sink.

When I come out, Max's already gone to his room to crash, and Luc has obviously done his best to cover up the couch with one blanket so that I don't have to lay directly on it. I give him a grateful smile.

"He promises me there aren't any roaches and there are mousetraps out. You gonna be okay?"

"Yes. Sorry," I say, and I mean it.

Luc turns off the light, double checks that the front door is locked, and stretches out on the couch. It's the tightest space we've had while sleeping in close quarters, but the couch is just wide enough that, lying on our sides, we can both fit. With Luc's chest against my back, I can feel the steady beat of his heart. His hands are folded against my stomach and I'm not self-conscious about it. I realize it doesn't make my heart race with anxiety, because he seems so content and calm and I feel *safe* when we're together like this. He nuzzles his face into my hair and breathes in deep.

We've been silent for a few minutes when I offer, "He seems nice."

Luc laughs softly against the back of my neck.

"What's so funny?"

"You hate it here."

"I don't *hate* it here. It's just…"

"Filthy?"

"Well, yeah. But I don't hate *him*. He seems really sweet. I mean, if a cousin I hadn't spoken to in years showed up at my house, I wouldn't be comfortable with them crashing on my couch."

He kisses a spot of skin, just below my ear, and it makes me shiver in a way that is both pleasant and a little embarrassing. "He's just that sort of guy. He's kind of the black sheep of the family since he's never been able to hang on to a job and has always been a stoner, but he's got a good heart. I've never heard him say a mean thing about anyone."

I tap my fingers against his arm in tune with *Mary had a Little Lamb*. Does Luc plan to tell Max that he's dying? Or that he plans on killing himself? Does he still *have* a plan? I don't know, and I still can't bring myself to ask. Which makes me a coward, I think, that I'd rather lie here and savor every breath against my neck, every gentle squeeze of his arms, and pray that I'm managing to sway his decision, than to risk upsetting this delicate balance between us.

How much time do we have left?

SIXTEEN

Luc

"You sure you'll be okay here on your own?" I ask Evelyn for the fifth time. She fusses with the collar of my jacket and smiles, leaning up to kiss me quickly on the mouth in a way that suggests she's still not used to being able to do that. Honestly, neither am I. I kind of hope I never get used to it, because it's awesome.

"For the last time, I'm good. You guys have fun."

She's making an effort to assure me it's okay, but Evelyn's an open book. I know this apartment creeps her out, but this is important, this outing with Max. I need to look around at some places, and who better to guide me through Vegas than someone who's lived here for years? I figured Evelyn would want to go along, seeing as this is a venue for *our* wedding, but she insisted she wanted to be surprised and have me pick something out.

"We won't be long," I promise, kissing her back before turning to follow Max out of the apartment.

When we're in the car, Max rolls down the window and lights up a cigarette. My eye twitches. I hate the smell, but given all of his hospitality, I can't bring myself to tell him to stop. "Have you ever considered one of those vape pens?"

Max rolls his gaze to me, blinking slowly. "Huh? Wassat?"

"Like the electronic cigarettes?"

"Ohhh yeah. I've seen those. Awesome, but, like, expensive."

I *hmm* in reply. Maybe before we leave, it wouldn't hurt to get him a little present as a thank-you.

Max says, "Evelyn seems cool. So you guys are really getting hitched, huh?"

"Seems that way."

"But your folks don't know?"

Ah. I haven't said as much, but Max isn't a *total* idiot. "No. I'd rather they didn't, if that's okay with you."

He holds up his hands with a smile. "My lips are sealed. Why, though?"

Really should have thought up excuses earlier. Maybe I'd counted on Max not asking questions. "Things are complicated. I'm not sure how to explain it. This is something she and I need to do on our own, though, I can tell you that much."

I hold my breath as I wait to see if Max will leave it at that, or will press for info. He puffs out a plume of smoke, shrugs, and reaches over to adjust the radio. "All right, cool. Whatever I can do to help, cuz."

Max guides me to eight different chapels over the course of the day. It's after lunch by the time he shows me the exact one I had in mind. Or, the one I think Evelyn will like. So I can't give her some huge ceremony, but I can make the best of our situation. Before we leave, I make a reservation and gather some pamphlets on what we'll need to do as far as getting ourselves a marriage license and all that. A ceremony alone isn't going to help Evelyn after I die when it comes to collecting any kind of financial help.

When we head back to the apartment, it's nearing dinnertime. I hadn't meant to stay out so long, and I'm hoping Evelyn hasn't gone crazy in Max's dirty place alone. Max opens the door first, pauses, and steps back. "Sorry, wrong apartment—"

"Dude, you used your key. It's yours." I push past him to step inside, and for a second even I'm almost convinced we're in the wrong place.

The living room is spotless. All the garbage is gone. While the carpets are stained and torn and in dire need of replacement, they've been vacuumed. Evelyn herself is passed out on the couch, bundled up in one of my coats, and doesn't stir at us entering.

"Whoa," Max says. *Whoa* is right. Not just the living room, but upon closer inspection the kitchen, the back balcony, the bathroom and bedroom…all spotless. She must have worked her ass off.

I sink onto the edge of the couch, brushing the hair from Evelyn's face with a crooked smile. She shifts and cracks her eyes open to look at me with a sigh. "Mm?"

"We're home."

She smiles sleepily and pushes herself up to sitting. When she sees the way Max and I are staring at her, a faint blush creeps into her cheeks. "Um…I'm sorry. Is it okay? I just figured it was a way to say thank you for letting us stay here."

"Lady, it's fuckin' awesome." Max laughs. "Even the floors are, like, clean. Did you vacuum? Do I own a vacuum?"

"No. I had to borrow one from a lady a few doors down. I don't think she spoke any English, but she was very sweet. She even brought me over some cleaning stuff and rags when she realized what I was trying to do."

Max is already turning to wander down the hall to his room, still muttering as he goes. "I don't think this place was this clean even when I moved in."

I chuckle, sliding farther onto the couch to let Evelyn curl herself up against my side. "Tell me the truth: were you just getting tired of the filth?"

"If that were the only reason, then I would've just cleaned up out here and not the entire apartment." She raises her eyebrows. "You guys were gone forever."

"Sorry, I know." I dig into my back pocket and offer her the brochure I grabbed from the Chapel of the Faeries. Stupid name, but whatever.

She takes one look at the image on the front and her face lights up. Like all the chapels we looked at today, this one was overdone and a little on the cheesy side, but it was pretty, in its own way. Outdoors. Lit with something the worker there called "fairy lights," with white rose bushes all over the place. Small and quiet. Nothing huge and flashy. I hadn't realized how tight my chest had been about making this decision without her until I see the pleased look on her face and know I chose right.

"This is beautiful, Luc. Is this definitely the place?"

"I got it booked, yeah." I fidget with the sleeve of my coat that she's wearing. "Night after tomorrow. Is that okay?"

Her eyes widen. "Two days?"

"Two days," I agree.

"We're really getting married in two days?"

"If you haven't changed your mind."

"Have *you*?"

"Uh, I just spent all day trying to find the perfect wedding place I thought you'd like and forked over the money for a hotel reservation. What do you think?"

Evelyn laughs—I really, really love her laugh—and throws her arms around my neck, pressing kisses to the side of my face. "We're getting married in two days!"

Any sadness, any hesitation she had that night in the butterfly house seems to be gone. For now. This is what I wanted to give her: happiness. Something to look forward to. Something to laugh and smile about…and something to remember me by when I'm gone.

Despite being small, the wedding isn't going to be free. There was the fee to reserve the chapel. I figure there will be a fee to get our marriage license, too, which I'm planning on doing the day of the wedding, first thing in the morning. There's also the cost of a hotel room, and I want to make sure it's a hell of a lot nicer than any other place we've stayed. I can't give her some grand wedding or honeymoon, so I'll splurge on what little I can.

The goal for today was to go dress shopping for Evelyn, so she could pick out clothes to wear. Even if it won't be an actual wedding gown, she deserves to have something nice. Me? Eh, I can get away with pants and a button-down shirt.

Before we're able to get out the door, though, Evelyn puts a hand to my chest. "Oh no. You can't go with us."

I pause, startled. "Why not?"

Max clicks his tongue and shakes his head solemnly. "Come on, man, really? The groom can't see his chick in her wedding dress before the actual wedding. It's bad luck."

My eyebrows raise. I guess it's only fair. Evelyn spent all of yesterday on her own, so if she wants to go out and do this part alone... I hand her one of my bank cards. "I guess I can keep myself entertained while you're gone." She smiles brightly and kisses me quickly on the mouth. She and Max head out the door, leaving me alone in the apartment.

It leaves me alone with my thoughts, too, which is something I've been trying to avoid the last couple of weeks.

When I'm positive they've left the parking lot, I take a seat on the floor and drag over my duffel, carefully removing the brown paper bag wrapped up in clothes inside. Smuggling it inside was tricky, but I didn't trust leaving them in the car while we're here. This isn't exactly the safest neighborhood.

The amber bottles are cold and heavy and I immediately break out into a nervous sweat. How am I supposed to feel, holding what is ultimately my death in the palm of my hand? I could drink it right now if I wanted.

I could be dead in minutes.

The thought is freeing and frightening all at once.

Before I realize what I'm doing, I've picked up my phone, turned it on, and called Mom's cell. She answers on the first ring, relief in her voice.

"Luc?"

"Hey." I stare at the bottle, turning it slowly from side to side, watching the liquid within rush like rolling ocean waves. "Just wanted to check in."

She heaves a sigh. "Baby... When are you coming home? Now you're in Nevada?"

How do I tell my mother I'm not coming home? "Mom, I wanted to ask you for a favor. A really big favor. You remember Evelyn, right?"

"Yes, I think so. Is she with you?"

I don't answer that. Not directly, anyway. "I need you to promise that if anything happens to me, you'll take care of her."

"What?"

"Promise me."

"You're scaring me, Luc. What's going on? What are you trying to do?"

The pain, the worry in her voice breaks my heart. I feel myself choking up, throat constricting, eyes stinging with tears, and I don't want to cry like a fucking baby over decisions I've already made.

"Please, *promise* me."

The line is silent for several long moments. Mom's voice is soft. She's crying. "Of course, baby. Whatever you want. Please, just come home."

I wish I could, but I know what waits for me back there.

Tests and doctors and hospitals and parents who are constantly afraid I'm going to break. I won't return to that again. "I love you, Mom. Don't worry about me, okay?"

I hang up before she can reply.

Evelyn

*N*embutal.

The stuff Luc is going to drink to kill himself.

I hadn't been snooping through his bag. I'd just been looking for any of his clothes that needed to be washed while cleaning Max's apartment, and—there it was.

It took everything I had not to dump both bottles down the sink. How stupid was I to ever think leaving Oregon meant maybe, just maybe, Luc had abandoned his suicide idea. I'd known that he'd ordered it online, knew that he had to have been in possession of it...and yet *seeing it,* holding it, was entirely different and made the situation far too real.

When he and Max got back yesterday, I wanted so badly to cry and beg Luc to reconsider. But I know that would only push him away, and that's not what I want. I want to support him, I want to be there for him, I want to love him with everything I have and hope he'll realize this isn't the end of the line.

I'm not feeling very hopeful.

For now, let's focus on the good: tomorrow night, I'm getting married.

God, that sentence sounds so totally bizarre.

Max offered to go with me dress shopping and I said okay because I thought it would be rude not to, and maybe a little because I don't know my way around the city and don't want to be alone.

As it turns out, being alone with Max isn't so bad. He lounges in the passenger's seat, playing navigator to the nearest mall, and makes small talk in between directions.

"So you and Luc have known each other a long time, huh?"

"Um… On again, off again, yeah. We were friends in school. I moved away for a few years and just got back."

He chuckles. "Love at first sight?"

I have to smile. "No, not really. It was different than that."

"What was it?"

If I tried to explain it to Luc, he'd call me a sap and roll his eyes, but… "Sort of like…I felt as though I knew him." Pause. "The day we met, I saw him sitting there in class next to me, and he was familiar. Even when he was pushing me away and being standoffish, there was something about Luc that felt right."

A sensation that has only increased with time. Maybe it wasn't *true love at first sight* or whatever. It was more than that. I've never thought he was perfect. I've never thought I could change him. Luc is one of the most flawed people I've ever met, and I adore him despite it.

"That's cool." Max bobs his head and smiles, pointing across the street to signal me to turn into the parking lot. "He's sick again, isn't he?"

The question sucks the air right out of me. Thankfully,

I pretend to be preoccupied with finding a parking spot before turning off the engine and answering. "What makes you think that?"

"He kept his phone off all day yesterday, and he's getting married without his folks here." Max tilts his head. In this particular light, from this angle, I see the family resemblance more. "I talked to his dad around the time he had his transplant and I researched it and stuff."

He's more observant than I gave him credit for. What do I say? How much has Luc told him? Max doesn't deserve to be lied to like I was. "He's sick again," I say slowly. "He figured his parents wouldn't approve so we took this kind of…impromptu road trip without telling anyone."

At that, Max actually laughs as he swings the car door open to get out. "That sounds like the shit I would do. Cool."

It's unlike anything Luc or I would do, really. Max seems complacent enough with that answer, though, so I don't elaborate.

We head into the mall, which is significantly smaller than the one back home, but then again I haven't gone to many malls in my lifetime. It occurs to me I don't really know what kind of dress I should be looking for, or even if I have some kind of budget. Ten dollars? Twenty? Fifty? Maybe I should've had Luc tag along after all.

I look up at Max. "Um… Don't suppose you have any idea where to start?"

He graces me with a crooked grin. "Lady, if there's something I know, it's weddings." He takes my wrist and leads me down the rows of shops and into a department store. I let him bring me to the women's section, immediately overwhelmed by all the choices.

"Do I have to wear white? Does it have to be a short dress, a long dress?"

"Okay, first, relax." Max clamps his hands on my shoulders and bows down so we're eye level. "Whatever you put on, Luc is going to think it's super hot on you. So worry about finding something *you* like. Who cares what color it is? This is your wedding. Go crazy."

Oddly enough, his words do relax me a bit. I take a deep breath. "What makes you so knowledgeable with weddings?"

"All that work at wedding chapels." He straightens up and turns to one of the dress racks. "Saw a shit ton of people get hitched. I mean, it's Vegas, so half the time they were just drunk and doing it on a whim, but…"

Sounds like my mother. Thinking about her makes me feel instantly guilty. Here I am, getting married, one of the only things she ever wanted for me, and she won't be here. She won't even *know*.

I shake it off and start riffling through dresses. Today isn't about her, it's about me. And I want to find a dress that I love and will make Luc think he's the luckiest guy in the world.

For the next two hours, Max and I start a system of picking out dresses, heading to the dressing room, and I try them on while occasionally slipping one over the door to him to let him know I need it in a different size. He's endlessly patient with me. Every couple of dresses, when I find one that looks okay, I step out to show him and get an opinion.

When I find the right dress, though, I don't need an opinion. Because the second I have it on and look in the mirror, I just…know.

"Max?"

I step out of the dressing room and stand in front of the mirror while Max lumbers up alongside me, nodding approvingly. "Is that your dress?"

The dress is, in fact, white. Which I guess is okay because there's nothing wrong with traditional. White, with an empire waist with thin straps. It falls to just above my knees, with lace appliques in the shape of ivy creeping up the fabric. I stare at myself for a few moments before my vision begins to blur, and suddenly the tears are pouring down my face and I can't seem to stop them.

Max startles, glancing around as though hoping Luc is miraculously here to take care of this. "Whoa, hey—c'mon, what're you crying for?" He takes me by the elbows while I'm burying my face in my hands, and leads me to a nearby bench to sit me down. Hopefully out of view of any customers walking by.

All I can manage is, "I don't know." I press my hands against my eyes, humiliated and desperate to stop crying. "I'm getting married and Luc is going to die and my mother isn't here and I just…I just…"

These last few weeks have been incredible and painful and agonizing. More than anything, it's speeding by so quickly I feel like I haven't had a chance to fully, truly react to so much of what's happened. I've been so caught up in the moment and wanting to enjoy every second with Luc, but the anger and the resentment are there beneath the surface.

I hate what he's doing. I love him so, so much, and I hate that I love him because all this would be so much easier if I didn't.

Max takes my hands in his, drawing them away from my face. "A girl shouldn't cry in her wedding dress unless it's happy tears. Luc's not gonna die—"

"You don't know that."

"He'd be stupid if he did." He considers his words. "Look, Luc and I weren't best friends or anything, but I like to think we were closer than I was with most of the family until I moved out here and we sort of lost contact. But he's a good kid, and I see how he looks at you like you're the coolest thing ever. So don't cry, okay?"

Poor Max. He has no idea, and he didn't sign up for this. He certainly shouldn't have to deal with me sobbing all over the place. I sniff a little and wipe at my eyes, forcing a smile. "You're right. I'm sorry. I do really like this dress." I don't feel any better, but I can't let Max take the brunt of that.

A wash of relief crosses Max's face and he grins. "Cool. Let's find some shoes and get out of here."

Mom and Dad,
      I'm writing this because I'm pretty bad at words, but I wanted you to have some sort of closure after all this is over. You're probably pissed at me, and that's okay.

You should be. As long as you aren't blaming yourselves.

I'm sorry I'm not a stronger person to be able to keep fighting this. I'm so exhausted, so tired of being sick, tired of doctors and hospitals. To think I almost had this beat once only to find out my heart is failing again? That was it. The last straw. I can't do it anymore.

And I'm so, so sorry for that.

You were the best parents I could've asked for.

Mom, I asked you if you'd look after Evelyn for me. To write everything out would take weeks or months, but let's leave it at this: this girl is amazing and I love her. I probably don't deserve to ask anything of you at this point, but I'm going to: just look after her. Make sure she's going to be okay. She made these last few weeks incredible for me.

I stop writing because it's getting hard to focus on the words. I'm not sure if the pain in my chest is because of my failing heart, or because I feel like a failure of a son. This might not be the right time to worry about saying good-bye just yet, but I would hate for something to happen and me to never get the words out. They deserve that much, and so much more.

I hear Evelyn's and Max's voices as they come down the hall toward the door, and I make quick work of folding up the letter and slipping it into a pocket of my backpack so I don't have to answer any awkward questions about what I'm doing.

Max greets me with a smile, but Evelyn has stayed outside even after he shuts the door. I rise to my feet. "Is she okay?"

"Yeah, man." He glances over his shoulder. "She had kind of a breakdown in the store. Not sure if I'm supposed to tell you that."

My blood goes cold. "Did something happen?"

"Nah, she's probably just got the jitters or something." He pauses. I'm waiting for him to say something else, to discover that Evelyn has said more than I wanted her to, but he just smiles and pats my shoulder before heading to his bedroom.

Dammit.

Breathing deep, I run my hands through my hair and step outside to the balcony where Evelyn is still standing, hunched over with her elbows on the railing. She has her phone in hand, staring at the screen.

"Expecting a call?" I ask, sidling up beside her.

She tilts her head, giving me a smile that is less than sincere. "No. I was debating whether or not I should call my mom."

"Yeah, I tried that this morning. Didn't go over so well." I lean into her a little, staring out over the parking lot and the mountains in the distance. "What would you say?"

Evelyn exhales heavily. Her head comes to rest on my shoulder. "I wanted to tell her that I'm getting married. I wonder if she'd be happy for me."

"If that's the reaction you're expecting, I wouldn't do it."

"I know, I know. Wishful thinking. She doesn't call much anymore. Maybe she's given up."

My parents have left a voicemail every single day we've been gone without fail. I'm not going to mention that part. "Seeing as she ran off with guys all the time, maybe she's trying to give you space."

That gets a real smile out of her. She turns to face me, shaking her head. "Don't try to be an optimist, Luc. It doesn't suit you."

She's right, but I hate seeing her upset about something. Especially her mother. Mrs. Abel isn't on my list of favorite people, especially the more I become aware of how her actions have affected her daughter.

My eyes lower to the shopping bags at her feet. "Did you find a dress?" When I reach for one, she swats my hand away.

"You can't see it until tomorrow! It's against the rules."

Tradition. Right. "Okay. Do you want to be alone to call your mom?"

"No, I don't think so." She pauses, and the way she draws in a breath and frowns tells me she has more to say and is trying to think of how to say it. "I saw the medicine in your bag."

Chills sweep over me like a cold blanket. She's not referring to my regular daily meds; she's seen all those already. "And?"

Evelyn hesitates. I'm hoping against hope I don't see any of that hesitation on her face tomorrow at the altar. I hope she really, *really* wants this and I'm not forcing her into something she'll regret later.

As Marilyn's husband lay dying, I wonder if she regretted marrying him. If she wished he'd taken the medication to end his life sooner to avoid all the pain at the end.

"Nothing, I guess. I don't know why I brought it up. I thought I should let you know that you can talk to me about it. You shouldn't keep it all inside."

A perplexed frown pulls at my face. Not the response I was expecting. Evelyn hates this, she hates the idea of what I'm going to do and yet... Then again, should I be surprised? Evelyn has always put others before herself. She'll swallow her feelings down and smile because she wants me to be happy.

It's for that reason I can't talk to her about it. I can't discuss anything I'm feeling about dying, because when I'm dead and gone she shouldn't have to shoulder the weight of all that for the rest of her life. Taking a deep breath, I force a smile and slide an arm around her shoulders. She relaxes when I press a kiss to her forehead. "Thanks. I appreciate the offer."

I just won't take her up on it.

This is the last night I will sleep as an unmarried man for the rest of my short life. How bizarre that statement sounds, rattling around in my head.

Evelyn fell asleep fast, holding tightly on to my hand where it rests against her stomach. I don't know how she's managing sleep at all. I feel like I'll never sleep again. How much longer do we have of this life? A week, a month, a year? I've already spent more money than I ever intended to. I figured two weeks, driving up to Oregon, and if I made the decision not to come back, that would be it. We've been gone more than a month. Evelyn is now eighteen so her mother can't force her to come home. We can get married.

And then what? Where will we go, what will we do? Some days, I feel like I could keep going for years. Then other days—like today—my entire body feels like it's lagging, reacting to things slower than it should. Days where my chest feels tight, where chills send me scrambling beneath the blankets, where I feel too nauseous to keep anything down.

At what point will that escalate? At what point will my bad days begin to outweigh the okay days? I don't ever want to see another hospital in my life. The longer this goes on, the more likely it is to happen. We had one close call already. I refilled my sixty-day supply of medications before leaving home, so I have another thirty days before I'll need more.

Evelyn shifts in her sleep with a sigh, dragging me from the depths of my thoughts and into the present.

Yeah, okay. Right now, I have to worry about her. She needs me, and I made a commitment to make sure that she's happy, that she's going to be all right when I'm gone. I touch my fingers to her hair, smoothing down a few singular strands that are ruffled and sticking out at random places. I should've left my Nembutal in the car where she wouldn't find it, but I was afraid of it getting broken in to in this neighborhood. Maybe I should've taken the risk.

Or maybe that's continuing my trend of being a coward. She was bound to realize I had it sooner or later and, as I've discovered, Evelyn reacts poorly to finding out "later."

I'm not going to let myself dwell on it. We're here, we've come this far. Looking at her sleeping beside me, I can no longer think that bringing her along on this trip was anything other than the right choice.

Maybe not the easy choice…but the right one.

SEVENTEEN

Evelyn

When I open my eyes and let the morning light in, there's only one thought on my mind: *I'm getting married today*. This comes to me with a wash of conflicting emotions. Excitement, fear, happiness, anxiety.

I'm alone on the couch. Vaguely, I can hear Max's and Luc's voices in the back room, so I give myself a few moments alone to gather myself.

Married.

Am I completely insane? No. Insanity was my mother running off with a trucker when she was sixteen. Is this a poor life choice? Maybe. I haven't figured that out yet. What I'm 100 percent positive about is that I love Luc, Luc loves me, and I want today to be perfect.

The blanket smells like Luc. I roll over and press my face into it, breathing in deep, and I wonder how long the scent of him will remain on his things after he's gone. My eyes squeeze shut at the thought. This is supposed to be a happy day, not one for tears and dwelling on things.

I force myself off the couch to steal away into the bathroom, get a shower, and do my morning routine, before finding the guys.

Max greets me with a sunny smile. "Hello, hello, bride to be. How's it going?"

"It's going." I pull my long hair forward over my shoulder, toweling it as dry as I can get it. "What's our agenda for today?"

"Good timing." Luc rises to his feet. "We need to get over to the Clark County Marriage Bureau office first to get our marriage license before we do anything."

My stomach lurches at the thought, but in a giddy way. I'm glad Luc knows how this works, because I have no idea. I look to Max. "Are you coming with us?"

He looks positively startled by the question, swiveling his eyes from me to Luc and back again. "Me?"

"Yeah, you." Luc turns to Max's closet, browsing through for a clean shirt, then turns to throw it at him. "You're coming to watch the ceremony, right?"

Max catches the shirt and stands, still looking surprised. "I'm not gonna be in the way? You have reservations…"

"It's not going to be a problem to bring you back here after the ceremony," I insist. Max helped us get this spur-of-the-moment thing together. He *should* be invited.

Slowly, his usual lazy grin returns. "Yeah? Well, cool. Lemme get dressed." He grabs some more clothes and we leave him to change while we gather our things from the living room.

"Getting cold feet yet?" Luc asks.

I zip up my backpack and cast him a flat look. "No. Should I be asking you that?"

Luc shoulders his own bag and comes to kneel in front of me, expression serious. "Don't be silly."

"Uh-huh. Look who's talking." I'm smiling, though, put at ease by familiar banter. Some things never change. Luc's mouth twitches up into a brief grin. He leans in, forehead resting against mine, and we remain that way, simply enjoying the sensation of each other's presence until we hear Max's bedroom door open.

Max himself slides into the room, arms open wide. I know from doing his laundry that his selection of outfits is limited, so he's just in a pair of jeans and a faded white button-down that he probably had left over from one of his jobs. The part that gets me to laugh, though, is the obnoxiously colored tie around his neck: mustard yellow with penguins in Christmas hats.

"What the hell is *that*?" Luc asks.

"The only tie I got, man!"

It's going to be an interesting day.

The line at the marriage bureau is out the door. During the hour that we wait, in between filling out paperwork, we listen to Max make conversation with anyone and everyone around us. Most of the couples are, surprisingly, locals. Others just rolled into town today with the intention of eloping. I don't think that's quite what Luc and I are doing, is it? We had some prior planning, even if not a lot.

When it's our turn to be called up, I hand over the

clipboard with both of our driver's licenses. The woman behind the counter adjusts her glasses. "Just turned eighteen, huh? Your folks know you're here?"

"Yes," I lie. Not sure how convincing it is, but I don't feel like being lectured by a stranger.

She asks us a few questions, and before I know it, we're walking out of the Clark County Marriage Bureau with our very own marriage license. I still feel like a little kid playing pretend. I'm not an adult. I don't *feel* like an adult. Judging by the look on Luc's face as we stare at the certificate together, I'd say he feels the same. Amused and nervous and excited and scared to death.

The three of us wander downtown. At some point we manage to shake Max long enough to slip into a smoke shop, where we pick out a vape pen. A parting gift, Luc calls it. To say thank you for being the one family member he ended up being able to act normal around, even if only for a little while.

We have dinner at a small hole-in-the-wall deli, where I'm too excited and impatient to do more than pick at my sandwich. The clock is ticking. Our reservation at the chapel is at seven o'clock, in just under two hours. Luc's nerves must be doing the same thing as mine, because he's hardly touched his food. I nudge his foot beneath the table with my own. He lifts his gaze to me and I smile, which he returns briefly.

"We should get going," Max says, scarfing down the remainder of his dinner.

Luc looks at the clock on the wall. "We still have some time."

"You don't wanna get married wearing that, do you?"

he says, gesturing to our clothes. "They give you an hour beforehand so you can get ready there."

I exchange looks with Luc. This is really going to happen. We're really going to do this. Actually, I'm kind of grateful we're not having some huge ceremony; if I'm this nervous about *eloping*, how would I react to getting up in front of a room full of people?

It's a short drive to the Chapel of the Fairies. From the outside it doesn't look like much, but Luc promises it's better than first impressions suggest.

Once inside, a clerk checks us in. He shows us to a quiet hallway with a few doors marked as dressing rooms: half for men, half for women. Max and Luc look back at me one last time before they're ushered into their dressing room, and I'm brought—alone—into the women's room.

It really is just that: a room. With a full-length mirror that was probably bought at Wal-Mart, a folding chair, a card table, and a tiny bathroom. It's barren but clean. Being left alone in the silence gives me a second to breathe because I don't have Luc to focus on, to wonder what he's thinking. I'm glad he has Max over there with him in case he's as bursting with excited anxiousness as I am.

I can't say I've really envisioned my wedding before. That isn't to say I didn't think I'd get married—I knew I would someday—but this has just come a lot sooner than expected.

And to a guy I never thought I'd have a chance with.

The paper shopping bag with my dress and shoes crinkles when I place it on the table. I begin to remove everything from inside. Not just my outfit, but some bobby pins I'd brought from home, and lip gloss.

The room is eerily quiet as I get changed, and I fill the silence with absent humming. Slipping out of my leggings and sweater-dress and tennis shoes. Thankfully I was smart enough to buy a strapless bra, though it isn't the most comfortable thing to put on. It'll look great, and that's what matters to me right now.

I slip on clean underwear and then my dress, turning to stare at myself in the mirror. While we were in the main lobby, I had flipped through some of their bridal magazines for ideas on what to do with my hair, and now I try to replicate some of those, twisting and tying and pulling and pinning.

And I'm suddenly struck with how lonely this is. Not the lack of people waiting for us or whatever, not that we're having a last-minute wedding, but that Mom isn't here with me. For all my life, I envisioned her being here on my wedding day, doing my makeup and my hair.

She doesn't even know where I am.

Before I realize it, I've picked up my cell and called her. Surely, she's been keeping an eye on the phone, waiting for me to call, right?

After three rings, it goes to voicemail.

Tears sting my eyes. I didn't want to cry today. This is supposed to be *my* day, a happy day, not a moment I should be allowing to be affected by my mother's absence.

I think about just hanging up, but instead I find myself speaking when the line beeps.

"Hey, Mom, it's me. Um, I just wanted to let you know that I'm okay. I'm in Vegas. Cool, huh? But, yeah, that's…not really why I'm calling." Deep breath. "I'm getting married. I wish I had let you know sooner. But here I am, telling you. I know it seems like it's out of nowhere and— Never mind. It doesn't matter."

I squeeze my eyes shut.

"I love you. I miss you."

End call.

I go back to pinning my hair back. In the end, my curls are still falling loosely around my shoulders, but I've twisted and fastened it all away from my face. I slip into my shoes—just a simple pair of white flats—and put on some lip gloss, the only makeup I have on hand. I finish the outfit with the butterfly necklace Luc gave me on my birthday.

The sadness of not having my mom here is shoved aside. It's my wedding day, and I'm going to enjoy every moment of it. I have a beautiful dress, the perfect groom, and even my hair looks pretty good for having done it myself.

Looking into the mirror, I think maybe I look like a bride now after all.

Luc

Max is already wearing his nicest outfit, which really isn't all that nice, but it's better than a T-shirt and ripped jeans. I don't know why I brought nice clothes with me. Something in my subconscious had told me I might need them or something, I guess. Just a black button-down and dress pants and shoes.

They could've buried me in these clothes. Instead, I'm getting married in them. Holy shit.

Other than getting dressed, washing my face, and brushing my teeth, I don't have much to do in order to get ready. So, really, it's a lot of pacing the room because there's only one chair and Max has claimed it, and I'm too anxious to sit anyway.

"Second thoughts?" Max asks.

"It's not that." I push my hands through my hair. My hair—should I have done something different with it? It's just shaggy and hanging there and stupid and…fuck, I don't know. This needs to be perfect. "Am I doing all this right? Evelyn deserves a better wedding than this."

Max tilts his head. "Then why not postpone it? I don't know what makes y'all in such a rush, anyway."

No, he wouldn't know, would he? "If something happens to me," I say slowly, turning to look in the mirror, "I need to know Evelyn's going to be taken care of."

He frowns, leaning back to open the nearby window so he can pull a joint from his pocket and light up. "Why are you two so morbid? It's not like you're gonna keel over and drop dead at any second, man."

"You don't know that."

"Neither do you."

My jaw clenches. "It's hard to explain. Let's just say if we don't do this now, we might never get the chance."

Max takes a long drag, exhales out the window, and shrugs with a small smile. "If you say so. It's none of my business."

It's not, and yet what he said sticks with me. All

those nightmares I've been having of Evelyn in a funeral dress…it makes my stomach clench. Those are thoughts I'm not going to entertain right now. This day is about Evelyn and me, and I'm not going to self-sabotage my happiness by getting ahead of myself.

Someone knocks on the door and announces, "Mr. Argent? The chapel is ready for you. You have five minutes."

Max rises to his feet, smudging his joint against the windowsill carefully before tucking it back into his wallet. I take one last look in the mirror before we step into the hall. No sign of Evelyn. Maybe she's in the chapel already. How does this entire thing work? I should've asked. Was I supposed to write some kind of vows or something? Max ushers me down the hall, following the signs for the chapel.

The chapel really isn't a chapel. It leads outside, where an awning serves as protection against the elements. There are three rows of chairs on each side and Max goes to occupy one of them; otherwise, they'll be completely empty.

Where the awning ends, the "garden" begins. It's really just a bunch of ivy, bushes, and plants that serve as a backdrop, complete with an arch decorated in fairy lights, or whatever they called them. Glorified Christmas lights, I guess? But it's pretty, I'll give it that. Greenery with sparkles. And now, in the darkness, it looks even better than it did in broad daylight or the pictures I showed Evelyn.

A guy steps in behind me, eyebrows raised and a courteous smile on his face. "Are we ready?" He moves around me to head to the front of the chapel without waiting for an answer.

I trail after him, glancing over my shoulder, anxiety

gnawing at my insides. What if Evelyn changed her mind? "We're just waiting on—"

"I'm right here, sorry!"

The sound of her voice sucks all the tension right out of me. I turn to look as she enters the room.

She's the most beautiful thing in the world, with all that dark hair around her bare shoulders but not hiding her soft face. She's trying not to trip over her own feet as she hurries down the aisle, cheeks flushed from either the cool night air or embarrassment, I don't know which. Max whistles and claps. I can't help but grin. Any of the anxiety is replaced with an overwhelming sense of fondness. Because whether it's for a day or a year, I'm going to be married to this really fucking awesome girl and I kind of want to pick her up and spin her around because *I do* sounds so stupid and not enough to express anything I'm feeling. I've never been great with words.

Evelyn slows and then comes to a stop beside me. One of the bobby pins is coming loose from her hair, and I don't want to fix it because it looks so *her* that I find it charming. Her smile is a nervous one, but there's a sparkle in her eyes that tells me this is *good*. She's excited. We're doing this.

I don't know whether the guy performing our ceremony is a priest or pastor or just someone who's legally allowed to do it, but whatever. He's a fairly short, squat man with white hair, mustache, and a suit and tie. His name tag reads WILBUR. He reminds me a little of Colonel Sanders or something.

Wilbur steps up to the altar and turns to face us, beckoning Evelyn and me to take our places. I find myself reaching for her hand without thinking, and her fingers immediately curl around mine.

The officiant looks over the top of his glasses at the paper on his podium. I'd think he's done this enough times he'd have all the vows memorized.

I have never been so still and yet so eager to jump out of my own skin.

"Luc Argent, will you take Evelyn to be your wife? Do you commit yourself to her happiness, to love and honor her in sickness and in health, in adversity and prosperity, and to be true to her as long as you both shall live?"

We're staring at each other so intently, so seriously.

I don't know which of us smiles first. But the second we realize the other has started to crack, we both laugh.

Wilbur blinks, puzzled. He wouldn't understand how silly this is. That, in the long list of things Evelyn and I have gone through together, this is, really, nothing to be serious over. After so much pent-up anxiety and nervousness, it's a relief to realize I had nothing to be afraid of. All that matters is the here and now, and right here and now, I'm with Evelyn.

I stop laughing, but I don't stop smiling. "Yeah, I do."

He clears his throat. "Very good. Evelyn Abel, will you take Luc to be your husband? Do you commit yourself to his happiness, to love and honor him in sickness and in health, in adversity and prosperity, and to be true to him as long as you both shall live?"

Evelyn is still smiling, too. The lights of the archway are reflected in her eyes like small galaxies I could stare at forever.

She says, "Yes. I do."

"Then by the power vested in me by the state of Nevada, I pronounce you husband and wife."

I don't wait for him to tell me I can kiss the bride. I gather Evelyn up and kiss her like it's our last night on earth.

Evelyn

It's ten o'clock by the time we drop Max off at home and arrive at our hotel. Immediately I can tell Luc spent more money on this than he should have. He's said this entire trip that he had a budget planned, that he wanted money left in his savings for his parents to use, and now I have to wonder how much of it he's blown through because of me.

My adrenaline is still going. I nearly lost it during the vows and broke down into tears.

For as long as you both shall live. How long is that?

But then I saw the crinkling of Luc's eyes and the twitch of his mouth, and his excitement had filled me with overwhelming happiness and love, and I couldn't help but laugh with him.

I want the melancholy to stay at bay for a while. This is our wedding night. I'm a married woman. I still feel like a kid.

We get our card-key from the marble-floored lobby and head to an upper floor. The top floor, actually. We must pass five aquariums in the halls along the way, and I have to inwardly lecture myself about wanting to stop to stare at all of them. Tomorrow, we'll have time to explore. The truth is, our night isn't over and I have all new reasons to be nervous.

Let's face it: I've never been with anyone. The last time we started venturing toward that territory, I panicked. While I like to think I've gotten slowly more physically comfortable with Luc touching me, I worry I'm going to ruin this whole thing.

Maybe it's just me, maybe I'm a hopeless romantic, but I never felt like it was necessary. Like the relationship we shared with each other didn't *need* sex to be complete. I don't know if I actually feel that way, or if it was a coping mechanism because I'm so nervous.

I've never been in a hotel room that served as anything other than a place to sleep for a night. At most, they might've offered a free breakfast of bagels and coffee in the lobby. The room Luc and I step into is huge, with a king-size bed facing a large, flat-screen TV mounted on the wall. There are double glass doors, which Luc opens to step out onto the balcony and take in the Vegas view. Meanwhile, I'm setting my bag on the table, taking note of the gift basket there with a tag that reads "Our gift to the newlyweds," and contains a pair of "complimentary" bathrobes, wine, and chocolate. I say "complimentary" because I'm sure there was an extra charge on Luc's bill for it.

I peek into the bathroom, taking in the hot tub—a hot tub, *in our hotel room*—before joining Luc out on the balcony. He looks over at me with a crooked smile. "What do you think?"

"It's really beautiful." I loop my arm with one of his.

"Are you sure it's okay, though? The money…"

"Don't stress over the money. This is important. I wanted it to be special. You only get married once."

I go still. Luc pauses. Breathes in, holds it, and exhales through his nose as he realizes the connotation of what he just said. *He* might get married once, but that doesn't mean I will. After he's gone, there might come a day where I meet someone else, where I move on. Does the thought hurt him? It hurts me. I don't want to imagine a day where Luc would not matter to me as much as he does right here, right now.

Which is why I'm willing to let the comment slide for now. I take his hand in mine and give it a squeeze, wanting him to know it's all right. He laces our fingers together, running his thumb across my knuckles before saying, "Do you want to get a shower? Uh, with me?"

A shower. With Luc. Me and Luc together, in a shower. Naked. I almost start giggling out of sheer nervousness.

Maybe I'm not the only nervous one, though. Luc pulls back and I think his cheeks are a little red. "I'm gonna get in. If you want to join or whatever." He doesn't even give me a chance to respond before he ducks back inside the room and heads for the bathroom.

Nervous or not, I already know the answer I would have given him had I been able to get the words out. Still, I find myself waiting until I hear the water going in the bathroom and the butterflies in my stomach are at full force, before I slip out of my dress and remove as many of the bobby pins as I can find from my hair. I stand there in my bra and underwear, looking at my reflection in the television screen, and take a deep breath before removing them, too.

This is okay, I tell myself. Because it's on my terms, and Luc is letting me set the pace and I love him for that.

When I work up the nerve to go into the bathroom, I find the shower stall has not one, but two shower heads. Luc has them both on. I can make out the outline of him, smudged by the crystalized glass and steam. The lights are on low, sapping most of the color from the room and causing my eyes to need to adjust.

Luc pauses when I shut the door behind me. "Coming in?"

"Yes." Well, I'm glad my voice sounds calmer than I am. Because as much as I want to rush out and cover up, I'm also itching to get into the shower and be as close to Luc as humanly possible.

He opens the glass door a crack, and I move forward to step inside. I wonder if he left the lights dim on purpose, to makes things a little less awkward. Maybe he just likes taking showers in near-darkness, I don't know. But it makes it easier to step into the shower with him, pulling the door shut. It's even darker in here.

Not to say that I can't see Luc, because I can. The darkness just…makes the outline of him softer, I guess. I stay under one of the showerheads and watch him with his back to me under the other, head bowed as he rinses the shampoo from his hair. His body is long and lean, skinnier than he should be, but beautiful, every angle pronounced and begging to have fingers traced along them.

It dawns on me that I've never even seen Luc shirtless. When he straightens up and turns to face me, it also dawns on me why that is.

I knew he'd have a scar from his heart surgery. Common sense. It never occurred to me what it might look like, or that Luc might be self-conscious about it. It starts at his clavicle and runs straight down his chest, ending at just below his ribcage. It's prominent. It's un-missable. And I see him absently touch a hand to it like, yes, he's aware this is the first time I'm seeing it and he doesn't like it.

I'm so busy watching Luc, so busy studying him, taking everything in to commit to memory, I don't even realize he's doing the same thing to me until he reaches out to touch his wet fingertips to my cheek. It startles me into looking up at his face. My cheeks flood with heat.

He smiles a little. "Hey."

Some of the tension eases out of my shoulders. "Hi."

"I think you missed some of those pins."

"Did I?"

Luc steps closer and I welcome it, letting my body press against his as my cheek comes to rest on his chest and his hands are slipping through my hair, searching out a few stray bobby pins I overlooked.

I can hear his heartbeat. I can feel his ribs against mine, the small of his back beneath my palms as I put my arms around him. When I turn my head to kiss his chest, I can feel the scar beneath my lips and Luc pauses, just for a heartbeat, before plucking the last pins from my hair and setting them aside on the soap holder. He winds his arms around me, smoothing his hands down my spine, tracing them slowly over my hips. Cautious, as though he expects me to jerk away. I have no plans of doing so this time.

He tries to help me wash my hair, making a perplexed face when his fingers continually catch on my curls and it makes me laugh softly. "Is it always like this?"

"Yep." I dip my head back beneath the water, running my hands through my hair with practiced ease, knowing how to untangle as I go. With my eyes closed and sound effectively drowned out by the spray of water as I rinse, it almost startles me to feel his lips against my throat, delicate and warm and perfect. As soon as he begins to draw away, I reach for him, pull his face to mine, and kiss him with all the eagerness I've ever wanted to.

The shower water is turned off—I think Luc does that—and we only stop kissing because I'm suddenly eager to dry off. The moment I've returned my towel to its hook, Luc is cupping my face in his hands and kissing me again. Every step forward for him is a step backward for me, until we've returned to the room, to the bed, and my calves are pressing against the edge of the mattress.

I go easily, lying back with Luc following after me, mouths still fitted together, and every time his tongue brushes against mine it sends a shiver straight down my body to settle between my thighs.

Everything moves along in slow motion and yet too fast to make sense of what's happening. My hands are moving over his shoulders and arms, smoothing down his chest and ribs, and his hands seem to be all over my body at once and his mouth following not long after. Luc kisses me everywhere that sends my heart into gallop mode, now and again searching my gaze for permission with his eyes until I touch his hair or arm or cheek to reassure him this is more than okay.

Even when he's settled between my legs and I can feel him pressed against me, he ghosts a gentle kiss against my mouth that tastes like heat, water, and desire, and he asks, "Good?"

"Good," I agree breathlessly.

Definitely good.

I have never been better.

EIGHTEEN

Luc

I wake with the sun and open my eyes to Evelyn asleep next to me. She's lying on her stomach, the dawn seeping in through the windows and cast across her bare back and shoulders. Her hair is in her face, fanned across the pillow, still damp in places when I reach out to touch it.

She's the most beautiful thing in the world.

When my fingers brush against her cheek, she stirs, stretching her arms slowly with a sigh. I don't really want to wake her up just yet, especially because I'm not feeling so great.

Physically, that is. Emotionally? I think I'm still on cloud nine.

I roll out of bed and grab my meds from my backpack, where they're tucked in the main pocket along with the Nembutal wrapped in one of my shirts. In the bathroom, I take a look at myself in the mirror. My eyes are shadowed and hollow, and my hair's a mess, but otherwise I've looked worse, I guess. I've felt worse, too. It's just been a busy last couple of days; no wonder I'm starting to feel it.

After taking my meds, washing up, and pulling on a pair of sweat pants, I return to Evelyn and lean over to press a kiss against her cheek. She makes a low noise in response but still doesn't budge, so I turn on the TV and take a seat beside her.

She sleeps for another hour and a half, until the sun is fully up. She's scooted closer to me, bringing her head to rest against my thigh. I busy myself tracing patterns down her back until her eyes open tiredly and she rolls them up to look at me with a sleepy smile.

"Good morning."

"Morning," she mumbles, draping an arm across my lap with a sigh. "What time is it?"

"Nine thirty." I stroke the hair back from her face, ignoring the faint, uncomfortable heat that has settled over my entire body since I woke. I'm not getting a fever. I'm just not. "Go back to sleep if you're still tired."

"Hungry, actually." She muffles a yawn against the back of her hand.

"We can hit the buffet downstairs if you want. It's supposed to be huge."

Evelyn makes a noise of agreement. Reluctantly she rolls away and out of bed, momentarily seeming torn between whether or not she should be self-conscious about strolling across the bedroom completely naked. She glances at me, gives a bit of an embarrassed grin that I can't help but smile at, and manages the walk to the bathroom without trying to cover herself up. I'm glad for it.

When she returns, it's with her hair tied back and looking much more refreshed and awake. Before she can move to get dressed, I catch her by the wrist and draw her to me. "You could just go like this. Everyone would be jealous of me."

She laughs, bowing her head to hide how pink her cheeks have gotten. "Don't be weird."

"I'm being honest." I duck down to press a kiss to the curve of her neck.

Evelyn squirms a little and tickles her fingers against my sides. "Get dressed. I'm starving."

Fifteen minutes later, we're dressed and heading downstairs. The elevator makes my stomach turn, a reminder of how not hungry I am, but I don't want to admit that to Evelyn. She'll know I'm not feeling good, and that isn't what this part of our trip is about. I'm not going to let my heart ruin it for either of us.

The buffet is by far the most impressive meal we've had this entire trip. Not only is there every breakfast food I could name in the span of an hour, but it's fresh and delicious. Even with as little appetite as I have, I try to force myself to eat what I can because it tastes so good. My stomach isn't happy with me after the fact.

If Evelyn notices anything is wrong, she doesn't comment on it. She eats with no problem, and we sneak a few sausages and pastries back up to the room for later snacking. Evelyn also grabs a few pamphlets and brochures from the front desk. Considering we're too young to hit the casinos, it couldn't hurt to look up other things to do while we're here.

While she takes a seat at the table to go through the options, I find my way back into bed and drape an arm across my eyes, exhausted. But when Evelyn settles on something she wants to do, I smile. I pretend everything is fine because if she realizes how shitty I'm feeling, she'll insist we stay in. Sleep isn't going to make me feel any better.

The hotel itself has plenty to look at. Architecture and art and shopping. Evelyn's easy to window-shop with; she doesn't even care about buying anything, just enjoys looking at everything in detail. The Venetian down the street has even more to look at, including the gondola rides, and I kind of regret that we didn't stay here instead.

We end the day with a Cirque du Soleil show. Even in my somewhat foggy-headed state, I have to admit the entire thing is fucking amazing. Evelyn watches the show as she watches everything: wide-eyed, amazed, eager not to miss a thing. I can't think of a moment during this trip where I've enjoyed anything quite as much as I enjoy watching her reactions to things.

The fun only stops when I have to cut out of the show early, rising from my seat and hurrying into the hall, muffling a coughing fit into my hand. Afraid Evelyn might follow, I disappear into the nearest men's room until I can stop. When it passes and I can breathe in properly again, I look down and see pinkish phlegm in my palm, and my chest constricts.

Not good.

I wash my hands and splash cold water on my face, taking a few deep breaths to ensure I'm not going to start hacking all over the place again. We've been out for hours, I'm exhausted, and my chest hurts. Maybe it's time to call it a night.

Evelyn's waiting for me in the hall, phone clutched in her hand like she was ready to call me. I do my best to give her a reassuring smile.

"Sorry, had the worst tickle in my throat. Is the show over?"

"Pretty much." She's staring at me like she clearly doesn't believe a word I just said. "Are you okay?"

"Yeah, sure." I take her hand in mine to begin heading out of the venue. "Hungry?"

"If you aren't feeling good, we should go back to the room. It's been a long couple of days."

"I'm *fine*, Evelyn."

Her mouth tugs into a thin line, unimpressed with my lie. "We'll go back to the room."

"Suit yourself." I can't bring myself to complain; if it means resting, I'm good with that.

It's a twenty-minute taxi ride to even get back to our hotel. By the time Evelyn is unlocking our door, I'm coughing again, exhausted from being on my feet. I breeze past her into the room, heading for the bathroom to finishing my coughing over the sink, pleading with my body to not cough anything else up. Maybe the last time was a fluke.

Evelyn follows me, of course. I feel her palm against my back, see her worried face in the mirror. Once I calm down again, she rubs her hand across my shoulders soothingly. "You okay?"

"Fine," I mumble. Admittedly, not convincing this time at all.

She takes in a slow, deep breath, and I brace myself for

what's coming. "Maybe we need to take you to the doctor."

I bite back the urge to snap at her, because she's only being concerned and it wouldn't help anything. I straighten up and twist around to brush the hair back from her face, forcing a smile. "It's been a long couple of days, like you said. I haven't been sleeping a lot. If it's okay, I'll call it an early night, and I'm sure I'll feel better in the morning."

Evelyn opens her mouth to protest but hesitates when I lean down to kiss her forehead. Her shoulders slump. "Yeah, okay."

It's a small victory, one that I hope results in me being able to take my meds and sleep this off.

I get changed for the night and Evelyn accompanies me to bed, although it's still relatively early and I figure she'll stay up after I've drifted off, maybe to do schoolwork. But she lies with me, stroking her hands through my hair, down my chest, and the touch combined with my exhaustion is enough to put me right to sleep.

I wake repeatedly throughout the night. Coughing. Sweating. Heart lodged in my throat. A few times I feel Evelyn's hand against my forehead or cheek, her voice murmuring to me, and I make sure to wake enough to respond to her each time. "Still fine, it's okay." The last thing I want is to find myself in a hospital again after an ambulance has been called.

When I finally get up for good, I stumble for the bathroom, figuring a shower will make me feel better. Lukewarm water does a little to wake me up, if nothing else, and soothe my heated skin.

I get dressed and wander back into the room, grabbing my phone and sinking onto one of the couches near the balcony doors. Evelyn is seated at the table, surrounded in paper birds. I feel her eyes on me and try to shrug it off, act like nothing's wrong, although I don't have the energy to go to her and kiss her, tell her I'm just fine.

Turning on my phone gives me a moment of pause. It's nearly twelve. In the afternoon. That can't be right. "How long did I sleep?"

"You can tell time. I'm sure you know," Evelyn replies.

Somewhere around sixteen hours, not taking into consideration the number of times I woke up because I was coughing or my heart was racing. I feel as though I've hardly gotten a regular night's sleep. To top it off, I can tell without a thermometer that I'm running a fever. Shit. I've been taking my medication like I'm supposed to. What else *can* I do? Obviously sleeping didn't do a damned thing to help.

When I glance up, Evelyn's standing with the car keys in her hands, a determined set to her face. My stomach drops. "Evelyn, no—"

"You need to go to the hospital. Come on."

"I don't *want* a hospital!"

"And I don't want you to keel over two days after getting married!" she snaps back.

Running my hands over my face, I try to breathe in deep and count to ten. "I'm fine. I promise. It's been an emotional couple of days, that's all. My body isn't used to it."

"Then the trip to the doctor's will be short and sweet, right?"

"*I said no doctors!*" I slam my hand on the coffee table hard enough that Evelyn jumps and I immediately hate myself for it. Her cheeks redden as tears rush to her eyes. She averts her gaze, foot tapping the ground like she's trying her best not to lose her temper. It doesn't work.

She throws the keys on the table and stalks across the room to our baggage on the dresser, immediately grabbing for mine to unzip it and begin rifling through it. I lurch to my feet, instantly unable to breathe. "What're you doing?"

"Where is it?" She pulls my shirts and pants out one by one, and although I know it's not in my suitcase, I know it's only a matter of time before she realizes it and goes for the backpack instead.

"Where is what?" I move up behind her and reach out, helpless; I don't want to grab her. It's a stupid answer; I know damned well what she's looking for.

She whips around regardless and shoves one of my T-shirts into my hands, tears streaming down her face. "Where is it, Luc?"

I chuck the shirt aside. Everything feels distant, disconnected. I desperately need to sit down. The dizziness is probably the only thing keeping me calm; I can't afford to get worked up right now. "You need to chill out. Do you see how you're acting?"

"How *I'm* acting? You're so full of it!" She turns away again, pressing her hands against her eyes and struggling to breathe in, breathe out. I hate this. I hate seeing her this way, when I know reaching out to hold her will only make things worse. Instead I give her a few moments to calm down, but the anger and hopelessness rolling off her don't dissipate. They're still written in every curve of her expression when she turns back around to look at me, and it's the hurt I see in her eyes that kills me the most. "I can't do this."

She may as well have hit me in the stomach. I suck in a breath. "Can't do what?"

"*This*. All of this." She wipes at her eyes, but fresh tears immediately replace the old. "This constant back and forth, never really knowing what to expect. I thought if I could really, *really* show you how much you have to live for, that you'd realize you have a reason to keep fighting."

I want to say her name, but my throat constricts. Extending a hand for her results in Evelyn stepping back, out of my grasp. Wherever this conversation is going, I don't like it. Don't want it.

"You like to say you're doing this for everyone else, but that's not it at all." She twists her fingers into her hair, at a loss for what to do with her body, and begins to pace the short distance between the bed and me. "You're doing it because you're scared. And there's nothing wrong with that—being afraid. I'd be afraid, too. But everyone else is scared, too, and we're scared because when you're dead, that's it. End of your problems, as you see them, because you're *dead*. What about everything that gets left behind? The loss, the pain, the guilt? The knowledge that I—that we—didn't get every last second with you that we could have?"

"I'm going to die one way or another."

Evelyn whirls toward me. "*You don't know that!* Stop acting like you *know* because you *don't*!"

My mouth snaps shut, biting back anything I could think to say. Slowly I step back and sink down into the chair by the table covered in cranes, and let her pace, let her talk and yell and anything that might make her feel better. I don't know what she wants from me. I don't know how to fix this.

Which is why it surprises me when she looks me in the eye and asks desperately, "What do you want from me, Luc?"

I open my mouth, stunned. "What? I don't…"

"I've tried to do everything. I've stuck by you every step of the way this trip, I've tried to understand—really, really understand—and nothing has been enough. Nothing is ever enough. Not for you or Mom or, or…" Her voice cracks and her expression crumbles. "I just wanted to be one of your options."

Her words are like a bag of bricks to my face. It shakes everything loose, including the fever-fog, and brings everything into sharp clarity that has me staring at Evelyn like I'm seeing her for the first time.

How long have I known how she's felt about her mother? Being second place, being runner-up. Never being the first priority. Evelyn has never felt like an option, a priority, with anyone in her life and I thought, I thought…

That I was different.

Pushing her away when she was in Arizona. Bringing her on this trip to protect her. Not telling her the truth about my condition. Marrying her to ensure she'd be taken care of when I'm gone.

I thought those were things I'd done with her best

interests in mind. I thought I was keeping her safe.

I wasn't keeping her safe from me.

So, so selfish.

Nothing about this trip has been a right decision, except for Evelyn. The one thing I thought was a bad idea—bringing her along—ended up being the only right decision I've probably ever made in my life. And this— her crying, her heartache, everything that *this moment* comprises—is completely my fault.

And I am the only one who can fix it.

Doing so means sacrificing my choice to go on my terms. It means fighting a fight I'm scared to take on because I don't think I can win. But Evelyn is still fighting. Mom and Dad are, too. I am the only one who has given up because, in the end, Evelyn is right; when I'm gone, my problems are gone with me. I've given up because I have nothing to lose.

Except knowing that I died doing everything in my power to make the girl I love happy.

When I rise from the chair, Evelyn turns away like she thinks I'm going to approach her. I don't. I head to my backpack, drawing out the T-shirt-wrapped bottles of Nembutal. The effort I went through to get these, what they've meant to me... A choice I've been deprived of since birth...

Evelyn turns then, eyes red and glassy and desolate.

Maybe a choice hasn't been taken from me entirely. My current choice lies between this amazing girl and these bottles, and it's a choice no one can make but me. I find some quiet sense of comfort in that.

She watches as I walk to the sink at the bar, breaking

the seal on a bottle and twisting the cap free. She watches still as I upend it, pouring it down the drain. But it isn't until I turn to offer the other bottle to her that she seems to realize the weight of this, of what I'm choosing right now, and she moves to me cautiously to take the bottle. There's no hesitation in how she opens it and dumps it into the sink, though her eyes don't leave my face.

Both bottles are discarded in the trash with a glassy clinking sound. This time when I reach for her, she doesn't pull away, just stares at me with impossibly wide, questioning eyes. I cup my palms to her cheeks, thumbs swiping away the wetness from beneath her eyes.

I say, "I'm sorry, Evelyn," and I mean it quite possibly more than anything else I've ever said to her. "I love you."

Her eyes tear up all over again, but she moves to me, burying her face against my chest with her arms winding around my neck to hold me tight. I nestle into her hair, murmuring it over and over, *I'm sorry, I'm so sorry*, and I'm glad she doesn't say *it's okay* because I know that it's not. Saying it's okay would suggest I haven't done anything wrong.

But she does say, *I forgive you*, and that's a thousand times better.

NINETEEN

Evelyn

I'm waiting for Luc to tell me he's joking. To say the bottles we emptied into the sink weren't really the Nembutal, that they're still hidden somewhere, waiting for him to get desperate enough to use them. I'm waiting for something to go wrong.

Because I can't wrap my head around it. The idea of Luc—of anyone—really choosing me.

No, I shouldn't take that credit. It isn't really just me, is it? I don't know. Maybe I'm afraid to ask. Luc could have had a change of heart—ha—for any number of reasons. But I would like to think something I said, some choice of my words, struck home and made him open his eyes to how broken his parents and Max and I would be when he died.

Perhaps it's an inevitable truth I will have to face someday. But not now, not today. I won't accept it.

We pack our things before checkout and turn in our card-key, cutting our stay short by two nights.

In six and a half hours, we will be home.

We debate whether or not to go to the hospital here. Luc looks at me, leaving the decision in my hands, and I decide that as long as we go straight to the hospital back home, it should be okay. There, he'll have his doctors and nurses, his medical records, his parents. It'll be better.

The driving we split in half: I handle the first three hours, from I-15 until CA-58, and the sun has started to set and it's threatening rain the closer we get to Bakersfield. I hear thunder off in the distance, and it sends a shiver down my spine and makes Luc cringe a little. He hates thunderstorms; I remember that fact from when we were younger. Still, he insists on me pulling over so he can take the wheel.

All around us, nothing. Sand and shrubs, mountains in the distance that become invisible as the sun sets. No street lamps for miles and miles. When lightning breaks open the sky, it's surreal. Like God himself reaching down to touch the mountaintops. I could go to sleep if I was not determined to keep Luc company.

A crack of thunder makes the world around us rumble and I see Luc shudder. I smile, reaching out to turn the music up a bit, though it won't really help much. "You sure you don't want me to drive?"

Luc rolls his eyes and chuckles. "I'm not letting a little rain scare me out of the driver's seat." He extends his hand to me, and I place my palm against his and lace our fingers together.

I have no idea what awaits us back home. What

Mom will say, what Mr. and Mrs. Argent will say. I don't know what news the doctors will have for us, if we'll be too late or just in time to fix everything that's broken, what toll this trip has put on Luc's heart. But the point is that we *try*, and Luc is willing to do that. For me.

Headlights come at us from the other lane, the first ones we've seen in miles. Luc squints; visibility already sucks because of the rain and the dark. I ease my hold on his hand in case he wants it on the wheel, but he stays put.

The next strike of lightning illuminates the moving truck veering into our lane.

Thunder follows.

Screaming metal on metal.

Luc's hand leaves mine even as I'm grasping for it. The movement pitches me forward, something solid cracking against the front of my head before the seat belt slams me back into the seat. Spinning, spinning, smoke and thunder and a blaring horn so loud the truck seems to be on top of us. I wait for the airbag to deploy. It doesn't.

Darkness blankets over my vision as we're pushed from the road.

All I can hear beneath it all is Luc.

"Evelyn, Evelyn—"

TWENTY

Luc

Fever swarms all around me. It's hard to breathe. Every time I open my eyes, it's to an onslaught of bright lights and unfamiliar faces, green scrubs, gloved hands. Voices asking me if I'm all right. Each time the gurney hits a bump in the linoleum of the hospital floor, it sends a jolt of pain searing up my left arm and into my chest.

There's a mask over my face. I paw at it with my right hand, wanting to ask *where is Evelyn?* But the nurse coaxes my hand away and holds the oxygen mask firmly in place.

I feel like I'm going to throw up.

Vaguely I remember the car. Rain pouring in from the broken windshield and driver's side window.

Smoke.

A blaring horn.

Sirens, somewhere in the distance.

I remember looking to my right and seeing that the passenger's side airbag had not deployed and Evelyn was slouched back in her seat, head turned away from me.

All I could see was blood. Blood on me, blood on her. I couldn't see the driver of the moving truck that hit us.

I remember paramedics. Voices calling to me, a brace being put around my neck as strong hands lifted me out of the car like I was nothing.

Evelyn, is Evelyn okay…

Someone shouted *this one's already gone!* and I squeezed my eyes shut, willing away the sounds and the sights as they loaded me into the back of an ambulance and reality began to fade out. No, no, no. They could have meant someone else. It had to have been the truck driver.

Not Evelyn.

Even after I'd passed out and came to again here and now in the hospital, I can't get the words out. My throat is dry. And, God, my chest hurts.

"Luc?" A man leans over me. A nurse, I'm guessing; he isn't dressed like a doctor. How does he know my name? They must have found my wallet. "Luc, can you hear me?"

How do I answer that? I blink blearily at him instead, vision still swimming.

"Everything's going to be fine, man. All right? Just need you to relax."

Relax. As though every nerve in my body isn't alight and screaming, like someone isn't having to hold on to my uninjured shoulder to keep me from trying to sit up.

Doesn't matter, doesn't matter… Is Evelyn okay?

I never do get my answers before I'm drifting back out of consciousness.

Evelyn

When I wake, it's to white walls, an IV in my arm, and a splitting headache. I've never been admitted to a hospital before. There were emergency room trips once in a while; a broken foot when I was six, pneumonia when I was twelve (chest x-ray, antibiotics, sent home again). But I've never lain in a hospital bed with a needle in my arm and a monitor attached to my finger. It's scary. Is this how Luc feels every time he's here?

Luc. Where is he?

I force my eyes open despite the lighting overhead that only serves to make my head throb worse. When I touch a hand to my forehead, I feel gauze and bandages. My body aches everywhere. Back, neck, shoulders, hips.

My fingers find the call button for the nurse's station and I push it. Directly beside it, on the guard rail, are buttons to adjust the bed and I make use of them to lift me up to sitting. Movement makes me wince.

A nurse with a name tag that reads LATOYA enters my room. She's motherly-looking. Something in her expression. She comes to my bedside and smiles. "Hello there, princess. Good to see you awake."

Doesn't feel good to be awake.

I gesture a little and Latoya brings me a paper cup

of water, which she helps me drink although I think I'm perfectly capable of doing it on my own. I hurt, but I don't think anything is broken. With some of the dryness in my mouth taken care of, I manage to ask, "The guy I was in the car with… Where is he? He's okay?"

"He's in recovery," Latoya says gently. "He went in for surgery not long after the paramedics brought you in."

My hands are shaking as I accept the cup from her and take a drink on my own, trying to steady my nerves. "Surgery?"

"I'm not sure on the specifics, but I can ask." She pats my arm and starts to move away, and the thought of being left alone with no answers makes me panic.

"I need to see him." I abandon the now empty cup in my lap and start fighting with the guardrail to lower it. "Please, I can walk. I can…"

"Hold on now." She catches my hands, expression patient. "I don't think you realize that if you'd hit that dashboard just a little harder, you might not be here."

An image of the car comes to mind when I close my eyes. My forehead slamming into something solid before the seat belt forced me back… Guess that explains the massive headache.

I grab hold of Latoya's wrists in turn, staring into her eyes imploringly. "His name is Luc Argent. We were driving home from Las Vegas. We'd just gotten married and he—he wasn't feeling well. He's been having some problems from a heart transplant. The doctors need to know that, right?"

Latoya relents. She leaves me with a promise that she'll go immediately to tell the doctors if they don't already know. Surely if he went in for surgery, they saw the scar on his chest, but that doesn't mean they'll have any idea about the complications Luc has been having. No one would.

For my part, I have to stay right where I am and try to assess the various points of pain on my body. Back and neck? That's sort of a given from a car accident. My legs hurt, possibly from bracing my feet against the floorboard on impact. My head? Dashboard. The raw pain across my chest, I discover, is a result of the seat belt; a red, rash-like mark over my right shoulder and neck, down across the left side of my ribs, and another across my stomach. The bruising has startled to settle in, making it look a hundred times worse than it probably is.

I'm going to be hurting for a bit. But given the alternative, I'm grateful for every ounce of pain.

Latoya returns with mixed news: Luc's surgery itself had nothing to do with his heart. He dislocated his shoulder, likely tore his rotator cuff, though the surgery was more to remove several shards of broken glass that had embedded themselves in his body.

"But?" I ask when she pauses.

"But he's being kept in recovery for now. Just to monitor him," she says. "They're concerned about the stress on his heart, is all. We'd like to send for his medical records but we'd need his consent, or…" She pauses, lifting up a clipboard and a form. "You said you two are married, right?"

That's right, we are.

Without a second thought, I take the form and sign. When I hand it back to her I ask, "Is my stuff here? My phone? I need to call my mom." Not just Mom, but Luc's parents. Maybe that's even more important.

Latoya retrieves a clear plastic bag containing all the items of clothing I was wearing—I startle at the surprising amount of blood on my shirt, and she explains that head wounds bleed a lot—my shoes, and my phone. I haven't spoken to Mom in nearly a week. Haven't honestly looked at my phone or listened to any messages she might have left me since I called to tell her I was getting married. I didn't want anything spoiling it.

Before she leaves, Latoya promises that as soon as Luc is out of recovery, she'll wheel me to his room and, in the meantime, she'll check his belongings to get his phone. I don't have his parents' numbers in mine.

Mom answers on the second ring. I don't let her get out more than a hello before my eyes are watering at the sound of her voice. "I'm okay, but there's been an accident."

Hospitals. Heart monitors. The hateful, erratic beeping trickles even into my dreams. Memories. I don't know what they are. I would rather wake up to find this had all been a bad dream, that I had just passed out back in the hotel in Vegas and Evelyn had called an ambulance again.

Except I'm aware of more than what is usually wrong with me in hospitals. Not just a sense of disconnection or exhaustion or achiness—though those are present, too—

but sharp pains reaching from the fingers of my left hand all the way up into my shoulder.

My throat burns. My eyes burn. I blink them open to turn my head, try to look to my left and figure out the source of the pain. All I see are bandages. I can curl my fingers but I feel too weak to lift my arm.

A nurse sweeps in to check on me. He watches the monitor with concern before looking down and realizing I'm awake. He smiles in that way that nurses do even when they know something is very wrong.

"Hey, Mr. Argent, how are you feeling?"

I open my mouth to speak. My voice cracks against the dryness of my throat. "Where's Evelyn?"

The nurse—I can't read his name tag, too blurry— raises his eyebrows and nods to the other side of me. I turn my head slowly and all the worry, the terror, rushes right out. Evelyn is seated in a wheelchair at my bedside, asleep.

There's a large bandage obscuring half her forehead over her right eyebrow, and I can see bruises blossoming from under the collar of her hospital gown. But otherwise, she looks okay. Alive. Safe. There are paper cranes crammed together on the bedside table, the hospital tray, and another resting in her lap. She's been waiting here for a while.

A sharp pain ticks in my chest and I close my eyes, waiting for it to pass. Now isn't the time.

"Mr. Argent," the nurse says, drawing my attention back to him. "We've sent over an urgent request for your medical records and history, but there's no telling how long it'll be for them to get it to us. Do you think you're up for answering some questions to help us better treat you?"

Yes. No. I don't know. I'm drawing a blank. Another sharp pain. Another jump in the heart monitor that makes the nurse glance toward it with a worried frown.

"I can try."

He wheels over a cart with a laptop seated on it. My hospital isn't so advanced. Clipboards and handwritten notes for them. Every question he asks me, I attempt to answer as best as I can. Doctors' names and information. Medications. Results of my last biopsy and stress test. Symptoms. How long have I been feeling unwell, why haven't I gotten treatment, am I feeling any chest pains, shortness of breath, swelling, nausea, lack of appetite... He doesn't have to ask if I've been suffering from an erratic heartbeat. The monitor tells him the answer to that.

When he leaves, it's with an assurance that a doctor will be in to see me shortly. "Shortly" in hospitals is rarely shortly. On the grand list of one to ten of how much of an emergency something is, I only rank about a six. Unless my heart gives out. The dying are always bumped up to an immediate ten.

Left alone, my attention returns to Evelyn and I bask in the relief that she's okay. I reach for her, but she's far enough away that I'm only able to brush my fingertips against the back of her hand.

It isn't enough to wake her, but the coughing fit I break into a moment later is.

The world swims out of focus around me. Evelyn is immediately up, her cool hand against my cheek, and the head of the bed is lifting until I'm able to find the air I couldn't get while lying flat on my back.

I open my eyes, taking in slow, calculated breaths.

Evelyn is leaning over me, and I see the same relief in her face that I was feeling a minute ago. At least for now, it blurs out the stabbing pain in my chest.

"I called my mom and your parents," she says, smoothing my hair back. "I hope that's okay."

"It's fine." Sort of an emergency, isn't it? Though I wonder how long it'll take them to get here and how long ago she called them. "What'd they say?"

"They're worried, of course." She smiles faintly. "Had a lot of questions for me, but I think they were mostly concerned with getting on the road."

"I'm sure we'll hear about it when they show up," I mumble, already feeling tired at the thought of it. Evelyn's voice sounds far away. I want to hold on to her hand, close my eyes, and go back to sleep. Maybe not a good idea right now. I should stay awake.

I've always been aware of my body, of how far I can push myself. I'd already gone too far, and the wreck pushed me clear off the edge. So when Evelyn asks, "How are you feeling?" I respond with, "Doing okay."

It isn't the truth.

This time, the lie *is* to protect her. Because there is nothing more she can do.

TWENTY-ONE

Evelyn

Luc listens as I tell him what I know about his surgery, that the man driving the moving truck died on the scene, and there's a quietness about him that I'm unaccustomed to. His hand reaches for mine, lacing our fingers together, and his skin is cool to the touch and clammy, unsettling.

I talk until I realize he's fallen asleep again and realize I was really only speaking because the sound made me feel better, made me focus less on the anxious knot of worry that's embedded itself in my chest.

I am not stupid. I know the doctors are concerned. I know the lines on the heart monitor are not normal and the sound of his breathing is off. I know I have every right to be worried.

But what else can I do but wait? Luc sleeps and I reach

for the scrap paper some of the nurses gave me in order to start my folding back up. Fifty cranes so far. Nine hundred and fifty left if I want to reach a thousand. I wonder if the cranes I've folded on our trip up until now would count toward the total, but I haven't been keeping track.

Each crane has a different memory associated with it as I fold. Our first meeting. My first day of freshman year, and I was one of the youngest students in our economics class. Luc sat beside me—Evelyn Abel and Luc Argent—and I spent the class staring at him. Or rather, at his hands. I'd never really seen a boy paint his nails before and at first I was confused, and then fascinated, and then curious. Until our teacher called me out on "ogling" Luc instead of paying attention. He was almost a year older than me and he hadn't even looked my way. I was so far under his radar that I could have screamed at the top of my lungs and he wouldn't have batted an eye.

At least, that's what I thought at the time.

Not wanting him to think I'd been staring because I had a thing for him or something, I left class after dropping an origami butterfly onto his desk with the words: *I like your nails.* In retrospect, it was probably stupid and childish, but it worked.

The next day, Luc left a bottle of nail polish on my desk. Not one of the cheap Walmart brands, either. Something with a fancy name in French. I don't know what happened after that. For as different as we were, for as standoffish as he could be, I couldn't stay away from him. Eventually, maybe, I thought that he felt the same. The days where we were having a great time, talking and laughing and just *being*. The days he would grab my hand and hold it in his, just for a few seconds, until he would pull away and act like nothing happened. Then the one time at the movies where I thought *maybe* he was about to lean in to kiss me during the ending credits and... That was Luc: hot and then cold. I could never get a read on him.

Then there was the first time I sought him out during lunch; I found him sitting alone somewhere and asked if I could join him. The cautious look he'd given me, and I think he'd been about to say no until his gaze flicked down and saw my hands. The nail polish he'd given me on my fingernails. He'd scooted over a little and looked away and said, *If you want.* I did want. Again and again. Until it was him searching for me, like under the bleachers where we listened to "Tiny Dancer" on repeat.

When I told him I was leaving for Arizona, it was over the phone because he was home sick. At the time, he said it was just a cold, but now I have to wonder if that was true. "We're leaving on Sunday to drive down there," I'd said, and Luc had gone silent for a very long while.

"That's...really sudden, isn't it?"

"Mom doesn't see a reason to wait. It's not like she has a job or anything to wrap up here."

Thinking back on it now, the last time I saw Luc, we sat on the swings in Grandma's backyard and hardly said a word to each other. Maybe neither of us knew what to say. I had tried to get the words out: *I'll miss you* and Luc had nodded and mumbled *yeah, me too.*

When he hugged me and said good-bye, I remember feeling as though it were the last time I'd ever see him.

Now I know it was because he likely thought it *would* be the last time.

I cried all that week. Arizona felt like a death sentence. How much different would things have been if we hadn't moved in the first place? Maybe I could have been there for Luc through his transplant. I would have had so much more time with him; the three years away from Fresno...it feels wasted. Wasted on Mom's flings, wasted on Robert...

Sixty cranes. My fingers are starting to hurt. I'm making them small, four out of a single sheet of paper, because I don't want to keep pestering the nurses for more. But Latoya comes in to check on me, startling at the growing collection.

"Child, what are you doing?"

I'm not embarrassed by this, but my voice comes out meekly. "Cranes... It's this Japanese legend. It says if you fold a thousand paper cranes, your wish will be granted and you can be healed." I glance at Luc. "I read it in a book growing up."

Latoya only nods to that, but she must think I'm crazy.

She comes back ten minutes later with a stack of paper, some water, and a tray of dinner for Luc and me. His looks a lot blander than mine. A special diet, due to his condition, I'm guessing. Even his water intake has to be monitored.

Luc murmurs in his sleep, quiet enough that it's hard to make out but enough that I continually lift my head every time I hear his voice. He's never talked in his sleep before. In any other situation I would find it cute, but now... It makes my heart beat up into my throat.

A coughing fit is what wakes him. I position his bed into sitting up a little more, but when he reaches for my cup of water, I hate having to tell him, "The doctor said only a little…"

"I know," he mutters, and drinks the entire cup anyway.

Once the coughing has subsided, he lays back again and presses a hand over his chest, above his heart. His eyes are shut but I can't tell if he's in pain.

"Do I need to get a nurse?"

Luc reaches for me instead, as though afraid I'm going to get up and leave. "I'm okay. Coughing made my shoulder hurt, that's all." He glances askance, noting the cranes all over the room. "You've been busy."

"I hit a hundred." I smile sheepishly. "My hands are killing me."

"No butterflies?"

"I can make you a butterfly, if you want one." And since he's watching me expectantly, I sit back in my wheelchair and begin to fold him one out of a full piece of paper.

While I work, Luc keeps his half-lidded eyes on me as he asks, "Back at the hotel, you said you couldn't do this anymore. Would you have left?"

I go still but don't lift my head. "I don't know. I was really upset at the time."

"Wouldn't have blamed you if you had."

"That isn't how things worked out, though, is it?" Finishing the last fold, I stand back up stiffly and offer him the butterfly. He takes it with a tired smile before letting his eyes meet mine.

"I love you. You know that, right?" he says.

I smile back at him, sliding my fingers through his

hair, relishing the way he leans into my touch. "I know. I love you, too."

"All things considered, have you had fun?"

A soft laugh escapes my lips. "All things considered, yes."

"Favorite part?"

"Mm… The aquarium, my birthday, I think. What about yours?"

Luc sighs, lifting the butterfly to hold it against his chest. "You."

There is nothing in all the world that Luc has ever said to me that hits me quite like that. My eyes glass over and I have to close them to force back the tears, although I can't stop smiling. "God, you're such a sap."

"I get it from you."

"Any regrets about the trip?"

"Would you believe me if I said no? I saw what I wanted to see. I had you." His fingers trace the folds of the butterfly. "Do you have my phone? Can you put on some music?"

I retrieve his phone from next to mine, buried beneath paper birds, and begin skimming through his music selection, which isn't as extensive as his iPod but still has plenty. "What do you want to hear?"

"Dunno. You pick something."

Easy choice. "Tiny Dancer" it is. As soon as it begins playing, he grins. "Now who's the sap?"

"Proudly so."

I start to sit again, figuring I'll keep working on cranes while we talk. Except Luc asks, "You've got my wallet, right? Is there a gift store here?"

"Probably. Do you want me to get you something?"

"A book. Something. I don't know." He closes his

eyes. "Would you mind?"

It's an odd request, but if it would make him feel better... I sink back down into the wheelchair. I'm not sure I can manage walking all the way down to the store, but if I bring the chair, I should be okay.

Taking Luc's wallet, I pause long enough to lean down and kiss him warmly on the mouth. His lips are as dry as mine are, and I think I'll grab us some chapstick while I'm there. "I'll be right back."

When I reach the door, Luc calls my name and I turn to look at him. He's still holding the butterfly against his heart. "What about you? Any regrets, about any of this?"

It's such a raw, honest question coming from Luc. Maybe the medicine is making him loopy. But it's a question I can answer without missing a beat: "No regrets. None at all."

It's the first time I've ever lied to him.

I have a lot of regrets. I regret not putting my foot down sooner. Not pushing him to tell me the truth. I regret not telling Mom about Robert, about not staying with the butterflies a little bit longer. Not kissing him more than I have. I regret so many little things that, perhaps, do not matter; the end result could have very well been the same, no matter what I did.

But the important thing is that I don't regret Luc.

I make the mistake of letting Latoya know where I'm going because I don't want someone thinking I'm a runaway patient. She insists on wheeling me down to the gift shop. The trek across the hospital to the downstairs lobby is long enough that I'm grateful I didn't argue it. The trip wouldn't have killed me, but it would have hurt like hell.

Latoya brings me to the shop and there, I hobble around on foot in order to find what I want. I have to look ridiculous, constantly reaching aside to make sure my gown is staying shut, my hair a mess, head in bandages. But I find a few books Luc might be interested in, a thing of chapstick, and a pair of earbuds in case he wants to use them at some point to block out the sounds of the hospital. I don't know where his have gone. I don't know where the car would have been taken, where our stuff could be... I should ask about that. Maybe Mom or Luc's parents can find out when they get here.

We head back upstairs, Latoya telling me about her kids, about how long she's worked in the hospital. It's a pleasant distraction from the aches and pains and dwelling on the drama that's undoubtedly going to unfold when my and Luc's parents show up.

Once we reach the ICU again, the halls are still busy with nurses and doctors moving to and from rooms, usually with some sense of urgency. It's so much different from my room, where it was moderately quiet and the nurses moved at a leisurely pace. I wonder if that's why Latoya has been by to check on me so often. I'm sure I'm keeping her from other patients, and that makes me feel bad.

We turn down Luc's hallway and the wheelchair comes to a stop. I glance back at Latoya and she shakes her head, begins to wheel me backward. "We need to go back for a minute..."

"What? Why?" I look toward Luc's room and notice the light above his door is lit. What does that mean? I reach down and lock the wheels, preventing Latoya from moving me any farther, and despite her pleading my name I shove the foot pedals up and haul myself from the chair, sending the books scattering to the floor as I limp quickly for Luc's room.

I hear the sounds, the orders being barked, the long, eerie monotone of a heart monitor flat-lining before I reach the door.

In the doorway is a man who immediately tries to block my path, catching my shoulders when I attempt to shove past.

"What's going on? What are they—"

"Ma'am, please, can I escort you down the hall so we can talk?"

I can't see Luc. Not through the crowd of people around him. An employee glances our way. She draws the curtain closed around the bed, around the chaos, and I can't breathe.

He doesn't understand. I need to be in there. If something is happening—

I didn't finish the cranes. I should have finished them. If I had, if I hadn't left to go to the stupid store, then he—

Latoya is behind me. She murmurs against my ear that I can't be in the way, that I need to let them do their work, and her gentle coaxing has me collapsing back into the wheelchair because my legs are going to give out if I don't.

But she doesn't make me leave.

Every sound, every chest compression, every attempt with a defibrillator, every order and question called by the crash team, every term used that I don't understand…

I hear it.

I hear Luc dying.

And I can do nothing.

...

Latoya wanted to stay with me but was getting paged to assist with other patients. I don't honestly notice her absence. Everything has faded into background noise.

After Luc's room goes silent and the heart monitor stops, several employees shuffle out, looking exhausted. One man is teary-eyed. He is young. No older than Luc himself, if I had to guess, and he catches my eyes and immediately looks away, ashamed. I wonder if this is the first patient he's lost, if he will eventually become numb to it.

The doctor comes to find me, crouching down to explain what had likely happened. Luc was already showing signs of heart failure, and the car crash put too much stress on him. I don't know why it matters now.

I was probably not halfway across the hospital when he went into cardiac arrest.

As the doctor speaks, I notice any other patients and families in the hall have been discreetly relocated. It's gotten quieter.

Two nurses wheel Luc from his room, clearing it for the next ICU patient in need. They let me in to gather our things, to collect every memory wrapped in paper cranes. His phone is still playing "Tiny Dancer," set on repeat. The origami butterfly lies trampled on the floor.

All of the cranes I shove into the trash.

I keep the butterfly.

TWENTY-TWO

Evelyn

I'm required to sit through one last examination by a doctor before they officially discharge me. The stitches on my head will dissolve on their own. I have nothing to wear that is not stained in blood or torn. My ripped jeans I pull on anyway, but can't bring myself to wear the shirt. At least I feel a little less exposed wearing more than underwear beneath my hospital gown.

They put Luc in an empty room outside of ICU to grant me some time with him, as well as his parents, when they arrive. I stand in the doorway to this room, thinking that it smells of death. Not that I've ever been around someone who has passed before, but this scent... Perhaps it's ingrained into our brains from millions of years ago. Perhaps it's instinct.

More than that, standing there staring at Luc, the

room is so silent and empty. I approach his bedside and his eyes are closed, expression lax. There's nothing anyone can tell me that would be comforting. He did not die peacefully in his sleep. Is this what Luc wanted to avoid? What he was afraid of? And yet the last image I had of Luc before leaving the room was one of tranquility, almost peace. He'd been calm, content. I don't know what that means. Is it too much to hope that he was okay with this, that he was ready?

If I had granted him his wish and let him end his own life, where would we be now?

The *what if*s will drive me insane, will break my heart again and again.

I take the butterfly and tuck it into Luc's hand, bringing it to rest against his chest. If I pretend really hard, I could convince myself that he's only sleeping.

Except Luc is not here.

The room is empty. I'm the only one here. Whatever made Luc *Luc*, whatever truly comprises a human being, makes them who they are, is gone. The body on the gurney is a shell, a piece of matter devoid of energy and life.

My phone buzzes. It's a text from Mom: *we're at nurse's station by your room, where are you?*

We? I'm surprised Grandma decided to come along. I text back that I'm on my way, figuring I can take my time. I'm still not prepared for any of this.

When I reach the door, I stop to look back at Luc. I don't touch him, I don't kiss him one last time because I want to remember the feel of his mouth against mine, kissing me back. Telling me he loved me. Telling me I was his favorite thing about this entire stupid trip.

I hobble down the halls of the hospital in a daze, carrying a plastic bag of Luc's belongings at my side. His wallet, the books I purchased, his clothes, and keys. I'll offer them to his parents if I see them. I wonder if they'll hate me. I wouldn't blame them. Grief can be easier to cope with if you have someone to blame for your loss.

"Evelyn!"

Mom's voice at the end of the hall makes me lift my head. She sprints down the linoleum toward me and despite myself, I find my legs hurrying toward her as best as they are able to meet her halfway.

Not once does Mom say *I told you so* as she holds on to me. Not once does she twist the situation around to make it about her. I cry quietly, but refuse to let it get any further than that. Crying makes my head hurt, which is the only reason I fight to keep from all-out sobbing. Mom pulls back, using her sleeve to wipe the dampness from my face.

"Oh, sweetheart, your head… Are you okay?"

I think to say *I'm okay*, like I always do, but I only shake my head mutely because if I start to speak to tell her all the ways that I am not okay, I'm not going to be able to stop. Instead I manage, "Where's Grandma?"

"Grandma?" Mom's hands drop, rubbing my bare arms instead, which are covered in goose bumps from sitting in the cold hallway for so long. Hospital gowns don't do much for warmth. "She's at home."

"But you said 'we'…" The moment the words leave my mouth, I know exactly who she meant. I jerk away from her, catching sight of Robert as he rounds a corner heading for us, a few vending machine sodas in his hands.

"He drove up a few days ago," she says, glancing back at him with a smile. "He's been so worried about you, too, you know."

"I'll bet he was." The sight of him after all this time makes me feel sick to my stomach as the anger wells up inside me. I welcome it, because it's better than this helplessness bearing down on me. I don't have to pretend to be nice anymore. What happened in Arizona wasn't my fault. Luc's words reverberate in my head, reminding me of that. Because of Luc, because of his life insurance, I don't *have* to go back with this man ever again. Now more than ever, I understand why Luc wanted so desperately for me to have that to fall back on.

Mom startles, turning to look at me, but I'm already stepping around her. Robert opens his arms when he's close enough to me, a gentle, sympathetic smile on his face. Once upon a time, I might have looked at that smile and been comforted, looked up to him as a father because I never knew my own.

Now, the second he's close enough to hug me, my cold stare is enough to root him to the spot. "You need to leave."

"Honey, what has gotten into you?" Mom steps up to my side, her hand against my back.

"You want to know why I won't go back to Arizona? Ask him." I don't move my stare from Robert's face and his smile slowly fades.

"Now, Evelyn... It's been a rough couple of weeks for you, I'm sure." Robert reaches for me again, and I shove his hand away when it comes to rest on my arm.

"Don't touch me."

An innocent man might look confused or hurt. An innocent man might immediately step back, not wanting to make the situation worse. Robert, however, only stares down at me, unblinking, unmoving, as though daring me to make a scene. I am prepared to make enough of a scene it'll be a whole damn movie if I have to.

"What's going on?" Mom asks quietly. This time, it's directed at Robert.

He tears his gaze from mine and shakes his head, shrugging. "No idea. Obviously she's been through something traumatic."

"You're right. You trying to watch me shower was pretty traumatic." As I turn to hobble away, I see the color has drained from Mom's face. I hear Robert speaking in hushed whispers, and when I reach the end of the hall, I hear Mom as clear as day: *What did you do to my daughter?"*

By the time I reach Luc's room again, my body aches all over and I am so exhausted I could cry. I'm so tired of crying.

I'm hoping I will eventually run out of tears, at least for a while.

I should eat something, I think. Food might make me feel better. Staring at everything in the cafeteria only makes me feel worse. Instead I settle on a bottle of water, because at least it's something and I'd feel dumb standing there without ultimately buying anything.

On my way back to Luc's room, I pass by a man in scrubs in the hallway that I recognize from earlier. The guy who was crying when he walked by me. He's standing on his own at the nurse's station; as I watch him, he brings his hands to his head and leans his elbows on the counter.

I don't know that I'm really in a position to comfort anyone, but my feet are moving on their own and a moment later I'm standing beside him. "Excuse me?"

He uprights himself immediately and spins in my direction, pausing when he lays eyes on my face. "Yeah, can I help you?"

His badge says his name is Jason. "You were with the team of doctors for Luc Argent earlier, weren't you?"

Recognition and guilt flash across his eyes and his shoulders square. "I was. I'm…really sorry for your loss, miss."

I've heard enough of that for the day; that isn't why I stopped to talk to him. "I just wanted to say thank you for trying to save him." The words start to catch in my throat a little and I have to duck my head, looking down at the water bottle in my hands. "You seemed pretty upset, and I didn't want you to think it was your fault. Was it the first person you lost?"

Jason lets out a heavy breath and runs a hand over his short-cropped hair. "It was my first code, period. I guess in training we're hyped up to keep going until we can save lives. So when it doesn't work…"

"It's part of the job, I guess." I look back up at him, though I can't stand the sympathy in his eyes. "Are you going to be able to get used to it?"

He smiles faintly. "I hope not. It pushes me to try harder next time."

It's a surprisingly endearing answer, one I'm sure a lot of his coworkers don't share. I won't tell him I don't think he'll last long in this job if he doesn't become numb to it somehow, because I think the world could use more people like him.

I place the unopened bottle of water on the counter for him, figuring he needs it more than I do. I thank him again and quickly turn to walk away before I start crying again.

When I return to the hallway of Luc's room, I see the woman I recognize as Luc's mother standing in front of his room, talking with a doctor. The man with her, I'm guessing, is his dad. I slow my steps. When the doctor catches sight of me, I see him say something and point in my direction, something that makes both of the Argents turn to look at me.

I freeze.

The idea of dealing with them in the raw aftermath of their grief is unbearable. I can't bring myself to move as they approach me, both their faces red and streaked with tears. I brace myself, fingers twisting into the plastic bag, and force myself to hold it out to them. Relinquishing hold of Luc's things once and for all is terrifying in and of itself.

The bag is ignored. Mrs. Argent draws me to her, hugging me tight. The moment her arms are around me, every emotion pours out of my eyes, past my lips, and I clutch at her for dear life and sob quietly into her shoulder while she cradles me against her and strokes my hair. I feel Mr. Argent's hand against my back, his other arm wrapped tightly around his wife's shoulders.

We cry. We grieve.

In the worst possible way I could have met Luc's parents, the Argents share with me their pain, and shoulder mine in return. It's more than I ever could have hoped for.

TWENTY-THREE

Evelyn

Jack and Amanda Argent are people to be admired. Maybe it comes from nineteen years of handling bad news, of being on pins and needles about Luc's health. Maybe they've even been preparing themselves since they realized Luc had left town. I don't know, and I'm not in a place where I can ask them.

But they do invite me to be a part of things. Legally, decisions are now left up to me regarding what happens next. Where he goes, how his body is treated. I defer these decisions to his parents, because these are steps he's discussed with them in the past, not with me.

Mom texts to ask where I am and I let her know. Surely, she won't bring Robert with her this time, plus I have the Argents here. Even though they have no idea about my situation, I find being near them gives me strength.

Whatever Mom has to say to me, I can handle it. I have to. I hope Luc would be proud of me.

By the time she locates us, Luc has been removed from the room to be taken somewhere to "await transport." The nurse didn't say as much, but I know what that means. They're sticking him in a freezer in the morgue until his body can be picked up and taken back home. I try not to think about it.

The three of us linger in the hall while I wait for Mom. "What happens next?"

Mrs. Argent—sorry, Amanda, as she wants me to call her—blots a tissue at her eyes. For the most part, she's managed to keep her composure. It hits her in waves, I think. "The car was in Jack's name, so we can go to the impound lot and collect his things from it. Your stuff will be there, too, won't it?"

As much as I hate to think that my belongings are important right now, I can't help but think of my laptop—I need that for school, for the pictures I've taken on this trip and moved from my phone to my hard drive, and the necklace Luc gave me on my birthday. I wasn't wearing it during the accident, which means it's still in my bag. Fingers crossed everything remained intact. "Yeah, I have a bag in there."

"You're welcome to come with us," Amanda says. "Otherwise we can get your things and bring them to you back home."

I want to go with them. I want to continue being around them, to help, to get to know them better. They've been so kind to me, and I don't want to go back to Grandma's where the only way to handle my grief is to hide away in my room alone. But I can't exactly ask them to let me accompany them all the way back home. I'm not in a position where I'm comfortable asking for anything. "I'd like to go with you, if that's okay."

She manages a smile and brushes a hand over my hair. I don't know what I've done to deserve this kindness from either of them, if Luc maybe told them something about me during their calls, but I'm grateful for it, whatever it is.

The brisk footsteps I hear behind me alert me to Mom's presence. I turn around instantly, relieved to see she's alone. Her face is scrunched up into something unreadable and I ready myself to hear that Robert convinced her I'm overreacting, that I'm emotional and lashing out.

She doesn't, however. She gathers me up into a crushing hug that makes me wince, and her voice against my ear comes out soft, shaky, guilty. "I am *so sorry*, baby."

I close my eyes and hug her back, letting out a heavy breath of pure relief. I pull away after a moment to ask, "Where is he?"

Mom swipes the tears from her eyes with a bitter laugh. "Hell if I know. I told him to go to hell and if I heard from him again, I'd kill him. So…you know. I imagine he's driving back to Arizona about now. I guess you and I are bussing it home."

Turning to look back at the Argents, who are politely trying not to stare or overhear the conversation taking place right in front of them, I step aside and gesture. "Jack, Amanda, this is my mom, Violet. Mom, these are Luc's parents."

The Argents shake Mom's hand. Jack glances at me. "Sorry to eavesdrop, but do you not have a way back home?"

Mom struggles to maintain her polite smile. "No, um. It looks like we just lost our ride."

"Well," Amanda says, "we have room for two more."

EPILOGUE

The room is virtually untouched.

There are still clothes in the laundry basket in the closet, a cup half full of water at his bedside. Amanda said she and Jack hadn't had the heart to go in and touch anything yet. That maybe they wouldn't for a while, until they were good and ready.

I've only been in this room a few times. Only once when Luc was alive. I've found comfort in putting myself in his surroundings, in looking through his things, in getting to learn stuff about him I hadn't gotten the chance to during our time together. He folded his socks, for instance. He made his bed every morning and kept his shoes lined up neatly beneath it. He had a habit of saving receipts for practically everything, crammed into his bedside drawer. I'm enjoying that I can still get to know Luc, even after he's gone.

His funeral was today. Exactly one week after the

accident. Not even ten days after we were married. The priest overseeing the service even introduced me as Luc's spouse, and it had felt strange, but not unwelcomed. Members of his family who I've never met, neighbors, a few medical professionals he's known since he was a child…they all look at me oddly, but I had Jack, Amanda, and Max—who immediately hopped on a bus from Vegas when he heard what happened—at my side.

I am not alone, no matter how lonely I may feel at times.

Afterward, the Argents held a reception at their home. They've insisted on keeping it light and easy, wanting happy memories in place of tears. I excused myself from it after a while in favor of coming up to Luc's room where I feel more at peace.

Amanda and Jack have given me many of Luc's things. His phone with his last selection of music, which I will probably never change. I claimed one of his band T-shirts he wore a few times on our trip, and his jacket. Sometimes when I wear it at night, it's as close as I can get to having his arms around me again.

I toe off my shoes by his door and cross the room to lie down on the bed. His pillows still smell like him. Or maybe it's my imagination, but either way, I find comfort in turning my head to bury my cheek against them as I place the earbuds into my ears and turn on Luc's playlist. I've grown to love some of his favorite songs. Janis Joplin, The Doors, The Beatles…

I think back to the last smile he gave me. The last kiss. The last conversation we had and I still wonder if he *knew* what was going to happen. If he sent me out of the room to spare me from watching him slip away. If asking me the questions he asked was his way of finding peace.

"Favorite part?"

"Mm… The aquarium, my birthday. I think. What about yours?"

"You."

He was my favorite thing ever. I should have told him that.

I hope he knew what it meant to me, that he went this way because of—for—my happiness. If I had known the end was this close for him, would I have thought differently about his choices? Would I have encouraged it? I don't honestly know.

Anger, sadness, grief, loneliness. Luc taught me all those things, and in the wake of his death, he will teach me how to cope with them.

"Any regrets, about any of this?"

God, a million regrets about so much, yes. But Luc?

Loving Luc will never be one of them.

Acknowledgments

This was one hell of a story to tackle, and having each other along for the ride made it twice as fun and exciting.

We had a majority of Luc and Evelyn's story written before pitching it to our amazing editors, Stacy Cantor Abrams and Tara Quigley Whitaker, but we were undecided where to go with the ending. In what way could we bring the story to a close that would be organic and real? It's thanks to them we went the direction we did. When we got one of the first rounds of edits back after submitting the ending, there was a note from Stacy that simply read, "I'm not crying, you're crying!" We took that as a sign that we didn't do too bad.

Thanks also goes out to Weston, who answered a lot of Kelley's questions about young transplant recipients and beta-read numerous scenes for us to make sure we were getting the right mood. Kelley can also say thank you to Nyrae Dawn, who wrote her more than once to ask,

"Have you decided on the ending yet? I need to know!" Sometimes those little notes can really pump you up and get you excited about what you're working on.

Kelley feels it important to mention that YouTube is a blessing. Thanks to various people who posted videos about the butterfly taxidermy process so that we didn't have to find a way to watch it in person because ew. Rowan feels it equally important to acknowledge every one of our cats and the dog who felt the need to lay all over us and make sure to get in the way as much as humanly possible while we were trying to plot, discuss ideas, and write.

Kelley would like to add: as always—thank you to my readers, who continue to support me and enjoy the words I put down. Every letter, tweet, Tumblr post, email, and Facebook message is truly inspiring and reminds me that I'm not just sending my words out into the void. Keep reading, my loves. Enjoy!

FALL IN LOVE WITH THESE OTHER FANTASTIC READS FROM KELLEY YORK

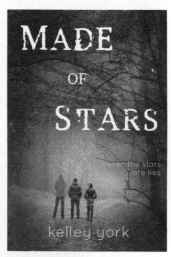

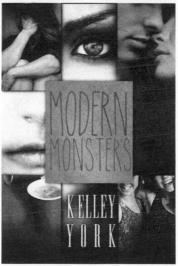

READ ON FOR A SNEAK PEEK OF KELLEY YORK'S *MODERN MONSTERS*, AVAILABLE NOW

CHAPTER ONE

Aaron Biggs leans over me to ask, "How's it going, Vic?"

His freckled face and dyed black hair obscure my light. I squint at the page of algebra equations on the cafeteria table, decide they aren't going to make any more sense to me whether or not I pause to see what Aaron wants, and look up at him. "Um. F-fine?"

"Super." He flashes me a grin. "My brother and his buddies rented out a cabin on the lake for a party this Friday. He said it would be cool if I invited a few people."

I'm used to playing receptionist. This invitation is not meant for me, but for my best friend, Brett. I am not important. I am tolerated by association. I am Vic Howard, Brett Mason's Best Friend, so while people don't always care to learn anything about me, they do recognize my face. Being cool to me, they seem to think, is a way to stay cool with Brett. At least Aaron knows my name instead of referring to me as "Hey, you." Of course, that's only because his mom and my mom are also best friends.

Aaron doesn't leave until I've written down his information: address of the party, phone number, and time. He stresses that there will be booze, food, and girls. Plenty of girls. College girls, even. The idea makes my throat dry. I can hardly talk to a girl my own age, let alone one older than me and with undoubtedly a great deal more life experience.

It's Wednesday, meaning I don't even see Brett until tennis practice after school. This also means I'm parking my butt on the bleachers outside the tennis courts and watching for the next two hours while Brett and a handful of others knock balls back and forth while wearing shorts that are way too short for my comfort.

When they're done, Brett slips through the gate, mopping sweat off his forehead and grinning my way. "Yo."

Sometimes when I look at Brett, I still see the chubby, pimple-faced kid with braces and glasses whom I befriended in third grade. Maybe that's why he doesn't impress or intimidate me the way he does everyone else. I knew him back when nobody else wanted to. "P-party invite," I say, short and to the point. Even though Brett has never made fun of my stutter, it's habit to keep sentences short. I hand him the information I took down.

Brett takes it and skims it over. "The lake, huh? Could be fun. Do you want to go?"

"The invite was f-for you."

"And you, by extension. I'm not going if you aren't

going." He crams the paper into his duffel bag.

Parties aren't my thing. More often than not, I end up being the loser sitting on the couch and watching Brett mingle and make new friends. Not that I'd want him clinging to my side the whole time—that'd be even lamer—but still…knowing he likes me to tag along is what convinces me to go to his social outings. No one else may care that I'm around, but Brett does. "Maybe."

Brett plops himself down beside me. "Do you have other plans?"

He always gets me there. "I m-might…"

"You don't." He laughs. "Come on. It's something different, yeah? Not some lame kegger while so-and-so's parents are out of town where we'll get yelled at for breathing on anything."

It is something different…except I don't like different. Brett nudges me with an elbow—once, then again when I roll my eyes and don't answer right away, and a third time, until: "Fine, I'll go."

"That's my boy." He claps me on the back, shoulders his duffel bag, and jerks his chin toward the parking lot. "Now let's get out of here."

Friday after school, Brett and I head to his place so he can get showered and dressed, all while lecturing me about the importance of wearing something nice and "at least run a brush through your damned hair, Vic," because my dark curls look unruly no matter what I try. Then we swing by my house so I can drop off my stuff and get changed. We're planning on grabbing a bite to eat on our way to the lake. I'm thinking the combination of a bunch of drunk people and a large body of water is a really bad idea, but what do I know? *Don't be a buzzkill*, Brett would say.

Mom is in the kitchen nursing a cup of coffee. As I'm heading out the door, I stop to tell her, "Going to the movies, then I'm s-staying at Brett's tonight. Be home tomorrow." This is more of a formality than anything. Mom doesn't care where I am if I say I'm with Brett. She assumes anyone with a 4.0 grade point average must be a good kid. A good influence. *Ha.* Since it's just Mom and me and she doesn't really care what I do as long as she thinks I'm not getting into trouble, I pretty much have free rein to do whatever.

Mom halfway twists around to smile vacantly. "That's good. Tell him I said hello." No further questions. Not that I expected any. Brett is outside, honking, so I leave without a good-bye.

Not counting the hour-long stop for dinner at a restaurant, the trip only takes about forty minutes. There are something close to thirty cars crammed haphazardly together outside the lake house already, because Brett insisted on showing up fashionably late. Everyone else has probably been here a good hour or two. Brett parks close to the end where it isn't as crowded. Even from here, I can make out the sound of music blaring, along with the shouts and cheers of people splashing around in the lake on the far side of the house. I should not have eaten that greasy cheeseburger and fries at the diner, because my stomach is in knots.

The lake houses are two stories, separated by a stretch of beach, so the noise from a party isn't likely to bother the neighbors. I looked this place up online last night (I like having a good idea of what I'm getting into before an outing) so I know they're pricy rentals. I know it has four guest rooms upstairs, two bathrooms, its own kitchen, and a hot tub out back. Shrubs line the walkway to the front door.

Brett leads me inside. It's one of the rare instances where I get to see him out of his element, because here he isn't Mr. Popular with everyone. (Yet. We'll see what happens by the end of the night.) Out of the sea of faces, I recognize maybe half. The rest must be friends of Aaron's big brother, students of the local colleges. The people who are familiar to me aren't people I've ever talked to much, anyway. Nearly everyone in the immediate vicinity is older than us, with the exception of Aaron, who just so happens to be making his way over from beside the patio doors with two plastic cups in hand.

"Glad you could make it!" He shoves a beer into Brett's hand and one into mine. "Got food in the kitchen with the keg. There's a chick in there mixing drinks, too."

Brett doesn't smile, but he looks around with an appraising nod that suggests he approves. He leaves my side and drapes his free arm around Aaron's shoulders despite being a good three inches shorter, and casts a look my way as though to ask if I'm coming. I don't particularly care for Aaron, nor do I want to trail on Brett's heels all night, so I shake my head mutely. Brett shrugs and they drift away from me. Brett is saying, "Why don't you introduce me to a few people?"

I give it twenty minutes before he's either making out with someone or getting into deep conversations about the merits of whatever college these people go to versus some of the colleges on his (or rather, his dad's) wish list.

Where does that leave me? Standing just inside the front door with a beer in my hand. I hate beer. It tastes like battery acid. Not that I've ever tasted battery acid, but it's what I suspect battery acid would taste like. I try a sip anyway, like maybe I've forgotten and tricked myself into thinking it tastes horrible.

Nope. Still battery acid.

I don't want to abandon my cup just yet, so I wander through the house, observing the various clusters of people talking, dancing, shoving their tongues in each other's mouths, mingling, having fun—everything I am not a part of. I'm in my own little bubble, unacknowledged by everyone.

In the kitchen, I discreetly dump my beer out in the sink and toss the cup into the trash. Before I can get far, someone spots me drink-less and shoves another red plastic cup into my hand. At least this one doesn't smell like piss in plastic. I'm pretty sure this drink consists of orange juice and vodka, with a little umbrella poking out to make it look fancier than it is.

The throng of people and the steady rumble of various conversations going on at once is making me claustrophobic. I make my way out back, which is much better. The air is cool and sharp and smells of water and sand. Paper lanterns hang from the trees, providing a dim but helpful glow to the stretch of rocky beach the house rests on.

There is no sign of Brett, which means he's still inside somewhere. I don't really care about finding him just yet. As long as he's having fun, then whatever. I'm not going to be the dude who puppies around after his best friend because he can't function socially on his own. If that means sitting here until he comes looking for me? Cool. That's sort of how these things go. Brett wants me to come with him, even in groups, but I never know how to interact. We've gone to the movies, bowling alleys, laser tag, arcades, and just hanging out at Brett's place with his friends from school or his tennis group. Some of them are nice enough guys; I just prefer to keep to the sidelines, out of the way.

My drink stays in hand while I people-watch. I spot Aaron's brother stripped down to his boxers, conversing loudly with a handful of people with lake water lapping at their legs. One guy I remember seeing at school floats around on a pink raft, tethered to the shore so he doesn't drunkenly drift away. A couple near the back door are arguing. By some miracle, despite their slurred speech, they're being quiet enough not to attract too much attention. A girl behind me is throwing up in the bushes.

My stomach rolls in sympathetic nausea at the sound

of her heaving. A quick look around tells me that either none of her friends are here, or they don't care that she's spewing her guts all by herself. I weigh my options: go inside and pretend I didn't see anything, or help her before she falls over and passes out. Possibly in the same bushes she's getting sick on.

In the end, it isn't really a question. Maybe I'd like to turn my head the other way, but I'm already setting my drink down and coming up behind where the girl is bent over, hands on her knees, long blond hair a tangled mess around her face. She's taking small breaths, shallow and quick, and whimpering. I squint. Now that I'm getting a better look, I recognize her from school.

"C-Callie?"

Callie Wheeler moved to town in the middle of last year. I knew her only because Brett and I have both shared classes with her at some point or another. She jerks her head around in my direction so fast she nearly falls over, and I catch her by the elbows. Her gaze floats across my face. She's probably trying to place my name. Most people don't pay enough attention to know it. Just as she opens her mouth to say something, I see the color drain from her face. I help turn her back around just in time for her to throw up again, and I rub awkward circles across her back, unsure what else to do. Only when she's done does she straighten up and slump against me. I hold on to her arm and place the other hand on her hip to turn her around to head for the house. Such is the joy of getting here late; everyone else is already plastered.

Callie wobbles on her feet, eyes closed to slits so small I doubt she can see where we're going. "Who're you 'gain?" she mumbles.

I have to hold on to her waist to make sure she doesn't stumble coming over the threshold of the back door. "Uh. V-Vic. Vic Howard?" Why do I feel the need to make it a question? As though I'm asking, *I'm Vic, is that okay?* "I'm a f-friend of Brett Mason's. We've had classes together."

"Oh," says Callie, and her eyelids droop and then close as we reach the steps that lead to the second floor. I'm left to haul her up them one at a time because she isn't lifting her feet much.

Given we aren't in someone's permanent home, I'm not worried about which room I take her to. I figure the first bedroom I come to on the left will do fine. Callie groans as I lay her down on the bed—on her side, in case she throws up again—and tug over a small wastebasket in hopes that she'll use it instead of, say, the floor. I lift her legs up onto the mattress.

When I straighten up to pull away, she paws at my arm. "Don't…don't call my dad…"

"I won't, I promise. But I'm g-going to leave you here, okay? Try to sleep."

Callie rolls her red and blurry eyes up to look at me. She manages a smile before shifting further onto her stomach, flopping her head against the pillow, and passing out almost instantly. She's going to be in for it with her parents if she stays here all night, I'll bet, but that isn't my problem. She's safe and she's comfortable. I've done my part.

Heading back to the party, I stop halfway down the stairs where I have a better view of the people lingering in the living room and near the back door. Callie isn't the only one passed out: the couch is occupied by a couple pawing at each other and a guy slouched back against the cushions, surrounded in plastic cups like he came here for no purpose other than to get as drunk as he could as fast as he could.

I'm searching for anyone who might go to my school and who might be a friend of Callie's so I can let them know to check on her. I see plenty of people I know, but I don't remember seeing Callie ever hanging out with any of them. Hell, even if I did spot one of her friends, I probably wouldn't know it. I see Chris Christopher (yeah, that's really his name) passing a joint around to Helen Barkley and Robbie Kurtis. Patrick Maloney, one of Aaron's best friends, bumps into me as I come down the stairs while he's going up, along with Eric and Jacob. Probably in search of a free bathroom or something, or to scope out the rooms to bring girls to later. Nobody looks twice at me.

The smell of weed is so strong at the bottom of the stairs that it almost makes me gag. I don't feel much like going out back again, so I wade through the crowd to the front door and squeeze outside.

It's amazing how much quieter it is from the front porch. The party is a world away, nothing but distant sounds of splashing and shouting, and I try to decide if there's something wrong with me that I'm incapable of mingling and having a good time like everyone else here. Like Brett. I've never "lived it up" at a party. I've never hooked up with a girl. I've never gotten so drunk that I threw up in the bushes. Given how much fun everyone seems to be having…am I missing out?

We got here two hours ago. Brett could be out in ten minutes or five hours. There's never any telling with him. It depends entirely on if he found something to entertain him: a conversation he enjoys or a girl he can flirt with. I have little else to do but utilize the abundance of games on my phone to entertain myself.

It's another two hours before Brett texts me:

you ok? where are you?

I respond, and in a few moments he emerges from the house with a smile. He's been drinking, but Brett never gets sloppy drunk, just happy drunk. Kudos to him.

He tosses me his car keys. "Ready to get going?"

They hit my knuckles and then the ground when I attempt to catch them. "Yeah. Meet anyone?"

"Nobody worth calling later." Brett crams his hands into his pockets and heads for the car. I grab the keys from the dirt and follow. Driving is always exciting. I've had my license for a year, but Mom doesn't have money to help me buy a car, and even after saving all summer I'd only ended up with enough cash for something I'd be humiliated to be seen in. Getting behind the wheel of Brett's semi-new hybrid is always awesome. Although I had planned to stay at his place, he informs me that he has things to do bright and early in the morning so we might as well drop me off at my house.

While Brett dozes in the passenger's seat, I focus on getting us home in one piece, letting my mind wander. This is my car. I'm driving home from a party I was invited to, not because of who my best friend is but because people wanted me there. I have the windows down and my sunglasses on, smiling at anyone we meet because I'm not self-conscious that my hair is a mess or I'm too tall, too skinny, too dorky, or too not worth looking twice at. When I get home, I'll have a bunch of texts waiting for me:

thanks for coming tonight, man! and it was great meeting you, let's hang out next weekend.

It's a common daydream of mine. One that ends when I pull up outside my house and Brett opens the door and circles around to the driver's side as I'm stepping out. My fingers curl around the keys. "You, uh, s-sure you should be driving yet?"

"Dude, give me my keys. I'm good. I'll text when I get home to let you know I made it in one piece, yeah?" He pries them out of my hand, claps me on the back, and gets into the car. "I'll see you Monday."

Then he's driving away, and I'm left feeling—not for the first time—that this is what the world has in store for me. Being someone's stupid, stuttering shadow. The designated driver. All of this is someone else's life. I'm just along for the ride.

...

Callie is a nagging concern in the back of my brain all weekend. Did she get home okay? Was she in trouble with her parents? How hungover was she the next morning? Does she even remember that someone helped her up to a room? I have no idea where she lives, so riding my bike past her house isn't an option. Instead, I have to wait for Monday. Second period, I work as an assistant in the front office. It isn't hard to take a quick peek at the locker assignments to tell me where I'm likely to find her between classes.

Brett meets me in the hall and on our way to the cafeteria for lunch, I tell him I want to take a detour. He gives me a quizzical look but goes along without question. My eyes scan the crowded hall for locker numbers and when I come across Callie's, I slow down but don't stop. There's no sign of her. Maybe she doesn't go to her locker between classes; some people keep all their books with them.

As we walk away, I notice someone who isn't Callie approach Callie's locker. She's about Callie's height, but with longer, darker hair. She messes with Callie's combination lock, pops it open, and begins clearing things out. Not just books but clothing, makeup, and miscellaneous junk.

I stop in my tracks, frowning. Why would she do that?

Brett shoves a finger into my ribs. "Hello? Earth to Victor, are we going to get lunch or what?"

Lunch. Right. I turn my gaze ahead and force my feet to move. Worst-case scenarios are running through my head. Did something happen to her? Alcohol poisoning?

Choked on her own vomit? Her parents were so mad they cut her up and stuck her in the freezer? Guilt is gnawing its way up my insides; if something happened to her, will it be my fault?

"What was that about?" Brett asks.

"N-nothing. Just looking f-for someone."

What happened to Callie?

GRAB THE ENTANGLED TEEN RELEASES READERS ARE TALKING ABOUT!

REMEMBER ME FOREVER
BY SARA WOLF

Isis Blake hasn't fallen in love in three years, forty-three weeks, and two days. Or so she thinks. The boy she maybe-sort-of-definitely loved and sort-of-maybe-definitely hated has dropped off the face of the planet, leaving a Jack Hunter–shaped hole. Determined to be happy, Isis fills it in with lies and puts on a brave smile for her new life at Ohio State University. But the smile lasts only until he shows up. The threat from her past, her darkest moment...Nameless, attending OSU right alongside her. Whispering that he has something Isis wants—something she needs to see to move forward. To move on.

Isis is good at pretending everything is okay, at putting herself back together. But Jack Hunter is better.

The Replacement Crush
by Lisa Brown Roberts

After book blogger Vivian Galdi's longtime crush pretends their secret summer kissing sessions never happened, Vivian creates a list of safe crushes, determined to protect her heart.

But nerd-hot Dallas, the sweet new guy in town, sends the missions—and Vivian's zing meter—into chaos. While designing software for the bookstore where she works, Dallas wages a countermission.

Operation Replacement Crush is in full effect. And Dallas is determined to take her heart off the shelf.

Proof of Lies
by Diana Rodriguez Wallach

Some secrets are best kept hidden…

Anastasia Phoenix has always been the odd girl out, whether moving from city to international city with her scientist parents or being the black belt who speaks four languages.

And most definitely as the orphan whose sister is missing, presumed dead.

She's the only one who believes Keira is still alive, and when new evidence surfaces, Anastasia sets out to follow the trail—and lands in the middle of a massive conspiracy. Now she isn't sure who she can trust. At her side is Marcus, the bad boy with a sexy accent who's as secretive as she is. He may have followed her to Rome to help, but something about him seems too good to be true.

Nothing is as it appears, and when everything she's ever known is revealed to be a lie, Anastasia has to believe in one impossibility.

She *will* find her sister.

Secrets of a Reluctant Princess
by Casey Griffin

At Beverly Hills High, you have to be ruthless to survive…

Adrianna Bottom always wanted to be liked. But this wasn't *exactly* what she had in mind. Now, she's in the spotlight…and out of her geeky comfort zone. She'll do whatever it takes to turn the rumor mill in her favor—even if it means keeping secrets. So far, it's working.

Wear the right clothes. Say the right things. Be seen with the right people.

Kevin, the adorable sketch artist who shares her love of all things nerd, isn't *exactly* the right people. But that doesn't stop Adrianna from crushing on him. The only way she can spend time with him is in disguise, as Princess Andy, the masked girl he's been LARPing with. If he found out who she really was, though, he'd hate her.

The rules have been set. The teams have their players. Game on.